Brimstone Bound

By Helen Harper

BOOK ONE OF
THE FIREBRAND SERIES

BOOK COVER DESIGN BY YOCLA DESIGNS

For Ruth, Tussy, Roch and David. Kampai!

Chapter One

There's nothing quite as satisfying as curling up on the sofa with a glass of red wine and chatting to your boyfriend about the best way to bring down a snarling six-foot-tall bloke armed with a machete.

'He had this crazed look in his eye,' I said, twirling my finger at my temple. 'I knew deep down that he was seconds away from spinning round towards the restaurant and slicing at as many people as he could. We were a hair's breadth away from total bloody carnage.'

Jeremy shook his head in dismay. 'You're still in training, Emma. I can't believe they put you in such a dangerous situation.'

I tried to act casual, as if the incident hadn't left me shaking uncontrollably for an hour afterwards, and took a sip of my wine. 'It's not like it was planned. And,' I added, 'this is the best way to learn.'

'By almost getting your head chopped off by a psychotic madman?'

'He didn't even get close,' I dismissed with the surge of invincibility that only comes after you've confronted your own mortality head-on and walked away still breathing.

I placed my glass on the table and stood up, tugging at Jeremy's hand to encourage him to do the same. Then I gave him the butter knife, which still had crumbs clinging to its dull blade, and stepped back about six paces. 'He was roaring loudly enough to wake the dead.'

Jeremy grinned, swishing the butter knife from side to side before letting out what could only be described as a remarkably feeble attempt at a roar.

'But,' I continued, 'he was expelling so much energy on the noise he was making, and was so focused on the weapon in his hand, that he didn't realise Williams was coming up behind him. I pulled out my baton and feinted left with it.'

I reached for a magazine and rolled it up, using it as a prop to act out what had happened. Jeremy responded, lifted up his butter knife to block my 'attack', and roared again. I beamed and nodded.

'And while that was happening, Williams got right up behind the perp...' I hustled round the table until I was at Jeremy's back '...reached round his neck with one arm, while at the same time slamming his free hand into his carotid artery.' In slow motion, I pretended to do the same to Jeremy. 'The blow caused the perp's blood pressure to drop instantly and he collapsed.'

Jeremy groaned and fell to his knees, releasing his hold on the knife. It clattered to the floor.

I stepped in front of him and dusted off my palms. 'Hey presto,' I said. 'One incapacitated criminal.'

He choked and spluttered melodramatically. Hollywood wouldn't be calling any time soon. 'This criminal might need the kiss of life to recover,' he told me.

'Well,' I said softly, lowering myself to his level, 'I'd better get onto that before it's too late.' I leaned towards him, my lips meeting his. For a moment he didn't react, then he opened his mouth and his tongue pushed towards mine. With both of us on our knees it was a clumsy clinch, and it wasn't long before discomfort overcame passion. We broke apart and smiled awkwardly at each other before returning to our previous positions on the sofa.

'Anyway,' I shrugged, 'it was all over within seconds. I was never in any real danger.'

'All the same, I'm glad that this rotation is over and you're moving to a new department on Monday. I'll sleep a lot better at night knowing that you're safe. I don't like the idea of my girlfriend putting herself in danger. It's certainly a far cry from accountancy. I could never do something like you did today. *You* should never do something like it again either.'

'You're underplaying the danger of spreadsheets,' I teased.

His eyes twinkled. 'The wrong data can be a killer. And that's not the only thing I have to worry about. This morning I forgot my brief-case with all the papers I needed for today. That's the third time this month. Brewster told me that if I do it again, he'll give me a formal warning.' He rolled his eyes. 'From the look on his face, I thought he was going to lop my head off. It's ridiculous. Everything is digitalized now. I think he just likes being the big, bad, scary boss.'

I laughed. 'There are risks and dangers everywhere.'

'Indeed.' He reached across and brushed my cheek with his fin-gers. 'You still reckon you'll be placed in Cyber Crime for your last rotation? That sounds considerably safer than the Criminal Investi-gations Department. I think you'll be much better suited to it.'

'CID has been an experience, but I do think desk work is my thing.' I ignored the twinge that told me I was lying through my teeth and squared my shoulders. Jeremy worried about me too much and the least I could do was set his mind at rest. Besides, it wasn't as if I didn't enjoy the office-based work I'd done so far. There was more to being a detective these days than patrolling the mean streets and physically running down criminals.

I set my jaw and met his eyes. 'I did well with the Fraud Squad, and DSI Barnes seemed happy when I asked to finish my training in Cyber Crime. My last two-week stint before final exams and then,' I spread my arms out wide, 'yours truly will finally be a real detective.'

Jeremy picked up his glass and clinked it against mine. 'I'll drink to that. Here's to London's finest.'

I beamed. 'Cheers.'

***

I strolled into the Academy building first thing on Monday morning wearing a plain white blouse and a black skirt suit. Ease of movement wasn't a consideration when I'd be sitting behind a computer for most of the day.

I nodded at Phyllis on the front desk before taking the lift up to the meeting room on the third floor. Most of my fellow recruits were already there, milling around in small groups, catching up on the details of their previous assignments, and anxiously anticipating the next one.

At this stage, there was little attrition in numbers. A few people had dropped out in the early days, but the selection process to attend the Academy was stringent and, as a result, there was a high pass rate. Our residency at the Academy might only last twelve weeks but achieving detective status was a two-year process that, unless you were already in the police, only started after you'd experienced life outside education. No one wanted detectives on the streets who had no direct knowledge of the real world. In any case, to get this far required considerable time and dedication; there was virtually no chance any of us were going to fail now.

That didn't mean I wasn't nervous about what was coming next. I'd received glowing reports from my previous rotations, and I wanted to keep it that way. The better I did here, the more chance there was that I could have my first choice of postings when I finally graduated.

I'd barely entered the room when Molly scooted over to me. We'd bonded on the very first day, when we'd been paired up during our first skill session designed to teach us how to find tell-tale evidence from grainy CCTV footage.

Molly had joined the police initially to flip the finger at her family. Her parents seemed to think that she should focus on finding herself a fella and settling down with a little part-time job in a shop or a school, rather than running around the grimy streets of London and infiltrating its underbelly. It hadn't taken her long to realise that, in the process of foiling her family, she'd found her true calling.

For my part, I'd dodged her questions about my reasons for signing up and mumbled something about it being a childhood dream.

Molly was smart enough to know there was more to it than that – and kind enough not to press me for more information.

'A little bird tells me that you had quite the day during your last shift with CID.' She punched my arm. 'You go, girl! I said you'd be great. You bagged a real bad guy.'

I smiled at her. 'It wasn't really me. The detective I partnered did all the heavy lifting.'

'Stop being so freaking modest, Emma. You held your own, and that means you did a good job. If it'd been me, I'd be crowing about it from the rooftops.'

'How did things go in the drug squad?' I asked.

She pulled a face. 'Grim. Very grim.' She held up her hand and crossed her fingers. 'Criminal Investigations Department next, though. Bring on CID.'

'Here's hoping,' I said, dropping my voice as Lucinda Barnes, the Academy's head, walked up to the podium at the front of the room.

Detective Superintendent Barnes, to give her full title, didn't smile although there was a warmth to her gaze as she looked round the room. For all that she'd been an experienced, hard-nosed detective before she took on the role as head of the Academy, she still retained something of a mother hen aura.

'Welcome back,' she said. 'I've been reviewing the reports from your last rotations and I can only say how impressed I am at all of your performances. You've done yourselves proud.'

Her gaze swept across our upturned faces, and I was certain I didn't imagine her eyes lingering on mine for longer than necessary. 'Now we are moving into the final phase of your training. You only have a two-week placement to complete, before final debriefings and testings. After that, you will be fully-fledged detectives, ready to take on the world. Rotation postings are going up on the noticeboard as we speak. I trust that you will continue in the same professional manner that you have done so far – but remember that being a police detective is not just about image.' She touched her chest briefly. 'It has to be part of your heart and your soul.'

I bit my lip, a tingle of pride rippling through me. It had taken me a long time to get to this point; the Academy was merely the tip of the iceberg in what had been a very long journey. I'd do it, though. Two months before my thirtieth birthday, and finally I was going to be in a position to achieve everything I'd ever wanted.

We bustled out into the corridor, eager to find out our new assignments. At half a foot shorter than most of my fellow trainees, I couldn't see the board for the other heads in the way. I knew from Molly's crow of delight, however, that she'd got her posting to CID. I pushed myself onto my tiptoes to get a better look, just as I heard several sharp intakes of breath and spotted more than one swift glance in my direction.

'Emma,' Molly murmured. 'Oh...'

I frowned at her and elbowed my way to the front. I scanned the sheet, searching for my name. When I finally saw it at the bottom, and my eyes tracked my assigned rotation printed next to it, I blinked. That didn't make any sense.

I rubbed my eyes and read it again. 'It must be a mistake,' I said, my voice sounding tinny. 'That can't be right.'

Molly's hand reached for mine and squeezed it. 'Yeah,' she said. 'It must be an error.'

I spun round, blindly pushing my way through the crowd and into the meeting room. I'd get this sorted out in a jiffy.

Barnes was still standing by the podium, frowning at some papers. She looked up when I entered. There wasn't any surprise in her expression; I had the impression she'd been waiting for me.

'Detective Superintendent,' I began.

'You've called me Lucinda until now,' she said. 'There's no reason to suddenly become so formal.'

I sucked in a breath and marched up to her, my arms swinging. The closer I got, however, the more my confidence leaked away. I stopped a few feet away and my hands dropped by my sides. 'Supes?' I asked, in little more than a whisper. 'I'm going to Supes?'

She regarded me implacably. 'It's very rare that trainees like you are given a rotation to Supernatural Squad. You should look on it as an honour.'

But it wasn't an honour. As green as I was, even I knew that nothing could be further from the truth. 'I'd been expecting Cyber Crime,' I said, aware of the tinge of desperation in my tone.

'That rotation is already full. You should consider this an excellent opportunity to hone your investigative skills, Emma.'

I straightened my back. 'I don't think it's a suitable department for me.'

'On the contrary, I believe it's the *perfect* department for you. And if it proves otherwise, well,' she shrugged, 'it's only for two weeks. Once you're done and you've got your full warrant card, you can request all the long-term postings to Cyber Crime that you want. For now, Supes is where you're going.' DSI Barnes nodded, indicating that the conversation was over. 'Enjoy it while you can. Not many people get this opportunity.' She picked up her pile of papers and walked out, leaving me gaping after her.

Molly edged into the room. As soon as she saw my expression, her face paled. 'It's not a mistake then.'

'No.' I bunched my hands into fists.

'It could be worse.'

I gave her a baleful look. 'Could it? Only fuck-ups get sent to Supernatural Squad, Molly. Isn't that what we were told in our first week? That the poor sods in Supes are the ones who haven't quite screwed up badly enough to be fired, or who are already well on their way to retirement. Why am I going there? I thought I was doing well.'

She swallowed. 'Supe Squad detectives are allowed to use weapons that the rest of us don't get access to. Crossbows with silver-tipped arrows. That's cool. Plus, you'll get to meet a lot of interesting people. If you play your cards right, you might be able to make some contacts that'll prove useful further down the line after you've graduated.'

'I don't need a bunch of vampires and werewolves in my address book!' I snapped. Then I immediately regretted it. 'Sorry. I'm just...'

'I know.' She tried to smile at me. 'It'll be alright, Emma. If anyone can excel at this, you can.'

It was an empty platitude and we both knew it. 'Yeah.' I lifted my head and pretended that it would be fine. 'It'll be great.'

Chapter Two

My new temporary partner-cum-mentor was waiting for me in the lobby when I returned to the ground floor of the Academy.

At first, I looked straight past him. He certainly didn't look like the other qualified detectives I'd met. It's all very well to say that you shouldn't judge a book by its cover, but we all do it. Detective Constable Anthony Brown possessed the sort of craggy, pockmarked, drawn face and shabby clothes that you'd be more likely to see on someone who belonged on the other side of law. If it weren't for the fact that Phyllis nodded towards him when she saw me looking lost, I'd have ignored him completely.

'Erm, hello?'

Brown's head slowly swivelled round. 'Is that a question?' he grunted. 'Or have we started recruiting people who can't speak English?'

My hackles rose immediately. The last thing I needed right now was a stereotypical hard-boiled detective who hated the world. 'I'm Emma Bellamy,' I said, more forcefully. I stuck out my hand. 'I assume you're Detective Constable Brown.'

He eyed my hand as if it were a strange foreign object before reaching out and shaking it limply. 'Tony. I can't stand all that official title malarkey. It's a pointless exercise, and a waste of breath.'

Okay, then. 'Tony it is,' I said with false cheeriness. 'Nice to meet you.'

He grunted again and looked me up and down. 'You look like you belong in an open-plan office in that outfit. Dressing smart won't help you in Supes. Quite the opposite. Do you see me wearing a tie? I don't even *own* a damned tie. We don't need secretaries or pencil pushers.' His expression took on a suspicious glint. 'You any good with computers?'

'Yes.' I folded my arms and glared at him. 'And I'm dressed like this because I was expecting to be placed with Cyber Crimes for the next two weeks. Not with you.' I sniffed. 'I'm not any happier about this than you are, but it's for fourteen days. I'd prefer it if those days weren't spent with a monosyllabic mentor who does nothing but gripe. And I'm sure you'd prefer it if I could actually be of some help to you. Which,' I added pointedly, 'I can be, if you let me.'

From behind her desk, Phyllis stared at us goggle-eyed. I wondered if I'd gone too far and had already blown my chances of getting a good report or learning anything useful during the next two weeks.

Then Tony threw back his head and laughed, before clapping me heartily on the shoulder. 'Well, well, well,' he chortled. 'So the little mouse can roar. Maybe this won't be so bad after all. What did you do, anyway?'

'What do you mean?'

He waved a hand. 'What did you do to get yourself lumbered with this gig? We never get trainees at Supes.'

My mouth tightened. 'I don't know what I did,' I muttered. 'But I'll make the best of it, regardless.'

He examined my face in a bid to ascertain the truth, then he shrugged. 'Okay, Emma Bellamy. I won't say it's going to be fun because it won't be. But perhaps it won't be a complete disaster either.' He gestured towards the door. 'Come on. I'm parked right out front.' And with that, he twisted round and strode out of the building. I swallowed and jogged after him.

Rather than using the conveniently located car park to the right of the Academy, Tony had left his beaten-up Mini parked on a double-yellow line. I gazed doubtfully at the lurid purple vehicle while he removed the sign from the dashboard which read 'Police. On Urgent Call'.

It was one of the old Minis which, judging by the number plate, had been in service since the 1970s. It wasn't the car's age that troubled me, however; it was the broken rear window, taped up with a black bin bag presumably to keep out of the worst of the wind. And the cracked side mirrors and the cloud of black smoke that the exhaust coughed out when Tony started the engine.

He leaned across from the driver's seat and, with what appeared to be incredible effort, wound down the window. 'Are you getting in or not?' he asked.

I wrenched open the passenger door while he shoved a small mountain of rubbish into the cramped back seat. The upholstery was marked with various coloured stains of dubious origins. Holding my breath, I clambered in. The interior smelled strongly of patchouli and something else that I couldn't quite identify. It wasn't entirely unpleasant, but it was strong enough to make my eyes water.

'How does this car even pass its MOT?'

Tony slammed his foot onto the accelerator and swerved into the road without checking to see whether anything was coming. I hastily clipped on my seatbelt and gripped the sides of my seat. It was clear this was going to be a white-knuckle ride. Literally.

'She doesn't.' He tapped his nose. 'But if you don't tell, then I won't.'

'But how...'

'Tallulah is special.'

Uh... 'Tallulah?'

'That's her name,' he said proudly. 'Don't wear it out.'

I was travelling in a tin can at breakneck speed with a complete lunatic by my side. I'd take machete-wielding attackers any day over this.

'Tallulah is special,' Tony repeated. 'Don't criticise her.' The tyres screeched as we took the next corner at high speed.

'I wouldn't dream of it,' I told him. Then I closed my eyes and began to pray for the first time since I was a small child.

'So,' Tony said, 'what do you know about the supes? Are you at kindergarten level, or do you have a master's?'

Actually, I did have a master's but it certainly wasn't in anything to do with the supernatural. With Tony seeming to warm to me, though, I was determined not to lose any ground and come across as a complete idiot.

I dredged my memory for what little I knew. 'The vampires live mostly in Soho, and abide by a feudal system of governance. They number around a thousand or so —'

'It's closer to two thousand,' Tony interrupted. He flicked his fingers in the air dismissively. 'But please. Continue.'

I drew in a breath. 'Their leader is a bloke called Lord – uh—' Damn it. What *was* his name?

'Lord Horvath.'

Oh yeah. That rang a faint bell, although the man could walk past me in the street and I wouldn't know him from Adam. Few pictures of him existed, and I'd never been interested enough in supes to look him up. I imagined he was a crusty old bloke – someone with yellowing fangs and thin white hair.

'What's he like?' I asked.

Tony's lips pursed. 'Annoying. What else can you tell me about the vamps?'

I tried to think of anything else that I knew for sure. 'They drink blood for sustenance...'

'Pfffft!'

'They're also considerably faster and stronger than humans.' I sneaked a side look at him. 'And they're immortal.'

Tony tutted. 'Unbelievable. What do they teach you kids nowadays?'

I bristled. I wasn't a kid. But I didn't know very much about vampires and, from Tony's reactions, it was clear that what I did know was wrong.

'The majority of vamps are only slightly stronger than us. They tend to use their physical attributes in other ways. Most of them rely on the fact that they become more attractive after they're turned into vamps. A pretty face and a flash of sex appeal encourages foolish humans to offer themselves up as food.'

I grimaced at the thought that, as a species, we humans were that shallow. I promised myself that I wouldn't be blinded by anyone's good looks.

'What about the wolves?' Tony asked. 'What do you think you know about them?'

'There are four groups,' I started.

'Clans,' he said. 'But alright.'

'They're all based in Lisson Grove, not far from St James's Park. During the full moon, all the wolves head there. The park is closed off to the general public so there's no chance of us humans getting eaten accidentally. Each werewolf has its own level of dominance, from wholly subservient to group – I mean, clan – alpha. Then there are the Others, the supes that live in between both groups. Their numbers are less significant, but they include the likes of ghouls, gremlins and pixies, each of which possesses different genetics and abilities.'

'And?'

And that was it; that was the extent of my knowledge. I shrugged. There was no point pretending otherwise.

Somewhat surprisingly, Tony looked pleased. 'Good,' he said. 'You know absolutely fuck all and that means you're not a groupie. There's been a few of those in the department. It's hard enough to do our jobs as it is, but when you've got police officers who go weak at the knees at the first glimpse of a fang or a patch of fur, it can become nigh on impossible.'

Tony had unwittingly given me the opening I needed. 'What is your job exactly?' I asked.

He slammed on the brakes, bringing Tallulah to a screeching halt. I was jolted forward, my forehead smacking against the windscreen despite my seatbelt. I rubbed it and winced. Tony frowned and reached across, using his shirt cuff to wipe away the tiny smear I'd left on the glass, as if it somehow damaged the aesthetic effect of the car.

'Welcome to Supernatural Squad,' he declared.

I glanced out of the window, noting the narrow grey building wedged between a small Waitrose and an expensive-looking hotel with a liveried bellman standing outside. 'Perfectly equidistant between – and within walking distance of – the vamps and the wolves, and close to all the others at the same time.'

Unable to stop myself, I let out a low whistle. In terms of postcode, it didn't get much more expensive than this.

Tony seemed to know what I was thinking. 'Yeah,' he said, turning off the engine. 'Don't think that the other departments haven't tried to take this away from us. They can't. Since the Supernatural Act of 1798,' he doffed an imaginary cap, 'Supernatural Squad has been entitled to this building. By law, it's funded in large part by the supes themselves – though they're not happy about having to pay for our existence.'

'Isn't that a conflict of interest?'

He just winked and got out of the car. I followed suit, casting a quick glance at the posh bellman outside the hotel. I half-expected a loud complaint that Tallulah was bringing down the tone of the neighbourhood, but instead he bowed at us.

'Good morning, Detective Constable Brown.'

Tony grinned. 'Good morning, Jeeves.' He joined me on the pavement and nudged me. 'Not his real name.'

No kidding. I smiled at Jeeves – or whoever he was – and glanced at the Mini. 'Aren't you going to lock the car?'

'Nobody touches Tallulah.' He walked up to the unmarked door and entered, leaving me to follow.

I stared after him for a moment, wondering what on earth I'd got myself into. I had the feeling it was going to be a very long two weeks. And Tony still hadn't answered my question about what his job at Supernatural Squad was.

***

The building that housed Supe Squad might have boasted a grand address, but it wasn't particularly grand inside. It wasn't one of those buildings that was bigger on the inside than it looked on the outside, either. The walls were a dirty yellow colour, presumably from the days when it was considered normal to smoke indoors. The corridor was narrow. I caught a definite whiff of stale coffee from deep within the bowels of the building, along with the same heavy, deep scent I'd noticed in the car.

'What's that smell?' I asked, as much to myself as to Tony who was striding ahead.

He stopped in his tracks and turned around. 'You got wolf in your family?' he enquired.

I was taken aback. 'No. Of course not.'

He raised an eyebrow. 'You can smell the herbs, though.'

'They're not exactly subtle. And when you say herbs—'

He rolled his eyes. 'Don't get your panties in a twist. They're nothing illegal. It's verbena blended with wolfsbane.'

'To ward off the supes?' I guessed.

'Yep.' He started walking again.

'Does it work?'

'No.'

'Then why—' Too late. He'd already vanished into a room at the far end of the corridor. I muttered a curse and went after him.

The room wasn't exactly a hive of police activity. There were four desks arranged haphazardly along one side. The nearest one was occupied by a woman not much older than me, with bright red hair shorn into a pixie cut, and pale skin that was accentuated by her blacker-than-black clothes. She seemed wholly intent on the crossword in front of her. A younger man in uniform was sprawled on a small sofa watching daytime television on the opposite side of the room. Neither of them looked up when I entered.

'Morning all,' Tony said. 'This is...' He glanced at me.

'Emma,' I supplied helpfully.

'Oh yes.' He pointed at the redhead. 'Moneypenny. She's our operations officer.' Then he switched to the policeman. 'Plod. He's our bog-standard police officer.'

'Liza,' the redhead said.

The man raised his hand. 'Fred.'

'Nice to meet you.' I looked around. 'Is the rest of the department upstairs?'

Liza snorted.

Tony smiled. 'This is it,' he said proudly.

I scratched my head. 'The ... morning shift?'

'No.' He gave me a patient nod. 'The entire department. As you can see, we're not exactly rushed off our feet.'

'This is it? There's only three of you?'

Tony ambled over to the corner to flick on the kettle. 'As I said, there have been others. They've come and gone – most people don't stick it here for long. There was a second detective for a while, but he retired in December.'

Oh. I relaxed slightly. It was only February. 'So you're waiting on his replacement?'

'He means December 2016,' Liza said.

I stared at her. That was almost five years ago.

She put down her pen and stood up, offering me a tired smile. 'Hi, Emma. Welcome to Supe Squad.'

I tried to smile back, I really did, but I couldn't manage it. The horror seeping through me was preventing so much as the tiniest twitch at the corners of my mouth. All I could think about was Lucinda Barnes confidently telling me that this was my perfect department. I sat down on the nearest chair, my shoulders sagging.

Liza slid open a drawer, drew out a small object and tossed it at me. I narrowly caught it before it smacked me in the face. 'Here,' she said. 'A key for this place.'

'Uh...' I turned it over in my hands. 'I'm only here for two weeks. I won't be staying.'

She shrugged. 'You never know.'

I *did* know. Once my rotation here was over, I wouldn't even look back.

Chapter Three

'No, I'm not in Cyber Crime.'

'But I thought that was going to be your next rotation?' Jeremy sounded about as unhappy as I was

'So did I. DSI Barnes pulled a fast one on me.'

There was a beat of silence. 'So where are you?'

'Supernatural Squad.'

'What?'

'I've been placed in Supernatural Squad,' I repeated.

'Shit, Emma. Won't that be dangerous?'

As far as I could tell, the only danger was that I might die of boredom. 'No. Definitely not dangerous,' I reassured him. 'In fact...'

'Hey!' Tony interrupted. 'D'Artagnan! Let's go!'

Crap. 'I have to go,' I said into the phone. 'I'll see you tonight.'

'Love you.'

'Bye.' I hastily ended the call and stuffed the phone into my pocket. 'D'Artagnan?' I said to Tony.

His brow furrowed, making the deep wrinkles in his face more pronounced. 'I can't possibly remember everyone's names. You're a trainee. I'll remember D'Artagnan.'

'And that makes you what?' I inquired. 'One of the Three Musketeers? You don't seem the swashbuckling type.'

Tony wagged a finger at me. 'Wait and see.' He swung a shabby coat round his shoulders. 'Come on. It's time we headed out.'

'Where are we going?'

'To do our jobs, D'Artagnan. The public expect their taxes to be put to good use and I'd hate to disappoint them.' He grinned at me. 'Hop to it.'

Anything was better than staying within these depressing walls. I grabbed my suit jacket, shrugged it on and headed out of the door.

'Don't we get crossbows with silver-tipped arrows to carry with us when we're out and about?'

Tony snorted. 'If you think I'm letting the likes of you anywhere near a deadly weapon like that, you're more naïve than I thought. Besides, those things haven't been used for years. We don't need them. I don't even know where they're kept any more.'

I looked him over. He certainly wasn't carrying any sort of weapon. So much for that perk, then.

'The vamps won't start stirring until around teatime,' he told me while we walked, 'so we'll start with the werewolves. Consider this Supernatural 101.' He patted his stomach. 'Plus, I'm getting a little peckish and there's a great sandwich shop next to the Sullivans' lair.'

'The Sullivans are one of the werewolf clans?'

He nodded. 'Currently aligned with the McGuigans. Or at least they were the last time I checked. With the wolves, anything is possible. They're mercurial bastards.'

I took a notepad from my coat pocket. 'How do you spell McGuigan?' I asked, wanting to get it right.

Tony stopped in his tracks. 'Are you taking notes?'

'I don't want to miss any details.'

He rolled his eyes and strode off again. 'It's not rocket science, D'Artagnan,' he called over his shoulder. 'Put that away before you embarrass us both.'

Tempted to refuse, I glared at his departing back. But scribbling notes while walking wasn't the easiest thing in the world, so in the end I gave in to the path of least resistance and tucked it away.

'Look, just relax,' he said, with surprising kindness as I caught up with him. 'I know you want to do well, and you want a glowing report so you can show off to Detective Superintendent Barnes and get the posting of your dreams after you qualify. Don't worry about it. This is the easiest gig in the world. I'll write whatever the hell you want when these two weeks are up. Whatever shit you pulled to end up here, I can tell that you're not a bad sort. It'll be fine. One for all, and all for one.'

I wasn't sure if he was expecting me to thank him or not. 'I actually do want to learn something while I'm here,' I said. 'I don't want this to be a time-wasting exercise.'

'Hence our little side trip. You'll learn lots.' Tony smirked. 'Trust me.'

We crossed the street, before turning right and heading down a wide road. This was a famous part of the city; even though I'd never been here before, I recognised quite a few of the buildings and landmarks. We reached Swain Street and the gigantic arch that stretched from one side to the other. It was fashioned out of various sections of sculpted wood, forming a large wolf's head at the apex. I couldn't stop myself from gasping.

Tony sent me a sidelong look. 'Impressive, huh?'

I nodded. 'I've seen photos of it, but it's so much bigger than I thought it would be.' I stretched out my fingertips, brushing them against the warm wood.

'Most people think that it's purely decorative, or to entice in tourists.' He gestured at a group of chattering sightseers who'd paused in front of the arch for selfies. 'But the truth is far more complex. Although there are several different types of wood forming the arch, at its heart is a large section of hawthorn. Legend has it that hawthorn is a vampire repellent. I don't know whether that's true or not, but you'll certainly never see any vamps walking around here. Not at any time of night or day.'

'They can come in daytime?'

'Sure. They just don't choose to do it much. Think of the vamps as students – partying all night, sleeping all day.'

'And the wolves?'

Tony pursed his lips. 'They're dogs. They mark their territory and are food obsessed.' He paused and his voice dropped slightly, as if he were afraid that he'd be overheard. 'Don't underestimate them, though. Any of them. No matter what anyone would have you believe, both groups are still predators. They're at the top of the food chain. They keep us at bay through some nifty lawyer tricks, but if they wanted to rule this city they could do it in a heartbeat.'

We passed under the arch and into the werewolves' quarter. I suppressed the shudder that ran down my spine and considered what Tony had said. 'So,' I said finally, 'Supernatural Squad is essentially window dressing?'

Tony nodded approvingly. 'Pretty much. Our presence appeases those humans who are intelligent enough to be scared of the supes, but we don't have any power. Any supes who step out of line are dealt with by their own kind. We direct lost tourists, stride around and maintain some sort of visibility and very, very occasionally convene meetings to ensure that peace is being maintained.' He sent me an arch look. 'You can see why most detectives don't stick around for long. It's not exactly a thrill a minute.'

'Why do you stay?' I asked, genuinely curious.

He smiled. 'I like a cushy, hassle-free life and a guaranteed pay check at the end of the month.'

I watched him. There was something about his tone of voice – something about Tony himself – that made me think there was far more to his existence in Supernatural Squad than he was letting on. Working out what that was would give me something to do over the next two weeks.

Before I could press him any further, a hulking figure stepped out in front of us, appearing as if from nowhere. 'Anthony Brown,' he growled. Definitely a werewolf then. 'What are you doing here?'

'Just taking a stroll,' Tony said cheerfully. 'Upholding the law and keeping the peace. Usual sort of stuff.'

Curiosity getting the better of me, I gazed at the werewolf. He looked human for most of the part – until you examined him more closely. His thick dark hair curled in a way that seemed unnatural, and his chest and shoulders were far too broad for his short legs. One thing was certain: I wouldn't want to meet him on a dark moonlit night.

'Who's she?'

'This is D'Artagnan,' Tony said. 'She's visiting for a couple of weeks.'

'Actually,' I said, 'my name is...' Tony elbowed me sharply in the ribs, and I gave a surprised oomph.

The werewolf looked amused. 'Giving her the grand tour, are you? You should bring her round to the club later. She's a tasty-looking little thing.'

I resisted the temptation to step back. The sudden hungry glint in the wolf's eyes was remarkably intimidating.

'What do you think, darling?' he asked. 'Do you fancy a bit of fur?' His skin twisted and undulated across his cheekbones. I couldn't stop myself gasping. A second later, muddy brown fur sprang up across his face. There were even whiskers.

Tony tapped his foot. 'Yes, yes. It's an impressive party trick. You should save it for the tourists.'

'Twenty quid for a photo.' The wolf opened his mouth, baring his sharp teeth. Then he lunged, snapping his jaws as if were attacking.

I blinked – but I remained where I was. 'No, thank you,' I said primly.

The wolf's fur melted away, his expression suddenly disinterested. 'You can't say I didn't try.' He glanced at Tony. 'Full moon in five days,' he said.

'I'm quaking in my boots.'

The werewolf returned to the shadows at the side of the pavement, and Tony and I continued on our way. I hadn't realised I'd been holding my breath until we were well past him. I expelled the air in a loud rush and felt a brief ache in my lungs.

'Was that your first face-to-face encounter with a wolf?' Tony asked.

I nodded.

'Then you did alright,' he said grudgingly. 'Marsh back there is all huff and bluster. He puts on a show and makes sure no humans veer into forbidden territory, but he's not a bad sort. He's one of the Sullivans. He shouldn't be out here doing this sort of low-level grunt work, but last week he got into a fight with a wolf from the Carr Clan so now he's doing his penance.' Tony's mouth flattened into a thin line, 'As I said, the supes sort out their problems in-house.'

'Why did you stop me from telling him my real name?'

'Because our job is to fit into the supes' way of doing things. Not the other way around. And the supes' way is that you don't tell an outsider your real name unless you absolutely trust them. They believe that names have power. Fluff-headed nonsense, if you ask me, but when in Rome...'

'He knew *your* real name.'

A trace of a smile crossed Tony's mouth. 'Yeah. But I'm a foolish old man who's been here too long. I gave my name freely in the hope that it would encourage the supe community to trust me. Needless to say, it didn't work.'

I frowned but, before I could say anything, he jerked his head towards the small shop opposite us. Sullivan Sandwiches. 'Here we go. The best roast beef you'll get this side of the Thames.'

The bell jangled as Tony pushed open the door, and the rich smell of well-cooked beef wafted towards us. A young woman smiled at us from behind the counter. I stared. She had very sharp teeth.

'Cassidy, baby! How are you this fine morning?' Tony cried.

Cassidy? Was that her real name? I glanced around and noted the wide array of meat on offer. Oh. Butch Cassidy.

She looked pointedly at her watch. As she did so, I caught a brief glimpse of an odd yellow tag on her raised arm. I realised that the wolf outside – Marsh – had displayed a similar tag, except his had been green. Interesting.

'It's nearly two, Tony,' Cassidy chided in a soft voice. 'It's a bit late for lunch.'

He spread his arms out wide. 'Two? Then it's no wonder I'm so hungry! Roast beef on rye with extra horseradish, please. D'Artagnan, what do you fancy?'

I scratched my head. 'Do you have any hummus?'

The woman and Tony exchanged glances.

'D'Artagnan.' He shook his head. 'This is the finest meat you're likely to get.'

'Or cheese?' I suggested. 'Do you have any cheese? And salad?'

Tony's shoulders sagged and he gazed at me in dismay. 'Oh no.'

'What?'

'Oh no, D'Artagnan. This simply won't do. Please don't tell me. Please don't say the word.'

I folded my arms. 'I'm a vegetarian.'

He held up his hands in mock horror. 'Just when I was beginning to like you. Supes is most definitely not the right place for you. Don't you dare tell anyone else.' He glared at Cassidy. 'Don't you go blabbing to anyone either, Cass.' He sighed. 'We're in the bloodiest, most meat-driven quarter in the entire City of London, and those idiots at Head Office send me a vegetarian. Unbelievable.'

I couldn't tell whether he was teasing me or having a real dig. I guessed this wasn't the time to tell him that I was considering going the whole hog, so to speak, and becoming vegan.

'I can make you up a cheese sandwich,' Cassidy told me, scanning her well-stocked display of meat, meat and more meat.

'That would be amazing,' I told her. 'Thank you.'

Tony nudged me towards the door. 'Go on. You can wait outside. I'd hate to offend your delicate vegetarian sensibilities by having you hang around in here with all this delicious flesh on offer.'

I wasn't that bothered, but I had sense enough to realise that he wanted to talk to Cassidy on his own. I headed outside again. The air was chilly. Spotting a splash of sunshine to my left, I walked away from the shop. My suit jacket wasn't much protection against the cold, and the patch of sunlight was better than nothing.

I looked around, wondering how many more werewolves I could spot. Despite the encounter with Marsh, I was surprised at the relaxed atmosphere on the street. There was no hint of menace or fear; to be honest, apart from the impressive arch at the entrance, the werewolves' quarter was no different to any other London borough.

My eyes were tracking an old man who looked to be his eighties, whose impressive grey sideburns and whiskers definitely proclaimed wolf, when something odd flickered in my peripheral vision. I leaned to the side to get a better look, then I straightened up like a shot.

Sprinting down a side street as if the hounds of hell were after her was a young woman wearing nothing except a scrap of underwear. And her pale skin looked like it had been smeared with blood.

Chapter Four

I didn't waste any time. Hiking up my skirt, and thanking my lucky stars that I wasn't wearing heels, I took off after her. Whoever she was – werewolf or otherwise – she was in trouble. I pelted down the street, ignoring the wide-eyed stares I received from passers-by.

Even though she was barefoot, she was moving faster than me. I forced myself to move as quickly as I could, air whipping at my short, bobbed hair as I ran. 'Police!' I shouted. 'Stop!'

Either she didn't hear me, or she was too scared to slow down. Within seconds, she'd disappeared round the corner at the far end of the street. I cursed and followed her, past rows of expensive parked cars and well-kept houses.

I knew that I should have waited for Tony. The last thing trainees were supposed to do was to go after crime-related matters on their own. But there hadn't been time to fetch him. I had to find the woman and help her in any way that I could before something worse happened to her.

Reaching the end of the street I spun to my right, my eyes searching for her fleeing, blood-streaked figure. There wasn't a single living soul to be seen.

With my stomach tightening, I slowed to a jog. My head swung from side to side as I scanned for a sign of her. A lone crow cawed overhead, its black body silhouetted against the weak blue sky.

Then I heard a shout. And another. I tried to pinpoint the source. Somewhere up ahead – I was sure of it. I held my breath and kept going. Where was she? Where had she gone? I pushed aside my anxiety in favour of professionalism. I'd trained for this. I had it in me to help her. I just had to find her first.

The cobbles beneath my feet were uneven; in my haste, my toe caught the edge of one that was jutting out, and I almost went flying. I staggered but kept my balance, more through luck than cat-like footwork. My arms flailed and stretched out – and that was when I spotted the splash of red. Blood. The woman had left a trail of blood.

With a renewed surge of adrenaline, I focused on the ground. There were more droplets forming a faint path from where I was standing up to the scarlet door of one of the houses that lined the street. I had no choice but to follow it.

The door was slightly open and I paused briefly. There was a strange, huffing sound from within, followed by a guttural snarl. Obviously, even if I were a fully-trained detective, I couldn't wander into random houses to have a poke around. But I didn't need a warrant if there was a genuine expectation of immediate harm to life – and a half-naked woman covered in blood fit that expectation perfectly.

I gulped in air and kicked the door all the way open. 'Police! What is...?' My words died in my mouth. Standing in the hallway, facing each other with hackles raised and gleaming white teeth bared, were two enormous werewolves.

Neither of them paid me any attention. The one closest to me, whose hindquarters reached virtually to my midriff, was growling, its entire body quivering. The yellow eyes of the werewolf opposite were fixed on it. Their muzzles were less than an inch apart.

I might not have been an expert on the supernatural, but I knew aggression and intimidation when I saw them. Whatever was going on here was about to escalate into a full-blown battle.

I wasn't armed – I didn't have a Taser or a baton or so much as a bloody pen. And I was only carrying a trainee's warrant card. I reminded myself that I wasn't without power; I'd trained for this sort of situation.

I stepped forward. 'You will stand down.' My voice rang out across the hallway, clear as a bell.

Neither werewolf moved, but I knew they'd heard me from the visible twitches in their fur-covered bodies. The tail of the yellow-eyed werewolf started to drop – and that was when the other one made its move. It leapt upwards, massive paws outstretched. I caught a brief glimpse of unsheathed claws. I just had time to register how lethally sharp they looked before they descended onto the body of its adversary and chaos ensued.

The vicious snarls emanating from both creatures would have been enough to make most sensible people run. That's exactly what I should have done, especially with the scraps of fur flying in all directions and the very real risk that I'd end up in the crossfire between two painfully sharp sets of teeth.

Neither wolf was holding back. As they collided, they crashed against the wall making the plaster crack and a picture frame fall. When the yellow-eyed wolf, who I could now see was the smaller of the two, howled in pain, I stopped thinking about my own safety. Enough was enough.

'I said,' I yelled, as I reached forward and grabbed the nearest wolf by the scruff of its neck, 'stand down! I am the police and you will stop this immediately!'

I'd acted without thinking. Even so, no one was more surprised than me when the pair of them immediately subsided. I could feel the vibrations from the growls of the wolf I was holding, but at least it had pulled away from the fight. I shuffled round its body until I was between the pair of them, noting that the smaller wolf's fur was matted with blood.

'Change,' I ordered. Nothing happened. I gritted my teeth and hardened my tone. 'Change!'

It happened quickly. One moment I was holding the scruff of a wolf's neck, its wiry fur tickling my skin; the next moment I was pinching the smooth skin of a woman – the same woman I'd seen running down the street. I immediately let go of her, wondering if I'd been wrong and she was the attacker rather than the victim.

I turned to the second wolf. He'd also transformed and was standing in front of me with his hands by his sides. His body was covered in cuts and gashes. Between the pair of them, he'd definitely come off worst.

If I felt strange standing between a naked couple who were glaring at each other with ferocious, simmering hatred, it didn't seem to bother them.

'Back up,' I said. 'Both of you, three paces each.'

They did as I asked, although it was clear from the woman's shuffling gait that she was none too happy about it. Tough.

'Now tell me what is going on here.' I pointed at the man. 'You. Explain.'

'That bitch fucking attacked me for no reason!'

'No reason? Are you kidding me? My sister—'

'I haven't done anything to your fucking sister that she didn't want me to do!'

The woman put her hands on her hips. 'Then where is she? Eh? Why hasn't she come home?' Her voice shook. From the fire spitting in her eyes, I knew that if I didn't get these two away from each other she was liable to attack the man again.

I scanned her up and down, realising what I hadn't been able to tell from a distance: the blood on her body wasn't hers. She wasn't the one who needed medical attention.

'This is your house?' I asked the man. He nodded, his skin pale. 'Right,' I said. 'Then here's what we're going to do. You'll put on some clothes while the two of us—'

'Yield.'

My head jerked up at the cold female voice that interrupted the proceedings. The two naked wolves dropped to the floor, while I stared at the face of an older woman framed in the doorway beyond them. She had steel-grey hair and iron-hard eyes. She was immaculately dressed in expensive, designer-label clothes. Even if she'd been wearing a sack, she'd still have had the sort of aura that demanded attention. She was standing perfectly still, but it felt that her very presence was sucking the oxygen from the atmosphere.

Behind her, I briefly registered Tony staring at me with a mixture of horror and grim admonishment.

'I am Lady Sullivan, Alpha of the Sullivan clan. I will deal with this.' The woman's tone brooked no argument.

I raised my eyes to Tony, who glared at me and bit out a nod. My mouth tightened, but I wasn't in a position to disagree. I was a trainee, it was my first day in this department and Tony had already made it clear that our role wasn't to interfere with supe business. It rankled so much that it was almost painful, but I wasn't hot headed enough to argue – especially when I knew that I wouldn't win.

I nodded in mute agreement and shuffled out of the house. Lady Sullivan moved aside an inch to let me past. I didn't need to glance at Tony's bunched fists to know that he was furious with me. As for the two wolves who'd been fighting, all they'd done was cower since she'd appeared. That was some hold she had over them.

The female wolf glanced in Tony's direction, her eyes meeting his. He cleared his throat and addressed me. 'Come on, let's get out of here before you start a damn war.'

'Wait.' Lady Sullivan's voice rang out again. 'Why did they stop?'

I stared at her, uncomprehending.

'Why did they stop fighting?' She asked the question casually, as if it were a trifling matter, but there was something about the look in her eye that made me answer.

'Er, because I told them to,' I said, baffled. 'I'm with the police.'

Lady Sullivan gave me a tiny frown then turned away. It appeared our conversation was over.

'Come on,' Tony hissed again, and marched away at considerable speed.

I did as he said, although my shorter legs struggled to keep up with his brisk stride. He didn't say a word until we'd passed under the intricate arch. I felt numerous pairs of eyes burning into the back of neck as we departed.

'What the fuck was that?' he said, as soon as we were out of the werewolves' quarter. 'What idiotic thoughts were going through your head that made you think you could confront a pair of brawling werewolves? I told you,' he ground out, 'I told you that we didn't get involved in supe matters.'

'I...' Shit. I dropped my head. 'The woman was running down the street covered in blood. I thought she was in trouble.'

'Why didn't you check with me first?'

'There wasn't time!' I protested.

He stopped in his tracks and glared at me, his blistering anger searing into me. 'The balance between us and the supes is incredibly delicate! We're here on their sufferance. The wrong action or word from us and Supernatural Squad will be shut down. We're hanging on by a thread as it is. No wonder you were sent here. You obviously don't have it in you to follow the simplest of instructions!'

I lifted my chin. I'd started to warm to the gruff old detective, and I'd thought the feeling was mutual. Now I'd undone all of that, but I wasn't ready to back down. 'If you're expecting me to apologise, I'm not sure that I can. If the same thing happened again, I don't think I'd react any differently. I saw someone in trouble and I went to help her. I don't see what's wrong with that!'

'There's nothing right with it, either!' His cheeks were mottled red. He cursed and spat on the ground. 'Go home. You've done enough for today. I'll leave it for a few hours then contact Lady Sullivan and smooth things over. But never – and I mean *never* – try anything like that again.' He glowered. 'Got that?'

'Yes.' I paused. Then, 'Yes, sir.'

If my acquiescence calmed him down, there wasn't any evidence of it. He stormed off, his spine straight and his arms swinging, the brown-paper bag containing our sandwiches thumping against his leg as he strode away. 'Tomorrow,' he snapped out over his shoulder.

I bit my lip. This had not been a good day. I twisted away and looked for a taxi to take me home.

Chapter Five

By the time Jeremy returned, I was considerably calmer. I'd spent a good hour pacing the flat, sorting through everything in my head, and I was beyond nervous about what the next day at Supernatural Squad would bring, but I felt more in control. I knew I'd been right to tell Tony that I'd do the same thing again. I hadn't gone into this job to stand back and let disaster happen, regardless of the bizarre culture and set of rules that had evolved around the supes and the police.

Several times I considered picking up the phone and speaking to Lucinda Barnes – and several times I stopped myself. I'd wait to see what Tony said tomorrow before I did anything else that might be considered rash.

At least Jeremy could be counted on for support. He poured me a large glass of wine, listened to my tale of woe and made all the right noises. Then he bundled me off towards the bathroom. 'Light a few candles and take a long soak,' he instructed. 'You'll feel better for it. I'll make dinner.'

'You're the best boyfriend in the world,' I told him. 'I don't know what I'd do without you.'

'Wither and die, I expect,' he said cheerfully. 'Go on. Off you go. Don't forget we're meeting Becky and Tom later for drinks.'

Damn it. I'd forgotten about that. They were Jeremy's friends, not mine, and the last thing I wanted was to put on my polite front and make tepid conversation with them. Crawling into bed and pulling the duvet over my head seemed a much better option.

'I don't think I'll be good company,' I said. 'And I've got a headache coming on. Why don't you go without me?'

He frowned. 'We planned this ages ago. They're looking forward to seeing you.'

I doubted that very much. 'Jeremy, I—'

'It's fine. I'll send our apologies.'

'No!' I shook my head. 'Just because I'm staying home doesn't mean you have to. Go out. Have fun.'

'I don't want to leave you alone when you're like this.'

I smiled at him. 'I'm a big girl. I'll be fine.'

He sighed. 'Alright.'

I reached up and kissed him. 'Thank you for being so understanding. I'll come next time. Promise.'

He gave me a grudging nod. 'Okay.'

I pushed away my flicker of guilt and kissed him again. The truth was that deep down we both knew he'd enjoy himself more without me. Conversation with his friends usually excluded me – not deliberately, but simply because they shared a history that I'd never be part of. This would be better for all of us.

***

When I finally emerged from the bathroom wrapped in a large fluffy robe, I knew I'd made the right decision. Jeremy had been right – the hot scented water had indeed made me feel a whole lot better – but also exhaustion was setting in. After an early night, I'd feel more prepared for whatever I was going to face at work the next day.

Unfortunately, the best-laid plans often come to naught. As soon as I sat down in front of the cumin-dusted cauliflower steak and chips that he'd cooked, Jeremy pointed to my phone. 'You got a message while you were soaking,' he said.

I forked some food into my mouth, reached across to pick it up and glanced at the screen. 'I don't recognise the number.' I thumbed it open and scanned it. 'It's from Tony,' I said slowly. 'He must have got my phone number from the Academy.' I stared at the message, then put down the phone. I wasn't sure what to think.

'What is it?'

'He said that he's sorry for coming down me on so hard today and that I should meet him tonight in the vampires' quarter.'

Jeremy stilled. 'And will you?'

I avoided meeting his gaze. 'I'll have to.'

'No, you don't have to. You're not on night shift, Emma, and you already said you weren't feeling well.'

I sighed. 'From what little I know of him, Tony's not the kind of guy who apologises easily. I messed up with the werewolves. If I can make amends by presenting myself appropriately to the vampires, maybe I can turn this rotation around. The vamps don't tend to come out during the day, so I'll have to go there at night if I'm to meet any of them.'

'If the vampires don't care what Supernatural Squad does, why does it matter if you meet them or not?'

I put down my knife and fork, reached across and squeezed his hand. 'I didn't choose this rotation and I don't want to do it, but I need to do well. Not just for the report that I'll get from Tony, but for my own professional pride.'

For a long moment, Jeremy didn't say anything. 'I don't suppose I can stop you going.'

'No.'

His jaw tightened. 'You'll take care? You won't go rushing after any vampires who run past you covered in blood? After all, that probably happens to them all the time.'

I laughed. 'I promise I won't. And I won't be out for long. I bet I'm home and tucked up in bed long before you return from the pub.'

'Hmm.' He rubbed his chin. 'What exactly will you bet on that?'

My eyes danced. 'Whatever you want.'

***

I dressed in jeans and a sweater, hoping they'd prove more suitable than my smart suit. I didn't want to stick out like a sore thumb in the centre of Soho. I also swigged down a strong coffee in the hope that the caffeine would keep me going; I didn't think that Tony would appreciate me spending the evening yawning in his face, not after he'd gone out of his way to reach out and say sorry.

Despite my earlier misgivings after visiting the werewolves, I was curious to compare them to the vampires. Before today, I'd barely given the supes any thought at all. I still didn't know if I'd learn anything useful on this rotation but, if nothing else, it was an opportunity to improve my diplomatic skills. And although I could tell that Jeremy was still irritated that I was putting work before him, he gave me a lingering kiss before I left. Things weren't so bad after all.

Tony's message had asked me to meet him at St Erbin's Church on the edge of the vampires' quarter. I guessed there was a reason for choosing that particular spot. It was consecrated ground, so it was all but guaranteed to be vampire free. Even with my woefully limited knowledge of the vamps, I knew that the Church – like the werewolves – despised their kind. I couldn't have told Jeremy, but I felt a ripple of excitement despite my fatigue.

I took the Tube to Piccadilly Circus and walked the rest of the way. The bright lights dimmed, and the crowds of tourists reduced in number as I drew closer to the quarter. Plenty of humans were drawn to this area, and lots of them relished getting close to the vampires at any time of night, but they were discouraged from staying for long. Sensible people stayed away; the more stupid ones occasionally became bloody snacks. Or so I'd heard.

Although I was aware that it was probably a daft thing to do, I'd wound a scarf round my neck before leaving home. There was no point in tempting fate and leaving myself unnecessarily exposed.

St Erbin's Church had been standing in this spot long before the vampires moved in and claimed Soho as their own. Although the tower was a more recent replacement, the rest of the structure had been there since the seventeenth century. Considering the seediness beyond, it seemed out of place even with its gothic overtones.

As I walked up to the gate into the small churchyard, I noted various posters pinned to the wall: Samaritans offering support to anyone seeking to join the ranks of the vamps; the NHS offering blood to those who'd lost several pints of their own; a few church groups offering salvation to anyone who'd been turned and now regretted it. It surprised and amused me that the vampires allowed these notices on the edge of their territory. Maybe they had a sense of humour; if they did, it would be more than I'd witnessed in the werewolves.

The iron gate creaked on its hinges when I pushed it open. As far as I could tell, there was no one waiting in the churchyard and no sign of Tony. I checked my watch. It wasn't quite ten o'clock, so I was a few minutes early.

I wandered over to a bench overlooking the graveyard. It had rained a lot recently and this area clearly didn't have good drainage. I didn't need to be able to see in the dark to know that my shoes were already caked in mud. I made a half-hearted effort at wiping the worst off on the grass verge and sat down.

Gazing out across the shadowy gravestones, I wondered what wisdom the dead would impart to me if they could. Probably that hanging around a graveyard in the dead of night wasn't a sensible thing to do. As the damp on the bench started to seep through my jeans, I reckoned they'd be right.

I waited five minutes. Then ten. Growing bored, I stood up and looked around on the off chance that Tony was waiting around the corner. A group of giggly women, dressed up to the nines and heading deeper into Soho, passed by. One of them sent me a curious look, but her friends were too absorbed in the excitement of their journey into vampire territory to notice me.

I shoved my hands into my pockets in a bid to keep warm and walked round to the front of the church. Perhaps Tony was waiting inside, where it was both dry and warm. I tugged at the heavy door handle and slid inside.

It wasn't much warmer inside the church. The empty pews seemed to mock me, and the candles dotted around the place cast long, flickering shadows that only added to the eeriness.

'Hello?' I called.

There was a loud thud from somewhere beyond the vestry, followed by an even louder, 'Fuck!' A moment later, a youngish man in his thirties wearing a dog collar appeared, rubbing his knee. He straightened up when he saw me, surprise flashing across his face. 'Good evening. Are you in need of sustenance, my child?'

'Uh...'

The vicar grimaced. 'Sorry. That sounded better in my head than when it came out. I'm new to all this, and I'm trying to appear professional. It doesn't always work. But it doesn't mean that I can't help you.' He looked at me kindly. 'Are you heading into Soho? You know that the vampires won't provide answers for you any more than God will. Quite the contrary, in fact.'

I smiled at him. I had the feeling that he didn't often get random people wandering in. 'I'm not looking for God or for vampires. I was supposed to be meeting someone here. A bloke in his late fifties?'

'No-one else has been here since the morning. Not to my knowledge, anyway.' He gestured to a pew. 'But why don't you sit down while you're waiting for him and we can have a chat? It's far safer in here than out there. This is a sanctuary, you know, and monsters abound outside at this time of night. I can put the kettle on, if you like. I'm William, by the way. William Knight.'

Reverend Knight was very earnest, and he obviously believed all the Church's hype about the monstrous nature of vampires. It wasn't as if I knew anything different, though I was prepared to keep an open mind until I was proved wrong.

'That's very kind of you,' I said. 'But no, thank you.' I twisted round, my ears twitching. I couldn't be sure, but I thought I'd heard something outside. 'That's probably him now. Nice to meet you.'

'Wait! What's your name?' he called out.

I opened my mouth to tell him, then thought about what Tony had said about names. I grinned. 'D'Artagnan.'

Reverend Knight seemed taken aback. I waved at him and walked out.

The wind was picking up, rattling through the bare trees and making the dry leaves that had collected at the corners of some of the gravestones skitter and swirl along the ground. I frowned and scanned the churchyard. I still couldn't see any sign of Tony. Even the streets were empty, with no more vampire-seeking groups wandering past in search of a good time.

I checked my watch again. It was twenty past ten. The thought that this was Tony's way of getting back at me for my misdemeanours with the werewolves itched at me. He hadn't struck me as the petty type, but I barely knew the man. Anything was possible. I'd give it until half past then I was going back home to my warm bed.

I wrapped my arms around myself and gazed up at the sky. It was cloudy, but it was possible to make out a few twinkling stars. I was squinting, wondering whether I was looking at the Milky Way or simply a passing aeroplane, when there was the sudden sound of a twig cracking to my left. I stiffened and glanced over. Nothing.

Frowning, I ambled over to the source of the sound. I didn't think I'd imagined it. Then I heard heavy breathing.

Freaked out now, I spun around. Where was that coming from? I clenched my jaw. I was being ridiculously jumpy – it was probably a cat. Maybe even a fox. I couldn't see anything or anyone. If I was really that worried, I could hop inside the church again. In fact...

Pain exploded in the back of my skull. I cried out, falling forward to my knees while white lights flashed in my eyes from the blow.

My fingers clawed at the ground, scrabbling in the dirt. I coughed, spitting blood, barely registering the shadow that grew from over my shoulder.

I tried to twist my head to see what – or rather who – it was. Before I could, whoever had hit me the first time did it again, smacking something heavy across the other side of my skull. This time I went face first into the ground, receiving a mouthful of dirt. I didn't even get a chance to scream.

Screeching agony was overtaking everything, and it was difficult to think clearly. Something grabbed hold of a hank of my hair and pulled my head up. My vision was blurred; no matter how hard I tried to focus, I could make out little more than the dim shape of a figure looming over me. He spoke – I was sure it was a man – but the ringing in my ears made it impossible to hear either the words or to recognise the voice.

I croaked and licked my lips, my fingers reaching desperately for my pocket. If I could just get to my phone, maybe I could get some help.

'Please,' I whispered.

The figure moved and gave a strange grating sound. It took a moment for me to realise that it was laughter. It sounded like it was coming from a long way off. Something flashed in front of my eyes. I barely had the chance to work out that it was a knife before the scarf round my neck was yanked away and the tip of the blade pressed into my soft flesh.

I felt it sliding in, but there was nothing I could do about it. My carotid artery, I thought dimly. I half gasped, feeling the hot blood – *my* hot blood – soak my skin. And then everything went dark.

Chapter Six

The first thing I heard was the buzzing. It tickled my eardrums at first then, as I gained consciousness, it became more insistent – and more annoying.

I moved slightly and there was a strange rustle. What the hell was I lying on? It felt like plastic, or rubber sheeting perhaps. There was an acrid tinge to the air that definitely smelled of rotten eggs, and there was an unpleasant taste of ash in my mouth. This didn't make any sense.

It took more effort than it should have done to open my eyes. It was like they'd been glued together and I virtually had to peel open my eyelids. I blinked, trying to adjust my vision. I was so *hot* – and what was this crap around me? I plucked at it. I'd been right: it was definitely some sort of white plastic sheeting, but it was singed and burnt like someone had taken a flamethrower to it.

I sat up, shoving it to one side. That was when I realised I was naked.

I jerked with such force that I fell off the table and landed with a heavy thump on the cold, linoleum-covered floor. I groaned and looked around. It wasn't a table, it was a metal gurney. That was when the memory of the attack came flooding back to me.

I must be in hospital. It was the only thing that made sense. The incessant buzzing was coming from an overhead strip light that cast a stark light around the room. I licked my lips and tried to call out to alert a passing doctor or nurse but I could only croak. If I wanted help, I'd have to go and look for it.

Staggering to my feet, I grabbed the remnants of the plastic and wrapped it around myself. This was a strange hospital room: for one thing, the bed wasn't a proper bed, it was just a slab. And there was no IV line or comforting ECG beeping next to me, although I could see a metal tray with various implements lying neatly across it. Several scalpels and ... I stared. Was that a rib spreader?

I backed up, colliding with another metal trolley and sending various bits and pieces clattering to the floor. Without thinking, I bent down to pick them up. When I saw the flames flickering around my toes, I let out a brief shriek and frantically slapped at them to put them out.

My heart was hammering against my ribcage. What in bejesus was going on? I straightened up. With shaking fingers, I touched the side of my neck where I'd felt the knife pierce my skin and slice through my artery. There was nothing there. No mark, no bump. It wasn't even sore. I reached up to the back of my head where I'd been thumped. There was nothing there either.

Breathing hard, and growing more and more convinced that this was some sort of crazy-arsed nightmare, I looked around for some kind of clue as to where I was and what had happened.

My gaze fell on the clipboard hanging on the side of the gurney. I grabbed it and stared at the words: *Jane Doe. DOA. Approximate age: 30. Identifying features: mole on left thigh. Apparent cause of death: exsanguination from knife wound on throat.*

The clipboard slid out of my hand and fell to the floor.

Dizzy and disorientated, it was a few moments before coherent thought returned to my brain. What was obvious now was that the plastic I'd wrapped myself in was the remnants of a body bag. What was also obvious was that someone somewhere had made a terrible mistake. I most definitely was not dead. I poked myself again just to be sure. Nope. Not a ghost. I straightened my shoulders. Heads were going to roll for this.

The door to the small room opened and a white-coated woman with dark hair tied in a tight bun strolled in, whistling tunelessly. She walked up to the gurney, stared down at it and blinked. Then her head slowly rose and her eyes met mine. Her mouth opened in a silent scream.

'Hi,' I said.

Her jaw worked uselessly.

'I'm Emma.' I glanced at the ID clipped to her coat. 'You're Dr Hawes? Have you been a pathologist for long? I gestured at myself. 'Because you might need some re-training.'

I'd never seen anyone look so pale. 'You were dead,' she whispered.

'Clearly not.'

She lifted her chin. 'No. You were definitely dead.' She shook herself, her hand automatically going to the small gold cross around her neck. Her gaze drifted to my neck and I knew that it wasn't the knife wound she was searching for – it was fang marks. But I'd never met a vampire in my life and, even if my attacker had been of the blood-guzzling variety, it took far more than one bite to turn someone into a vamp. Even I knew that much. You had drink at least half a cup of the blood of the vamp who bit you to be turned.

'You made a mistake,' I told her.

'No. I didn't.' She remained where she was. I had the sneaking suspicion that she was actually frozen to the spot. 'You were definitely dead. Deader than dead.'

'Then how do you explain this?' I asked. My voice hardened. 'And where the fuck are my clothes?'

Her tongue darted out, wetting her lips. 'Stay there.' She turned and almost ran out of the door.

Fuck that. I tightened my grip around the body bag-cum-latest-fashion-item and marched after her. I wasn't going to let Dr Hawes out of my sight, not until I got my stuff back and received some sort of explanation – and apology – for whatever had happened to me.

She moved quickly down the corridor and into a room on the right. I followed. Unfortunately for the good doctor, she didn't realise that I was behind her. When I coughed, she jumped about a foot in the air. 'Don't come any closer!' she shouted.

I held up my hands and the body bag slipped. Adjusting myself, I tried again to show her that I meant no harm. 'I'm not going to hurt you,' I said, exasperated. 'I just want to find out what happened and get out of here.'

'That makes two of us.' She picked up a brown manila folder and thrust it at me. 'You. Were. Dead.'

I sat down on a chair and flipped open the folder. When I saw what it contained, I drew in a sharp breath.

'We wouldn't normally work so quickly on a case like yours,' Dr Hawes told me. 'But due to the location of your body, and the fact that you were obviously murdered, you were moved to the front of the queue.'

I didn't speak. I couldn't tear my eyes away from the contents of the file.

'I didn't make a mistake,' she said. 'And I wasn't even the first person to declare you dead.'

All I could do was offer the tiniest of nods. The first document in the file was a printout of various photos. It was clear they'd been taken at St Erbin's Church.

'When were these taken?' I asked, my voice barely audible as I stared at my very own corpse lying across two graves. It wasn't pretty. My eyes were glassy and bulging, and I was soaked in blood. All the photographic evidence pointed to one single fact – that I had indeed been dead. As the lady had said, deader than dead.

She pointed to the time stamp. 'Just before midnight.'

'Last night?'

Dr Hawes nodded.

My eyes flicked to the clock on the wall. Assuming it was correct, it was now a cat's whisker before 11am. That meant I'd been out of it for twelve hours before I'd been ... resurrected. I touched the pulse point on my wrist. My heart was definitely still beating.

'May I?' she asked.

Swallowing, I held out my arm. With only the briefest tremor, she checked my pulse. 'Hmm. It sounds normal to me.' Her brow furrowed.

'I'm not a vampire,' I said unnecessarily.

'I know,' she answered quickly. 'I've had a vamp in here before, and you're not one of them.'

'How do you know?'

'You're not pretty enough.' She smiled, the colour starting to return to her cheeks. 'And the heart rate of vampires, even newly turned vampires, is very slow when compared to humans. Werewolves' heart rates are very fast. Yours is normal.'

I gazed at the photographs. 'It doesn't seem possible.'

'You don't remember anything?' Professional interest was replacing her shock. For my part, I just felt sick.

'I remember getting attacked,' I replied. 'I didn't see my attacker's face. I don't know who it was, but I remember what it felt like.'

She was openly curious. 'And?'

'It fucking hurt,' I said frankly.

She met my eyes. I turned away, unable to cope with the sympathy in her gaze. Then she snapped her fingers. 'There is something that might help,' she said suddenly. She grinned. 'Come with me.'

She took off, marching out of the room and down the corridor. I padded after her, the half-ruined body bag that was covering my modesty flapping around my ankles.

'The desk is usually manned,' she said, as much to herself as to me. 'But Dean is taking advantage of a quiet period and having an early lunch.' We turned a corner to where the morgue's small front desk was located.

'Where exactly are we?'

'Fitzwilliam Manor Hospital,' she answered. She went to the computer and started tapping at the keyboard. Then she paused and looked up. 'Sorry. I was too shocked to take in your name the first time around. What is it again?'

'Emma,' I told her. 'Emma Bellamy.'

'You can call me Laura. I think we deserve to be on first-name terms now, don't you?' She tapped away some more then gave a crow of delight. 'Here. You're right here.'

I joined her and peered at the screen. 'Is that...?'

Laura nodded proudly. 'Yep. CCTV. It's the footage of where your body was.' She coughed. 'Where you were. Not your, uh, body.'

I squinted. This wasn't the time for semantics. 'Why does a morgue need CCTV?'

Laura made a face. 'We've had lab assistants in the past who haven't been entirely respectful towards the bodies. And when I say they weren't respectful, I mean we've had assistants who—'

I hastily interrupted her. 'I don't need to know.'

She glanced at me. 'Yeah. Fair enough.' She swivelled the screen so I could get a better look. 'Anyway, if we rewind the footage maybe we'll get some clues about what happened.'

I wasn't sure I wanted to watch; unfortunately, I knew I had to. I put my hand out, steadied myself on the desk and drew in a breath. 'Let's do it.'

Laura clicked on the footage. 'There,' she said. 'That's you.'

2.16am. I was already in the body bag so thankfully I didn't have to look at my corpse again. I watched as I was wheeled into a narrow room. There were several shelves and what looked like several other bodies. I shuddered. 'Where's that?'

'The cold chamber. Fortunately not the negative one.'

'Pardon?'

Laura explained. 'We have two cold chambers for storage. One is maintained at four degrees. That temperature doesn't halt decomposition, but it slows it down. It gives us time to conduct post-mortems, or to hold bodies until families can collect them for their own funeral arrangements. The other chamber is for when bodies remain unidentified and we need to hold them for longer. It's essentially a freezer.'

Goosebumps rose across my skin and I rubbed my arms. I felt cold just thinking about it.

Laura ran the footage forward. 'There,' she said, jabbing at the screen. We watched her enter the room and slide out my body bag again. She unzipped it, allowing the camera a clear glimpse of my unnaturally still body. She paused at my face for a moment and then zipped up the bag. 'That's me coming to get you to prep you for the post-mortem. I didn't need to feel your pulse to know that you were dead.' She whistled. 'Baby, you were *gone*. I was just double checking that I had the right corpse before I moved you.'

Something else I didn't want to think about too closely. 'Post-mortem? I thought it was pretty obvious how I'd died,' I said, frowning.

She shrugged. 'You were murdered. A post-mortem is protocol.'

I knew that. It didn't prevent me from shivering.

We watched as she wheeled dead Emma from one room into another. She busied herself getting her equipment ready, then the door opened and a man popped his head round the door.

'That's Dean,' Dr Hawes explained. She sounded eager now. 'He was telling me I had a phone call.'

'Related to me?'

'Nah. The geriatrics ward. They wanted to confirm that the body of one of their deceased patients had been moved.'

On the screen Laura nodded and walked out of the room, leaving my bagged corpse on its own. She smiled at me with morbid excitement. 'Five minutes later, I walked back in and you were standing up. So this is the part where things are going to get really interesting.'

My stomach was churning. 'Is there any chance that I was still alive? That I was just in a kind of coma or stasis or something, and nobody noticed?'

'No. There is no chance.' She ticked off her fingers while keeping her gaze on the screen. 'Paramedics saw your body. A doctor signed you off as dead. Last night's morgue crew checked you over when you came in. There are the photos.' She sucked in a breath. 'And now there's this.'

We both stared. There was no denying what we were seeing. The body bag – *my* body bag – was on fire. The stench of rotten eggs that had been in the room had been from me. Sulphur. Or rather...

'Brimstone,' I whispered. 'Fire and brimstone.' My mouth felt dry. 'Rewind the tape. Play it again.'

Laura swallowed. 'On it.'

We watched again. To all intents and purposes, it looked as if my corpse simply spontaneously combusted. Flames appeared out of nowhere, licking upwards through the white plastic from my head to my toes. It was only when the fire had flickered out that I began to twitch, then move, sit up and fall gracelessly off the gurney.

'I've seen a lot of shit in here,' Laura told me. 'But I've never seen anything like that before.'

Chapter Seven

'You were brought in with nothing on you. No bag, no wallet, no phone. Whoever killed you took whatever you had, presumably along with the murder weapon because it's not been found anywhere nearby. Your clothes are ruined as well – they've already been sent to the incinerator.' Laura looked me up and down. 'You can't walk out of here like that.'

'No kidding.'

She smiled. 'Fortunately, I can provide you with an entire wardrobe.'

I pulled a face. 'You mean dead people's clothing.'

'That's not something to get squeamish about,' she told me.

Probably not, but I had to get squeamish about something. I couldn't pretend that any of this was normal. I sighed. Unfortunately, I didn't have a whole lot of choice. 'Dead people's clothing it is.'

'I should report all of this, of course,' Laura said. I started to shake my head in alarm, but she was already there. 'However, I reckon you've got enough problems as it is. The faster you get out of here the better. Someone tried to kill you, Emma. Hell, someone *did* kill you. We can worry about the whys and wherefores of your resurrection later. Right now, you need to work out who sliced open your throat so you can stop them from doing it again. There's no guarantee that you'll wake up a second time.'

I couldn't deny that thought had been bothering me, too. 'I might have been in the wrong place at the wrong time. Or I might have been targeted.' I clenched my teeth together so tightly it hurt. 'The best way to find out who did this to me is to pretend I'm actually dead. If I go home, I might put Jeremy in danger.'

'Is that your husband?'

'Boyfriend.' I ran a hand through my hair. 'He'll be out of his mind with worry, but I can't risk his life too.'

'You were probably just unlucky and were targeted by a mugger.'

'Probably.' Except it didn't feel like an opportunistic crime. It felt like I was killed for a reason. It felt like it was personal. I shuddered. 'Once I know for sure, I can tell everyone I'm alright. I'll have to hope that Jeremy understands.'

'Do you have other family?'

'My parents are dead. I've got no siblings.' I thought about my uncle. I'd barely spoken to him in years. I sent him a Christmas card every year out of a sense of duty – after all, he'd taken me in when I was nothing but a snotty-nosed kid. But he'd always kept his distance and we weren't close. He wasn't a bad guy, but he wasn't a family man either. This wasn't the time to bother him.

Laura squeezed my arm. 'I'll hold the fort here. I won't manage it for more than a couple of days, but I can postpone your post-mortem and make up something about other cases when the police come calling. It actually helps that they weren't able to identify you immediately. With nothing else to go on, your case will be put on a back burner.' She nodded decisively. 'And if the worst happens, I can always pretend to lose your body for a day or two. I can't keep it up forever, but it'll buy you some time.' She hesitated. 'I should draw some blood from you.'

'To test for vampirism or signs that I'm turning furry?' I guessed.

'Yeah.' She looked apologetic. 'There's no sign that you are, but then I've never seen a corpse reanimate before.' She peered at me. 'You don't feel the sudden urge to eat brains, do you?'

I tried to smile. 'No. But I could murder a cheese sandwich.'

'Then you're absolutely fine.'

We exchanged looks. 'You're the only other person in the world that knows what's happened,' I said quietly. 'If this is only temporary and I drop dead again in three days or something...'

'I'm sure you won't.'

'But if I do,' I persisted, 'keep this to yourself, if you can. Chalk it up to the weirdness of life or something, and forget about me. I don't want Jeremy knowing that I didn't go to him for help. And I don't want my corpse dissected by government scientists.'

Her gaze was solemn. 'Your secret will be safe with me. But keep me posted with what you discover. And let me know if you start feeling ill.'

I nodded. 'I will. I promise.' I bit my lip. 'Thank you. Not many people would have dealt with this as well as you have.'

'I might say the same thing about you, Emma.'

I managed a smile. 'It's still only early days.'

***

Less than an hour later, I walked out of the front doors of Fitzwilliam Manor Hospital wearing jeans that were so tight they could have been sprayed on, an over-sized man's T-shirt with a warm sweater and a large puffy jacket on top, and scuffed trainers on my feet. It was an interesting get-up but it would have to do for now.

Surprisingly, I felt full of energy. There were no strange aches and pains, and there was nothing to indicate that a few hours earlier I'd been at the rainbow bridge. I had no memory of what being dead was like. There was no tunnel with a pinprick of light at the end, no harp-strumming angels, no sign of my parents.

I sucked in a sharp breath. This was not the time to get maudlin. Somehow, I'd survived my own murder. The only way forward now was to solve it to ensure that it didn't happen again – and that meant staying focused and returning to the scene of the crime.

Despite my feeble protests, Laura had emptied her purse and given me all her loose cash. It wasn't a huge amount, but it would keep me going for a day or two. I hopped onto the Underground, travelling a mere three stops until I reached Piccadilly yet again. Then I retraced my steps from the night before.

Everything looked very different in daylight. The glitz and glamour of night time had yielded to a seedier sheen, although the big screen at the Piccadilly Circus corner continued its incessant flickering of images, and there were plenty of people around.

Once I left the main tourist area, however, the crowds thinned and my apprehension grew. My eyes flicked from left to right as I examined the faces of the other passers-by. Was it one of these people who'd slit my throat? Were any of them surprised to see me? I stared so hard at one man, whose clothes and expression looked shady enough to belong in hell, that he waggled his eyebrows at me seductively. No. This was not a come-on.

I ploughed on, winding my way through the narrow streets until the spire of St Erbin's Church was visible. Rather than stop and gaze at it, I forced my feet to keep moving. If I stopped now, I'd never manage to move again. Despite my lack of fatigue or injury, this wasn't easy; I was trembling from head to toe and it took every bit of will power I possessed to walk up to the church gate and push it open. I can do this, I told myself. I *have* to do this.

Police tape cordoned off a large area of the graveyard. It flapped gently in the breeze, an unpleasant indication of what had happened. My mouth was dry, but I kept going and ducked under the tape. My feet squelched in the wet mud as I made my way to the slightly firmer grass. I didn't stop until I was standing next to a patch of discoloured ground. There. That was my blood. That was where I'd died.

I crouched down, doing my best to remain dispassionate. I didn't do a very good job. I reached out, brushing the sticky blood that coated the grass with my shaking fingertips. It wasn't even completely dry. I swallowed hard. We'd covered bloodwork at the Academy and, while I only knew the basics, I still reckoned that from the size of the bloodstain I'd lost a good six pints. Whoever had slit my throat must have ended up covered in it.

I raised my head and glanced at the nearest gravestone. Thomas Santorini. Born 1826, died 1899. Sorry, I mouthed. I didn't mean to sully your resting spot.

'Who are you?'

I jerked upwards at the sound of the cold voice then I spun round, ready to defend myself to the death again if I had to. Standing less than five feet away was a man. He was a few inches taller than me, with inky-dark hair, liquid black eyes and high cheekbones. His skin gleamed; if that wasn't enough of a clue, he was coat-less despite the cold February air. I gaped at his immaculate white shirt with its frilly cuffs.

'Vampire,' I murmured. I lifted my chin. 'This is consecrated ground. What are you doing here?'

He gave a mild snort. 'There is no such thing as consecrated ground. We go where we please.' He waved a hand. 'Even in daylight.' He took a step forward. 'And right now, this is where I please.' His voice hardened and his eyes raked my face before dropping briefly to my exposed neck. 'I will repeat my question. Who are you?'

'I'm with Supernatural Squad.' It wasn't really a lie. 'A woman died here last night, and I want to make sure that supes weren't involved.' I met his gaze, challenging him to argue with me. I had more of a right to be here than he did – and if he was looking for a fight, I'd give him one. I could do with the distraction.

'There are only three humans currently with Supernatural Squad,' he said. 'And none of them are you.'

He didn't know as much as he thought he did. 'I'm a trainee detective on temporary rotation,' I told him, with only a faint sneer.

The vampire quirked an eyebrow. 'Are you indeed? And they let you out on your own?'

'Apparently so.' I glared at him. 'Why are you here?'

'For the same reason as you. A woman died here. I've been ... tasked with finding out more. Sudden violent deaths aren't good PR for our kind.'

Except it wasn't a vampire who'd killed me. A vampire wouldn't have used a blade. 'Well,' I said briskly, 'you can stand down. Supernatural Squad will take things from here.'

His gaze flickered with amusement. 'Will they?'

I opened my mouth to answer him but, before I could, the main church door opened and Reverend Knight appeared. 'Hey!' he called sharply. 'Stop disturbing that spot! The police—' He looked at me and his voice faltered. 'You.' He paled. 'But—'

I interrupted before he could say anything else. 'Reverend Knight. Good to see you again. I'm just scanning the area for evidence or clues that last night's crew might have missed.'

He didn't move a muscle. I wondered whether he was the person who'd found my body. Probably. It had to be quite a shock seeing me again. He should try walking in my shoes.

I looked from him to the vampire and back again. 'Well,' I said briskly, 'I've seen all that I need to for now.' I raised my eyebrows at Reverend Knight. 'I'm with the police, Reverend. Can I come inside and ask you a few questions?'

I wasn't foolish enough to wait for his answer; instead, I took advantage of his shock and ducked under the police tape again. I needed to interrogate him before he recovered his equilibrium and refused to talk to me.

I'd barely taken three steps when the vamp's hand shot out and curled round my forearm. I stiffened at his touch.

'I think you and I need to talk,' he said.

I snatched my arm back, wrenching it away with surprising strength. 'That makes one of us then.' I sniffed, and sent a meaningful look in Knight's direction before walking into the church. The reverend stumbled in after me. Thankfully, the vampire chose not to join us. Small mercies.

'I ... I ... don't understand,' Reverend Knight stammered, once the heavy church door had closed behind us. 'I thought I saw you... I thought you were... I...' He sat down on the nearest pew, clutching at the armrest for support.

'I know what you saw,' I said. 'And I'd like to be able to explain it but right now I can't.' I injected a mysterious edge into my voice, hoping that Knight would draw his own conclusions and stop freaking out.

'You said you were with the police.' His words were slow as he did his best to come up with a rational solution for what he'd witnessed. 'Is this some kind of sting? An undercover police operation? Because you were dead. I was sure you were dead.' He shook his head, whether in disbelief or amazement I wasn't sure. He reached out and poked me gently, checking that I was solid and not a figment of his imagination.

'As I told you,' I said without flinching, 'I can't explain it right now.'

'Of course.' He blinked rapidly. 'Of course you can't.' He inhaled deeply. 'I spoke to your colleagues last night and told them I hadn't seen anything or anyone. You and I met and chatted. I left the church an hour or so later to head home, and that's when I saw you lying on the ground.' He lifted his eyes to mine. 'You were very convincing.'

I put my finger to my lips in an elaborate gesture of sharing a secret. In theory, he could be a suspect; he certainly had the means to kill me, if not the motive. However, he would have been thoroughly questioned last night and I didn't sense any sort of threat from him. The fact that he'd deluded himself into thinking I'd deliberately faked my own death as part of some crazy police plot helped with that. It's fascinating what we can make ourselves believe when we need to.

'Did you see anyone else hanging around the church last night?' I asked, focusing on facts rather than forced delusions.

He didn't hesitate. 'No. Only you.'

'And afterwards? After you found me?'

'There was no one. I checked your pulse and couldn't feel anything, so I called an ambulance straight away. The sirens drew a small crowd. As soon as the paramedics went to work on you, I came in here to give them space. The police spoke to me, but I wasn't much help. You'd only given me a nickname and they had nothing else to go on.'

I gazed intently at him. Reverend Knight might have been only feet away when I was being murdered, but he hadn't seen a thing. He knew even less than I did. 'Thank you for your time,' I said finally.

Relief spasmed across his face; he couldn't wait to get rid of me. He was in shock right now, but that shock would turn to fear as soon as I left. And quite possibly fury. My very existence would threaten him.

He glanced around and then, his voice quavering, said, 'Him. Outside. Is this to do with him?'

'The vampire?'

Reverend Knight flinched.

I thought of Tony and his text message. 'No,' I said quietly. 'This is all about humans.'

Chapter Eight

Further investigation of the crime site would have to wait until I was certain of solitude. At this point, it didn't really matter – it was obvious where I had to go next.

The only reason I'd been at St Erbin's Church was because Tony had lured me there. Then he'd failed to show up. It didn't take a detective to know that he was suspect numero uno – a child would have sussed that. I might not want to believe that he'd killed me, but I wasn't naïve enough to think that the police were all shining heroes. Corruption existed everywhere.

The only thing that gave me pause was lack of motive. Try as I might, I couldn't think of any reason why the old detective would want me dead. One minor werewolf fuck-up wasn't sufficient reason for murder. Still, I knew I'd learn a great deal from the expression on his face when I walked in through the door of Supernatural Squad. It was quite possible that I'd solve my own death within the next ten minutes.

I was also aware that I should be careful. Tony might well try to attack me again. At this time of day, though, both Liza and Fred would also be in the building. It wasn't remotely credible that all three of them could be involved.

I furled and unfurled my fists as I ran through various scenarios in my head. Whatever happened next, I was ready for it.

I strode into the Supernatural Squad building, marched down the corridor and burst into the main room on the ground floor. Liza glanced up with nothing more than vague interest; Fred didn't bother removing his eyes from the television screen.

'Where's Tony?' I demanded.

'He's not come in today,' Liza said. 'I thought he was out with you.'

I stared at her. She didn't look anything more than mildly surprised to see me – and neither did she look like she was lying about Tony.

'Fred, have you seen Tony today?' I demanded.

He barely stirred. 'Nope.'

I stalked forward until I was standing between the sofa and the television. With considerable reluctance, Fred met my eyes.

'I have not seen him,' he said, enunciating every word. He sighed. 'Look, I know you're full of enthusiasm and excitement, and you want to do great things, but this,' he flicked his hand around the room, 'this is what life is like in Supernatural Squad. You should enjoy the peace and quiet while you can.'

I stayed exactly where I was. 'Have you phoned Tony to see where he is?'

With what appeared to be a great effort, he pushed himself up to a sitting position. 'A woman was killed last night at St Erbin's Church,' he said. 'A Jane Doe. He's probably over at CID right now, arguing why we should get the case. He'll lose.'

I couldn't stop myself. 'You don't care that some poor person was killed right on the edge of our territory?'

For the first time I saw a flicker of emotion on Fred's face. 'Of course I care. But if it was a supe that did it, then the supes themselves will find the perp and deal with him – or her. If it was a human, CID will take the case from us. There's nothing for us to do. There never is.'

I ground my teeth together and counted to ten. 'I've lost my phone,' I said. 'Is there a landline I can use?'

Liza shrugged. 'Over on that desk. Your temporary Supe Squad warrant card is there as well. It arrived this morning.'

I nodded my thanks. She dropped her gaze back to her magazine and Fred slumped back into the sofa. So much for London's finest.

I found the phone under a pile of papers on the desk near the window and picked up the warrant card. The number was the same one I'd been given when I entered the Academy, but the symbol was different: the card was emblazoned with a small red crucifix on the bottom and a silver crown at the top. The card still had 'Trainee' stamped across it in big red letters. So much, so different. I slipped it into my pocket. At least I now had some form of ID.

I tapped my mouth thoughtfully, picked up the receiver and dialled my own number on the bizarre off-chance that my murderer would answer. It didn't take long to hear the click that told me my phone was turned off. Oh well – it had been a long shot. I glanced at the helpful list of numbers taped to the desk. It was time to get creative and call someone else.

'Hi,' I said into the receiver, as soon as the operator answered. 'I'm looking for one of your detective trainees, Molly Brigant. I need to speak to her urgently.'

'Who is calling?'

I glanced over at Liza's name tag. 'Liza Faulkner at Supe Squad.'

Liza's head snapped up and she frowned. I gave her a vague smile.

'One moment please.'

'What are you doing?' Liza hissed.

I covered the mouthpiece with my hand. 'I told you,' I said. 'I've lost my phone. I need to speak to my friend as soon as possible, and using your name seems the best way to go about it. It'll be fine.'

'Why don't you use your own damned name?'

Because at least one person believes that I'm dead and, right now, I don't want to dissuade them from that belief.

'You're more likely to be put through,' I told her.

The expression on Liza's face put me in mind of sour milk. Fortunately, I didn't have to continue explaining myself because Molly came on the line. 'Hello?' she said uncertainly.

I breathed out. Praise be. 'Molly, it's me.'

'Emma? What on earth are you doing calling me? I was told it was someone else.'

'I've lost my phone. Long story. Look, I need to ask you a favour. It's important.'

'Go on,' she said, confused.

'A woman was killed at St Erbin's Church last night. It's just on the edge of Soho. I need you to find out whether CID has been tasked with the investigation, and what details they already have on the murder. In particular, if there are any suspects. I know you're busy, but I wouldn't ask if I had any choice.'

Molly let out a short laugh. 'Right now I'm reading a manual on search and seizure regulations. I could do with the distraction. I'll nose around. Let me see what I can find out and I'll get back to you.'

'Thank you so much.' I read off the Supe Squad number and she noted it down.

'Anyway, how are things with you, Ems? You sound different. Is Supernatural Squad really all that horrific?'

'Honestly, Molly? I couldn't even begin to explain. Don't tell anyone you've spoken to me.'

'What? Why?'

I couldn't give her a quick answer, so I played chicken and pretended I'd not heard her before I mumbled a farewell and hung up.

'We won't get the case,' Fred said. 'There's no point looking into it.'

'It won't do any harm.' I wrinkled my nose. 'What's Tony's number?'

'Are you going to call him and pretend to be me again?' Liza asked. The corners of her mouth turned down disapprovingly.

No, I didn't want him to know I was in the office. 'Why don't *you* call him? Find out where he is.' I paused. 'And don't tell him I'm here.'

Her eyes narrowed. 'What exactly is going on?'

'Please, Liza?'

She watched me for a moment. 'You're very strange.'

I couldn't disagree. 'Will you call him?' I persisted.

She threw up her hands. 'Alright.' She reached for her mobile, fiddled with it for a moment then held it to her ear. 'His phone's turned off. It's not ringing.'

I swallowed. 'Is that normal?'

'No.' She jabbed another set of numbers and tried again. 'He's not picking up his home phone either.' She looked at me. 'What aren't you telling us?'

'Nothing. Do you have his address? If he doesn't show up, I'll nip round to his house and see if he's there. Maybe he's just not picking up the phone – although he's probably at CID, like Fred said. The thing is, I've got some paperwork that needs signing off.'

It was clear that Liza didn't believe me. 'You seem like a nice person, Emma, and I'm sure if Tony were here, he wouldn't mind you knowing where he lives. But until he tells me otherwise, I don't feel comfortable passing information on. I can give you his mobile number if you want to call it again later. He might pick up in an hour or two.'

She was loyal; that was a tick in both Liza and Tony's favour. It didn't particularly help my cause, but I knew that I couldn't argue with her.

'Okay,' I said. 'I'll take his number for now and wait here until he puts in an appearance.' I gave her a brief smile to show there were no hard feelings.

Liza scribbled it down on a scrap of paper. 'Is this his only mobile?' I asked.

Fred shrugged. Liza pursed her lips. 'He probably has another phone. We're supposed to have separate ones for work and home. But I don't know what the other number is.'

I rubbed my arms. Without my own phone to compare the records, I couldn't tell if this number matched the one on the text message that had lured me to the graveyard. It wasn't like I possessed a photographic memory, more's the pity. Had Tony taken my phone after the attack so that it looked like I'd been mugged – and so he could also delete his text?

'What's going on, Emma?' Liza folded her arms and frowned at me.

I avoided her gaze. I had to come up with something to explain my odd behaviour and my obvious anxiety to them. I certainly couldn't tell them the truth – I barely believed it myself – but I had to give them something.

'The reason I've been sent here on rotation is because I fucked up. This is my last chance to make things right or I'll be out on my ear and I'll never make detective.'

Even Fred perked up at that.

'I think I'm onto something that will turn my fortunes around,' I continued. 'In fact, it'll turn all of our fortunes around.' My murder was probably enough to get Supe Squad shut down for good, so in that sense I wasn't lying. 'But I don't want anyone to know what I'm up to. So if anyone comes looking for me, no matter who they are, can you tell them you've not seen me? I know it's a big ask and that—'

'Yeah,' Fred said. 'No problem.'

Liza pursed her lips but then she nodded. I must have looked surprised because she explained, 'We've been where you are. If this is what you need, Emma, we'll do our best. I didn't give you Tony's address out of respect for him. I can extend the same courtesy to you and stay mum on your behalf too. You should know that the only people who've escaped Supe Squad in the past have either died or retired – but hope springs eternal.' She gave me a meaningful look.

'Sooner or later, you'll need to tell us what's really happening. We don't know you well enough to trust you completely.'

'I'll tell you everything as soon as I can. I promise.' I lifted the receiver to make one last call. I knew this number by heart, and I also knew that at this time of day it would go straight to voicemail. Big brave policewoman, that was me.

'Hi, Jeremy. I'm going to be away for a couple of days for a work thing. I'll be too busy to get in touch and I've lost my phone, so don't call. Look after yourself and don't eat too much junk food. Big kisses.' I put down the receiver.

Liza was watching me. 'I hope you know what you're doing,' she said.

I smiled confidently.

I didn't have a fucking clue.

***

Tony declined to show up. As I waited, my tension grew with every passing minute. To pass the time, I Googled 'resurrection' and 'supes', and searched the police database for any similar attacks on women. I came up short on every front.

I checked my pulse every twenty minutes or so, and every time it was still there. Liza caught me on more than one occasion but, while her eyes clouded with deepening suspicion, she didn't utter a peep.

We were only interrupted once, when an American tourist who'd lost his wallet dropped by to see if it had been handed in. Unsurprisingly, it hadn't been. As the bloke with the twang from the Southern states wouldn't give Fred any more information to go on about where he'd last seen it, there was little we could do.

'He was probably in one of the vamp strip joints,' Liza said disdainfully.

'There are vamp strip joints?'

She raised her eyebrows in a particularly patronising fashion. I couldn't blame her; I was starting to feel that up till now I'd led a very sheltered life.

'There are very few real vampires in them,' she told me. 'Most of the strippers are human women hoping to catch some highly placed vampire's eye and get themselves turned. Not that you'd catch someone like Lord Horvath frequenting such an establishment.'

I had a sudden image of the head of the vampires as a stern old bloke with a grey moustache and a neatly trimmed beard who would never demean himself by lolling around a bar, let alone one filled with near-naked women.

'Yeah,' Fred agreed. 'The last thing he needs is to go trolling for birds.' Birds?

'Sorry,' he continued, seeing my expression. 'Women.'

'Is that because he's already in a committed relationship?' I asked.

He barked a laugh. 'No! Because he's got women of all ages and types throwing themselves at him all day long. The man's virtually got his own harem.'

Oh. That made more sense.

'The vamps are all about fun,' Fred said. 'And the wolves are all about seriousness and stiff upper lips.' There was a wistful note to his tone. I cast him a sidelong glance and wondered if he had a hankering to be turned. I thought he seemed far too lethargic to fit in with either group.

'How old is Lord Horvath?'

'About seventy, give or take. And no,' Liza continued, before I could ask my next question, 'he's not immortal. Vamps live for longer than we do, but they can't avoid the circle of life forever. Their lifespan is about double ours.'

'What about the wolves? How long do they live?'

Her brow creased. 'It's difficult to say. Best guess is about the same as us. But due to *accidents*,' she drew quotation marks in the air, 'when they're in animal form, the wolves' average life expectancy tends to be lower.'

'Do they ever come here? Any of them?'

'No. I doubt it would occur to a supe to drop by. The biggest groups – both vamps and werewolves – think that we're too weak, too stupid and too sentimental to be bothered with. Both of them turn humans when they need to boost their numbers, but they're very picky about who they take on. That,' she conceded, 'and the fact that their numbers were capped by the government at the turn of last century.'

I dredged up what I could remember from my history classes. 'The 1901 Limiting Act?'

Liza snapped her fingers. 'That's the one. It's next to impossible to be turned into a supe by accident either. There are a lot of rules around bites and a lot of safeguards in place to prevent mistakes from being made.'

I picked up a pen from the desk and twirled it. Casual, Emma, I told myself. Act casual. 'Tell me more about the other supes. Are any of them immortal? Or, uh, undead?'

Fred blinked. 'Undead? What, you mean like zombies?'

I managed a weak laugh.

'Or like ghosts?'

I did my best to look uninterested. 'It was just a thought.'

'You've been reading too many horror stories,' Liza said. 'Believe me, things are shitty enough around here as it is without dead supes walking around.' She paused and looked at me. 'Why? What have you heard?'

I was saved from answering by the ring of the telephone. Picking up the receiver, I was relieved to hear Molly's warm, familiar voice.

'Alright,' she said briskly, 'I haven't been able to find out a huge amount. The DC in charge of the investigation has several other cases on the go, and apparently there's a delay on Jane Doe's post-mortem, which is holding everything up.'

I sent out a brief prayer of gratitude to Laura. 'No leads then?'

'Not so far.' She lowered her voice. 'I get the impression that the folks around here are inclined to let it go because of the location of the murder.'

I sucked in a breath. 'Let it go? She was a *person,* Molly. Just because she died near the supes' areas shouldn't mean that she's forgotten!'

'Whoa, Emma. I agree with you but it's hardly my call. Once she's identified, I'm sure more will be done.'

Except by that point, any trail would be cold. A trickle of doubt ran through me. Was I shooting myself in the foot by not coming clean? What if all this smoke and mirrors malarkey meant that my murderer got away scot-free?

I took a breath and reminded myself that none of this was Molly's fault. I had to stay focused. 'Do you know if DC Anthony Brown from Supe Squad has been in to check on progress?' I asked.

'Yes.'

I straightened up. 'Is he there now?' I demanded.

'Sorry, Emma. I mean yes, I do know if he's been in and no, he hasn't. Everyone here has been waiting for him to show up and cause problems – supposedly that's what he always does when there's a crime related to his turf. But there's been no sign of him yet.'

Was that because I'd somehow scratched him during the attack? Maybe he was hiding until his wounds healed. Or was it because something terrible had happened to him, too.

'The general consensus,' Molly continued, 'is that Tony Brown is a pain in the arse. I heard he was sent to Supes for attacking a superior officer. What's he been like with you?'

I barely heard the question. All I could think about was that Tony had a history of violence. I'd not provoked him – but maybe he hadn't needed to be provoked.

I shook off my doubts. He was definitely the most likely suspect. Regardless of motive, there was no point hearing hooves and then expecting zebras. Tony was the one who'd lured me to St Erbin's; Tony was surely my killer.

'Jeremy has been texting me, you know,' Molly said, changing the subject abruptly. 'He wants to know what's happening with you.'

I stiffened and focused back on the conversation. 'What did you tell him?'

'Nothing yet. What the hell is going on, Emma? I thought you two were tight.'

'We were!' I protested. 'I mean we are. I just ...' Shit. 'I just have a lot on my plate at the moment, and he doesn't understand how important this training is to me.'

'It's only going to get worse after we graduate.'

I grimaced. *If* I graduated. I wouldn't bank on any certainties any more. 'Yeah.'

'You're too good for him,' Molly said. 'He knows he's punching above his weight.'

I rolled my eyes. As if. Job aside, I was the most ordinary person in the world, whilst Jeremy possessed the sort of blond, white-teethed, wholesome good looks that many women went for. 'Hardly.'

'Whatever you say.' She said it good-naturedly, but I couldn't stop myself feeling a twinge. If I couldn't wrap my head around what had happened to me, then Jeremy certainly couldn't. And I couldn't risk the possibility that he'd also become a target. I had to find Tony and speak to him. And quite possibly arrest him. Then I'd deal with the fall-out with Jeremy.

'Thanks for calling, Molly,' I told her. 'And thanks for finding out that info for me. If Jeremy bothers you again, tell him that I'm busy working. And if you hear anything else to do with Jane Doe...'

'I'll keep you posted.' She hesitated. 'Stay safe, Emma.'

I swallowed. 'I will.'

Chapter Nine

Both Liza and Fred clocked off early. Considering the lack of activity around the Supernatural Squad office, I didn't blame them. I waved them off, mumbling something about doing the same very soon. Then, as soon as they'd gone, I scooted over to Tony's desk.

His workspace was far tidier than his car. The only things sitting on the top of his desk were his computer, an old silver paperweight and a tub filled with some chewed pens.

I sat down in his chair and started to open the drawers. I wasn't sure what I'd find but, given his lack of appearance today and the way he'd lured me out last night, my suspicions had grown into near certainties. Although it was unusual for him not to answer his phone, neither Liza nor Fred seemed concerned about his absence. But it was too much of a coincidence for me. Coupled with the juicy titbit about his violent past, I could longer deny that he was involved in my murder. That thought was more than enough to quash any guilt I felt at snooping through his stuff.

Not that there was much to snoop through. Most of it seemed to be little more than filched office supplies. From the vast collection of pens, each with a different logo, taking equipment from other places appeared to be something of a hobby of Tony's. I guessed it was one way to pass the time.

I rifled a bit more and found an old envelope with an electricity bill inside. The address wasn't for Supe Squad but for a flat not too far away. Given that it was in Tony's name, that had to be his home. I allowed myself a small smile of satisfaction. It was better than nothing; at least now I knew where to go once I'd run out of leads in the office.

Turning on the computer, I crossed my fingers in the hope that I'd be able to access his files. He'd enquired about my computing skills when we first met, so I doubted that he spent much time on his machine. I'd already come across a few old-school detectives who avoided them like the plague.

The computer whirred into life and Tony's login screen appeared. I chewed my bottom lip and gazed at the blinking password cursor. Three attempts and then, without further IT support, I'd be locked out. I wrinkled my nose and did my best, my fingers flying across the keys. *Tallulah*. It was as good a guess as any. Alas, it was wrong.

I made a face and abandoned the computer for now. Perhaps inspiration would strike later. Instead, I glanced again at the electricity bill. Confronting Tony in his own home might not be the smartest of moves, but I was running out of patience. I wanted to know for certain that he had killed me – and why.

I grabbed the puffy jacket which Laura had given me and pulled it on, then picked up the paperweight on Tony's desk and slipped it into my pocket. It wasn't a great weapon but, if I did end up having to defend myself, it would be better than nothing.

The solstice might have been two months behind us, but it was still winter. At that time of day in London, the sky was already dark. I'd lived in the city all my adult life and usually it didn't bother me; the long summer days more than made up for the long winter nights. However, getting myself murdered in a dark graveyard at night had made me very jumpy.

I scanned the road as soon as I left the Supe Squad building. I couldn't see anyone shady hanging around – but I hadn't seen anyone last night, either. Not until it was too late.

'Evening!'

I only just managed to stop myself from screaming.

The smile on the bellman's faltered when he saw my expression. 'I'm sorry. I didn't mean to scare you.'

I gulped in air and tried to get my breathing under control. I forced the corners of my mouth into a smile. I could do this. I could be normal. 'Hi.' Relax, Emma, for goodness' sake. 'It wasn't your fault. I was surprised, that's all.'

Kindness twinkled in his eyes. 'You don't have to worry. This street is about as safe as you can get. Nobody comes near Supe Squad. Both this office and you are off limits. You'll be safer around here than anywhere else in London.'

It was a shame that I knew that was a lie. 'Thank you,' I said. 'It's Jeeves, right?'

'You can call me Max. I don't bother with all that secret name stuff. Tony insists on it, even though he's perfectly happy to use his own name all the time.' He grinned. 'But then again, the man's a co-nundrum.'

I couldn't let that comment lie. 'In what way?'

'Dresses like a tramp, acts like a gentleman. He's a good guy through and through.' Max blinked at me. 'But I'm sure you've worked that out for yourself.'

'Yeah.' I nodded. 'Sure.' I wasn't sure what else to say so I gave him a tiny wave. 'Well, I'll be seeing you.'

'Sure thing.'

I put my hands in my pockets, feeling the heavy paperweight nestling there. I touched it for comfort and lifted my head. The last thing I wanted to do was to look like a victim. I was nobody's damned victim.

I marched down the street, forcing myself to look straight ahead. I didn't need to keep looking behind me every five steps, I just had to listen for the sound of footsteps and keep my wits about me. It was only about five o'clock and there were plenty of people around; I'd be fine. I glanced over my shoulder anyway. No-one was there. No-one was there. No-one was—

'Good evening.'

Goddamnit! I swung round. The paperweight was half out of my pocket when I realised who was standing there. 'Is sneaking up on people a habit of yours?' I snapped with more force than I'd intended.

The vampire's black eyes flicked down, noted the paperweight, and slid upwards again. 'My apologies,' he murmured. 'It wasn't my intention to scare you any more than it was Max's.'

He'd been watching my interaction with the bellman? Alright. If I wasn't nervous before, then I was now.

'Leave me alone.' I side-stepped in a bid to get past him. He moved with me.

I felt fear bubble up inside me. Maybe I'd been wrong; maybe it was a vampire who attacked me. Maybe it was this guy.

'Calm down.' He raised his hand and cupped my face.

I let out a silent shriek, my stomach clenched, and I tightened my grip on the paperweight. Then I looked into his eyes and instantly my tension eased.

'You have nothing to worry about with me,' he murmured.

An odd warmth spread through my body. He was right: I was safe here. He would look after me and ensure that nothing hurt me. Everything was going to be alright.

'There now,' he soothed. He leaned further in until our noses were almost touching. A slight smile played on his lips. 'You have the cutest freckles across your nose.'

I wasn't sure if it was the compliment that brought me back or if I merely came to my senses. I yanked myself backwards and glared at him. 'What did you just do to me?' I demanded.

He held up his hands. 'I was only trying to keep you calm. You had a hunted look in your eyes and an elevated heart rate that suggested you were moments away from a full-blown panic attack. There's nothing sinister about my actions, I promise you.'

I folded my arms. 'Stay the fuck away from me.'

He tilted his head and examined my face. 'That's not the sort of response I usually inspire in people. It's not what I'd expect from a detective, either.'

His words annoyed me because he was right. Under normal circumstances, I'd never speak to a member of the public like that, whether they were vampire, werewolf, gremlin, human or damned alien. But these weren't normal circumstances.

I softened my stance and dropped my arms down by my sides. 'I'm still in training,' I said stiffly, as if that were an excuse. 'I apologise. I have important police business to conduct and I need to get on my way.'

The vampire gazed at me for one long moment. Finally he bowed, like we were in some Jane Austen novel, and stepped to the side. 'Heaven forbid that I should delay important police business.'

If his expression hadn't been so serious, I'd have sworn he was making fun of me. 'Thank you,' I said, determined to bring this conversation to an end. I held up my head and started walking again.

'Would this police business have anything to do with the fact that you were murdered last night?' he called out.

My feet came to a stuttering halt. Slowly turning round, I met his black eyes again – but this time I made no secret of the paperweight. I pulled it out of my pocket, tugging at it when it snagged on the material, and hefted it from hand to hand.

The vampire's gaze didn't drop. He continued to watch me, clearly waiting for me to make the next move. It wasn't gallantry, it was pure predatory instinct. I was sure of it.

A gust of wind picked up, sending a few dead leaves and a flyer for happy hour at a nearby bar spinning past us. It lifted a curl of the vampire's dark hair and flapped at the edges of my over-sized coat. Neither of us paid any of it any attention.

'Was it you?' Oddly, I wasn't scared any longer although I should have been. I didn't raise my voice. My training was finally kicking in;

it was about time. Whether he was about to attack me or not, the chaos that panic would induce wouldn't help. Maintaining calm confidence was the only chance I had of walking away unscathed. I didn't brandish the paperweight threateningly, but I was more than ready to throw it at the vamp's head if I had to.

I wasn't the only one who was calm. The vamp didn't blink – he was like a damned lizard. 'You're asking if I killed you.' It wasn't a question. 'I can assure you that I did not.' His eyes glittered suddenly with dangerous intent. 'Why? Do you have reason to believe that it was a vampire who slit your throat?'

I ignored his question and stared at him hard, attempting to reconcile his figure with the blurry, indistinct image I had of my attacker. It was no good. It could have been the Queen herself who'd slit my throat and I wouldn't have been able to tell.

The vampire understood instantly. 'You didn't see who killed you, did you?'

I gritted my teeth. 'Not properly.' Barely at all, if I were being truthful. 'How did you know that it was me?' How did you know that I'd risen from the dead, I screamed silently.

'A human woman was brutally murdered on the edge of vampire territory,' he said. 'It was my job to investigate and discover if vampires were involved. I saw your body before it was taken away.' His eyes narrowed slightly. 'Unless you have an identical twin, which I very much doubt given your scent and what I smelled from your blood last night, then that body was yours. You were definitely dead.'

'Tell me something I don't know,' I muttered.

'What are you?' he asked, sharp steel lacing his question.

'Was it a vampire who killed me?' I countered.

He didn't flinch. 'No.' He nodded at me, indicating that he'd answered me, so now it was my turn to answer him.

'I don't know what I am,' I bit out. 'All I know is that last night I was killed, and this morning I woke up in the morgue.' I declined to mention the strange fire. I wasn't about to give up all my secrets to a complete stranger. Especially one as threatening as this one.

'Injuries?' he inquired.

'None.'

He seemed to relax slightly. 'You're not a vampire. You're not a werewolf. You don't fall into any other known supe categories. And you're definitely not human. So,' he asked again, 'what are you?'

This time the question wasn't addressed to me; he seemed to be thinking aloud.

'If you're so sure that my killer wasn't a vampire,' I said, 'does that mean you know who did kill me?'

He shook himself, his eyes refocusing. 'No. But the graveyard was all but flooded with the scent of your blood. The tang of it – of you – filled the air. I could smell it from half a mile away. We might not have the same acute senses as the werewolves, but we know blood. *I* know blood. Instead of taking advantage of the impromptu buffet your death provided, whoever killed you walked away. I followed the scent. It led straight to Piccadilly Circus and then disappeared, either in the crowds or the Underground. There are less than a dozen vampires who could have shown such restraint and left so much blood behind without taking even a sip. All those vampires have already been accounted for.'

I felt sick. 'Impromptu buffet?'

'Sorry.' He didn't look in the least apologetic. 'With a healthy diet, we only have to feed on blood once a month or so to survive. But that doesn't mean we can withstand the temptation of fresh blood when it's splattered in our faces.'

His explanation didn't make me feel any less nauseous. 'Fine,' I said distantly. I turned away. The way he'd accosted me had raised my suspicions, but I'd never really expected my killer to be a vampire. I didn't trust him, but I didn't disbelieve him either. Unless he was doing that weird calming thing on me again. My skin prickled.

'I can help you,' he said. 'I assume your important police business involves finding the real murderer. I can help you with that.'

I glanced over my shoulder. 'Why would you want to do that?'

'I told you. Your murder took place on the edge of vampire territory. That makes it as much my business as yours.' He smiled, amused at himself. 'Well, almost as much.'

The last thing I needed was a dodgy vamp tagging along with me, whether I trusted him or not. 'I don't need your help.' In other words, fuck off before I decide that you *were* my murderer after all.

'What if you're attacked again?' He nodded at the paperweight. 'That ridiculous thing you're waving at me won't do you much good, even against a wolf.'

'I'll be fine.'

'There are appropriate weapons in the Supe Squad building. On the third floor. As long as you're a member of Supe Squad, you're permitted to carry a crossbow. There's not much else that will stop both vampires and werewolves in their tracks.'

Huh. How did he know where the crossbows were kept?

'Thanks for the tip,' I said grudgingly.

'I'm Lukas, by the way.'

'Yeah. I'm sure that's your real name.' I started walking. It was time to get out of there. 'I'm D'Artagnan,' I muttered. 'It was nice to meet you.'

I held my breath, waiting for the vampire to catch up with me or continue the conversation in some way. He didn't. I picked up speed. When I reached the end of the street and looked back, he'd already gone.

Chapter Ten

Despite being dumped in Supernatural Squad to live out the rest of his career, Tony had done well for himself. Not only was his flat in central London, a mere stone's throw from the office, it was in a pleasant street and hidden behind the façade of a well-maintained, eighteenth-century building. He was in 2A, from which I surmised he was on the second floor. I couldn't see any lights on from my spot in the street, and there was no indication that he was home. His flat might look out onto the back of the property, however.

Rather than jiggle the door or attempt entry by other means – and potentially alert Tony to my presence or upset his neighbours – I banked on the fact that it was the end of the working day. Other residents would be returning home. Sure enough, I barely waited ten minutes before a car drew up and a young woman stepped out, walked up the steps to the door and used her key to open it.

I crossed the street and reached the door before it locked shut again. Catching it with my fingers, I nipped inside. So much for security. The woman's heels were already click-clacking up the stairs and she was none the wiser.

I double checked that I had my trainee's ID in case I was stopped and questioned, then I started up after her. By the time I reached Tony's flat, she'd vanished into her own home.

Pressing my ear against his door, I listened for signs of life from within. The walls were thick and, considering the upmarket nature of the building, it was entirely possible they were also soundproofed. If this had been an action film, I'd simply have raised my foot and kicked my way in, but I suspected that trying that here would only result in me breaking my ankle.

I pursed my lips, wishing I had my phone so that I could text Molly and tell her where I was in case things went wrong. Then

I gripped the paperweight with one hand and knocked sharply on Tony's door with the other.

There wasn't any answer. I knocked again, more loudly this time. Still nothing. I was about to give it yet another shot when the door across the landing marked 2C opened and a bloke about my age peered out. When he saw me, he seemed to relax slightly. I guess I didn't look much of a threat. 'Is everything alright?' he asked.

'I'm Tony's niece,' I improvised. 'I've not heard from him for days and I'm getting really worried.' I widened my eyes and did my best to look anxious. 'You've not seen him lately, have you?'

'Yesterday morning,' he said. 'We bumped into each other on the way to work.'

I noted the man's starched shirt and plain suit before I spotted the gold ring adorning his little finger. It was difficult to be sure from this angle, but it looked to be engraved with an XP. Chi Rho. I sent a brief prayer of thanks to my old Religious Studies teacher for having a penchant for old symbols. Chi Rho was formed by putting together the first two Greek letters for Christ, and it was one of the earliest symbols of Christianity. A man whose only extravagance was a religious gold ring was not the sort of man who would approve of supes.

I wrung my hands. 'You must know he works at Supernatural Squad. I worry about him so much. All those vampires and werewolves...' I shook my head. 'Forgive me for saying so, but it's not natural. Any of them could turn on him. We were supposed to meet for lunch today. He didn't show up, which isn't like him at all.'

The man's expression softened. 'You're from Melissa's side of the family?'

I had no idea who Melissa was. 'Uh-huh. I'm Emma.'

'I'm Will. I was sorry to hear about what happened to her.'

I dropped my gaze. 'Yeah,' I mumbled. 'Me too.'

'Well, you're in luck, Emma. It turns out that I've got a spare key.'

My head snapped up. My daft ploy had actually worked. Unbelievable.

'We swapped copies of our keys when I moved in. I'll use it to
check that he's in and he's okay.'

Tony's neighbour was a damn sight more trusting than Liza.
Tony should have had more sense than to give his key to a bloke like
this. 'That would be great!' I burbled. 'Thank you!'

'It's the least I can do. Just wait a minute and I'll grab it.'

I did as he asked, banging on Tony's door a few more times for
effect. He wasn't at the office and he hadn't been into CID, so he had
to be home. Unless he was propping up a bar somewhere, drowning
his guilt at having murdered his own mentee. That thought turned
my blood to ice and I swallowed.

If he wasn't in, I'd make up some excuse about waiting for him
inside until he showed up. Hopefully his gullible neighbour trusted
me with the key. Stranger things had happened.

'Here we go,' he said, waving a small silver key. 'This should do
the trick.'

I stood back, calculating the possible outcomes of entering
Tony's flat like this. I still had the paperweight, not to mention Will
by my side as back-up. He didn't look like he'd be capable of much
if Tony was hiding inside with a sharp knife in his hand, but it was
good to be prepared for every scenario.

As Will wiggled the key and turned it in the lock until there was
a click, I tensed my muscles. You can't hide from me forever, Tony.
I'm coming to get you – one way or another.

The door swung open. 'Tony, are you—' Will called. He swallowed the rest of his question in stunned shock when we saw what
was awaiting us inside.

It was complete devastation. Either Tony was the world's messi-
est man or a tornado had whipped through his home. Papers were
scattered everywhere, a mirror was lying smashed on the floor and

a long sofa had been upturned. I leapt forward, all my earlier suspicions vanishing in an instant. I wasn't the only one who'd been attacked; Tony had been targeted too – and that put a completely different spin on everything.

I darted from room to room, my heart in my mouth as I searched for a body or bloodstains. I was desperate for anything that might provide a clue about what had happened to him. There was nothing helpful; each room was in a worse state than the last. Whoever had been in here had been thorough.

Paintings had been ripped off the walls and it looked as if a machete had been taken to the mattress in the bedroom. Huge gouges marred its surface and fluffy white stuffing was spilling out in all directions. Tony's clothes were strewn everywhere. I glanced down at a fallen photo frame. The picture of Tony with his arm round a pretty blonde woman was just visible through the cracked glass. Both of them were beaming at the camera and he had a stain on his cheek that perfectly matched the shade of her lipstick. I swallowed. Bloody hell. What was going on?

Will's face was white. 'You were right to be worried about him,' he whispered. 'We have to call the police.'

I could only nod; there was no point in telling him that technically I *was* the police. What good could I do on my own? My legs felt weak and jelly-like. I'd got it all so wrong. 'I don't have a phone on me,' I said.

'Mine is in my flat.'

'Okay, let's call from there.' I moved shakily to the door. 'Don't touch anything. We don't want to mess with the crime scene.'

If anything, Will looked even paler at my words. I walked past him and gestured for him to follow.

He was distraught. 'It was those fucking supes. I bet they're responsible for this. Those vampires have got hold of him – he's probably lying in a ditch right now with fang marks in his neck. His bones are going to be gnawed by werewolves. That poor man.'

I rounded on him. 'Enough! This isn't helping! We don't know that supes did this. It could have been anyone.'

'It was them.' His eyes were as wide as saucers. 'It had to be.'

'We don't know that yet.'

'They'll get away with it. The supes get away with murder whenever they want. They're ungodly! Tony Brown is a bastard, but even he doesn't deserve this!' His voice was rising with every word.

I resisted the temptation to grab him by the shoulders and shake him as hard as I could. And then his words filtered through.

I might have only been in Supe Squad since the previous day, but I already knew how it worked. Everyone had told me the same thing. Fred's words echoed in my head. If the supes were involved, then this was their case; if they weren't, it would belong to CID. Either way, the investigation would be taken away from me.

I'd been killed and now something had happened to Tony. The two things had to be related. If I called the police now, my own death would be out of my hands. I'd have no control over anything.

I wasn't normally reckless. Procedures were there for a reason and, fast track or not, I was still only a trainee detective. But yesterday I'd died, and I wasn't the same person I'd been twenty-four hours earlier. Nobody would have known Tony was in trouble if I hadn't come here. Questions would be asked about my own involvement, and I wouldn't have any answers. If I was to remain in control of my own narrative – and my own fate – I had to tread very carefully.

I thought quickly. I couldn't guarantee that calling the police now would help Tony. But if I remained free to investigate on my own, I still might be able to save him. My hands trembled. I'd be crazy if I did this; I'd be crazy if I didn't.

'*I'll* call the police,' I said. My voice sounded like it was coming from a great distance. 'I'll deal with this from here.'

Will stared at me. I was pretty certain that I didn't imagine the relief that flashed across his face. Even though he had Tony's spare key, he had no desire to get involved with the old detective's shenanigans, especially when vampires and werewolves and other beasties might be involved.

'I don't know,' he said slowly. 'They'll want to talk to me, won't they?'

'I'm sure they will, but the priority will be to locate Tony. It might take a couple of days before they question you.'

He twisted the ring on his finger. 'Whoever did this got into the building without anyone noticing. What if they come back? What if they target other residents?'

It wasn't his fellow neighbours that he was worried about; Will's concern was purely for himself. He also wanted me to convince him that I could take care of things so he could remain uninvolved – and his anxiety about his own well-being gave me the avenue I needed.

'You're right.' I nodded vigorously. 'If your name is attached to Tony's in any way, the people who did this might see you as a threat and come after you. It's how these bastards work. I'm his niece, so the police will expect me to be involved. There's no need for you to put yourself at risk. Perhaps it's best if we keep your name out of it for now, at least until the police have found who's responsible and Tony comes back.'

I wasn't going to mention that it was possible Tony might never return. To say it aloud would be to give it credence.

'I ... I ... I barely know him,' Will said. 'He's a passing acquaintance. We exchange greetings in the hall, that's all. I don't have anything to do with supes.'

I clicked my tongue in sympathy. 'That's why it's best if you don't get mixed up in this.'

His head drooped. 'I knew moving here was a mistake. It's too close to those heathens.'

Yeah, yeah. I stayed silent. I'd said enough to persuade him, but he had to take the final step. If I pushed him too far, he'd push back.

'Here.' He pressed Tony's key into my hand. 'You have this. It's logical that Tony's niece would have a spare instead of some neighbour he barely knows.' He looked at me anxiously. He didn't seem to be aware that he'd just suggested I lie to the police. Omission was one thing, deliberate deceit was entirely different – at least to my mind, anyway.

'Go to your flat. I'll call the police now.' And then, because I knew he'd be keeping an eye out, 'It might take them a while to get here. Even if they do show up quickly, they might do it on the sly so that anyone watching this building doesn't realise that we're onto them. A big show of force could put Tony in more danger.'

I was talking out of my arse. If I reported that a detective's flat had been trashed and the occupant was now missing, half of the police in London would descend. But Will didn't know that; he simply looked more terrified.

'You're right. Yes.'

'Go into your flat, turn up your music and act like you don't know about any of this. I'll take care of everything from here. I promise.' As far as that part was concerned, I wasn't lying.

Will grasped my hands, squeezing them tight. 'Be careful.'

'I will be,' I told him. 'Have no fear on that score. And I'm sure Tony will reappear soon.'

Chapter Eleven

As soon as Will disappeared, I got to work. The faster I worked, the faster I'd discover Tony's whereabouts, and that might make all the difference to him. I was damned if my need to stay in control of my own investigation was going to risk his well-being. I already felt guilty enough for suspecting that he'd been my killer.

My first port of call was the kitchen. I found a pair of luminous pink rubber gloves by the sink and pulled them on. Then I went to the fridge. Its door was hanging open and its contents had been strewn across the kitchen floor: brie, grapes, milk, spilled orange juice – even a few healthy-looking vegetables. Tony wasn't quite the straightforward carnivore he'd made himself out to be.

There was also a half-wrapped sandwich that seemed to have been thrown at the wall by the burglar in a fit of pique. I peeled it away from the linoleum to take a closer look. A cheese sandwich, *my* cheese sandwich, judging by the sticker. That meant Tony had returned here after he'd stormed off yesterday. In terms of time frames, that helped considerably. It didn't answer the question of whether he'd texted me last night, or whether someone had taken his phone to message me and make it seem as if the text had come from Tony. It was, however, a start.

Abandoning the fridge and the kitchen, I started searching for Tony's mobile. If he'd left in a hurry, or it had been dropped during the burglary, maybe it was still here. Unfortunately, there was no sign of it, although I spotted a landline telephone on the floor in the living room. I left it alone and continued my search of the rest of the flat.

I couldn't work out what, if anything, had been stolen. And I couldn't find so much as a scrap of paper that gave me a clue about Tony's whereabouts. I could have been looking for a white cat in a snowstorm for all the good this search was doing me.

Eventually, I returned to the living room and stared at the phone. I picked it up and dialled 1471. The disembodied voice of the computer chanted at me: 'You were called today at 3.24pm by 020 7946 0800. If you wish to return the call, press—'

I hung up. That had been Liza calling from the office. If I'd known then what I knew now, I'd never have asked her to call. I grimaced then reluctantly dialled another number.

'Good evening. This is Dean at the morgue in Fitzwilliam Manor Hospital. How may I help you?'

'Hi Dean,' I said. 'Is Laura still there? Dr Hawes, I mean. This is Emma. I'm—'

I didn't get the chance to finish my sentence.

'Emma!' Laura interrupted. 'I was hoping you'd call! I stayed late at work just in case, and I've been hovering over poor Dean and bothering him all day. Are you alright? Have there been any strange side effects? Have you found any clues about what happened to you?'

I wasn't sure which question to answer first. 'I'm okay, Laura. No side effects – not physical ones, anyway. As to what happened to me, that's why I'm calling. I have a question that I'm hoping you can help me answer.'

'Go on.' She sounded desperately eager. That made one of us.

I didn't want to ask my question but I didn't have much choice. 'One of my colleagues is missing. I need to know whether he's shown up at your morgue or one of others in the city.'

For a long moment, Laura didn't answer. 'Oh, Emma. I'm so sorry.'

The sympathy in her tone almost finished me and a mist of tears descended. I clenched my jaw and held back the tide. Just. 'He's in his late fifties. Caucasian, grey hair, clean shaven but with pock-marked skin. Average height and weight. His name is Anthony Brown.'

'No one of that name has come in here, and we have no John Does of that description. Wait a minute – I'll check the computer. It'll tell me if he's shown up elsewhere.'

'Thank you.' I clutched the phone through the kitchen gloves. It felt reassuringly substantial, as if it were the only thing in the world I had to cling on to. Seconds that felt like minutes ticked by. Then I hear Laura's voice again.

'He's not been taken to any of the morgues in the city.'

I closed my eyes. There was still hope. 'Good.' I breathed out. 'That's good.'

'It sounds like you're in over your head.' Laura sounded worried. 'Maybe it's time you reported what's happened, Emma. I've delayed your post-mortem for another forty-eight hours but, if both you and your colleague are in danger, that might not be a good thing.'

I fixed my gaze on a hairline crack in the ceiling. 'If I'm no further forward by then, I'll come to clean to whoever I need to. Right now, I need some time. I know you're taking a risk but—'

'Pah! Risk-shmisk. I've not had this much excitement for years. The dead aren't as interesting as most people think. I'll follow your lead, Emma. Just remember that what happened to you might not have been a one-off. You cheated death once. That doesn't mean you'll cheat it again.'

A fact that I was grimly aware of. 'Thank you, Laura,' I said again. 'I'll be in touch before the forty-eight hours are up.' I replaced the receiver, Laura's warning ringing in my ears.

I couldn't stay out on the streets armed with nothing more than a paperweight. Lukas had told me about the weapons housed at Supe Squad. If I was going to find Tony quickly, I had to return to the office anyway. I straightened my shoulders. I had a plan. Of sorts.

***

I made it out of Tony's building and all the way to Supe Squad without seeing Will, Lukas or any knife-wielding maniacs. At that point, I was prepared to count that as a win. Max the bellman's shift must have ended; he'd been replaced by another man in similar livery but with an entirely different disposition. He glared at me as I walked up to the Supe Squad building and fumbled with the key.

I leaned back from the door and met his irritated gaze. 'Were you working here last night?' I asked.

I could tell from his expression that he was no fan of the police and that he wanted to tell me to piss off. Fortunately, he also knew that it was in his best interests to answer me, so reluctantly he bit out a nod.

'Did you see anybody coming and going from here?'

'No.'

'No one at all?' I pressed.

'No.' He folded his arms across his chest. 'Nobody is ever around here at night. Your lot are part timers.'

I wondered what he expected, given that there was nothing for us to do. 'Well,' I said, offering him a dazzling smile, 'I'm here now.'

The bellman grunted and turned away. I didn't take it personally and let myself into the building.

The familiar hallway was shrouded in darkness. I found the light switch by touch, flicking it on and exhaling with relief when the weak lightbulb overhead lit up. I didn't feel comfortable in the dark any more. I wondered if I ever would.

Although I was itching to investigate the third floor and the weapons Lukas the vampire had mentioned, I restrained myself and headed into the main room on the ground floor. I glanced at Tony's silent computer before walking over to it and, without sitting down, tried to enter a password. This time I typed in 'Melissa' and pressed return, holding my breath. I cursed when it didn't work. Damn it – I only had one more try before I was locked out.

Fortunately, accessing Tony's files was only one of my ideas. There was another computer and, trainee or not, I could use it to get the information I needed because we'd been set up with our own logins during our first week at the Academy. Anything I searched for would leave a trace, but this was all about risk versus reward.

The easiest place to begin was Tallulah. Tony's grubby car was far too old to possess a GPS tracking system, but there was more than one way to skin a cat. Within moments, I had the Automatic Numberplate Recognition system up and running. If Tony had driven anywhere in London, the ANPR programme would find him. It didn't matter that I wasn't looking for real-time data; ANPR held its records for two years. Tracking Tallulah for the last twenty-four hours, especially within the city, would be ridiculously easy.

I didn't have a photographic memory, and I'd not paid attention to the grubby Mini's numberplate yesterday, but she'd been used to pick me up the previous day. It was a piece of cake to plug in the Academy's address and the time that Tony had arrived. You have to love technology – and Tony's shoddy, borderline illegal parking methods. In less than five minutes, I had Tallulah's numberplate.

I typed it into the ANPR system, then picked up the phone while I was waiting for the computer to do its work. Tony's mobile might be switched off but that didn't mean it wasn't still useful.

Every mobile has its own International Mobile Equipment Identity number, one that is unique to each handset. Even if the SIM card is changed, the IMEI remains the same. Whenever the phone checks in to a local base station, it transmits that number. I couldn't pinpoint the location of Tony's phone, but I could find out roughly where it was when it was last turned on – and that might make all the difference.

'Good evening,' I said into the phone. 'I'm calling from Supernatural Squad. I need a mobile number traced and tracked immediately.'

'I need your name and warrant number before I can authorise that action.'

I screwed up my face. I'd hoped that calling from a police department would pass muster. Apparently not. I crossed my fingers and reeled out the information.

'That's a trainee number.'

'Yeah,' I said quickly. 'My mentor wants me to practise. It's his phone that I'm tracking. He seems to think that practising real skills like this will make me a better detective when I finally graduate. It's just playacting, really.'

'This isn't nursery school,' the woman said, clearly irritated. 'This service is for genuine police business.'

'I know, I know. I'm sorry – but I need to do well at this. I'm a hair's breadth from graduation. If I can get through this last rotation…'

She sighed. 'Give me his name and number and I'll see what I can do. I have to contact the network directly, so it might take some time.'

I exhaled. 'It's DC Anthony Brown.' I gave her his number.

'Wait a moment and I'll verify that information. I'll put you on hold.'

As I waited, I checked the computer. The system had done its work. A list of different locations, including several photographs, had appeared on the screen. I ran down them and focused on the last one. Then I frowned. Tallulah had last been registered on St James's Street just after eleven o'clock last night. That was less than ten minutes' walk from St Erbin's Church – and it was around the time when I was being murdered.

I stared at the photo. It was grainy and the image was far from perfect, but that definitely looked like Tony sitting in the driver's seat.

The phone clicked and the woman spoke again. 'Take down these coordinates,' she said. '51.5069N, 0.01416W.'

I scribbled them down.

'He's certainly messing with you,' she said. 'DC Brown's phone was last pinged by the mast at that location at 11.33pm last night. What's the bet he's putting this on expenses?'

My brow creased. 'What do you mean, putting it on expenses?'

'Those coordinates are for the DeVane Hotel. I bet he sat in a plush corner and had a champagne cocktail, chuckling to himself about sending you there to look for him. Honestly.' I could almost hear her rolling her eyes. 'No wonder Supe Squad has such a bad reputation if it's full of detectives who swan around one of London's poshest hotels instead of doing any real work.'

I ignored her last comment and thanked her. The DeVane Hotel made no sense. It wasn't far from here, but it might as well have been a million miles away in terms of the sort of place I was used to. It certainly wasn't where I'd expected Tony to hang out. I shook my head briefly. It was within a stone's throw of St James's Street, so it had to be right. At least I knew where to go next. Now all I needed was a real weapon to take with me.

I cracked my knuckles and walked into the dimly lit hallway. A wooden staircase with a threadbare carpet runner that had definitely seen better days led upstairs. I gazed up, took a deep breath and followed it upwards.

In the last three months, I'd been fully trained in the correct way to use both a police baton and a Taser. Molly had been keen to go a step further and request firearms training but it wasn't something that interested me. Police in the UK didn't routinely carry guns, and gaining admittance to firearm training involved a barrage of tests.

I wondered how difficult it was to get training in the use of crossbows. I had a vision of a teacher dressed as Robin Hood, and a hysterical giggle threatened to bubble out of me. I gulped it back. My emotions were on the edge. I needed to keep my baser instincts at bay if I was to find a way through this mess.

The higher I climbed, the more the stairs creaked. Rather than adding to my unease, the noise was oddly comforting; it gave a touch of normality to my very abnormal day. I focused on each creak and felt myself calming down. In fact, I was so absorbed in the sounds that I almost didn't hear the knock at the front door. When it filtered through my consciousness that someone was out there, my whole body stiffened.

I took the rest of the stairs two at a time, then swung round the third-floor landing into the nearest room and headed for the window. When I peered down and saw who was standing in the street and frowning at the front door, my heart rate went into overdrive. Again.

Every atom of my body told me to whirl round, sprint down the stairs, fling open the door and throw myself into Jeremy's arms. The worry etched on his face sent tiny spears of anguish through me. He'd come here late at night to look for me, despite my messaged instructions to the contrary.

I gazed down at him. I didn't deserve him, and that was why I so determined to keep him out of this mess. I wasn't about to risk his well-being – his life – even if I desperately wanted his solid, comforting presence. He'd never understood why I wanted to become a police detective, and he certainly wouldn't understand what was happening now. I twisted my fingers and stepped back so that he wouldn't catch sight of me if he looked up.

He stepped to the side, his mouth moving as he spoke to the gruff bellman outside the building. I held my breath. If that cantankerous bastard told him that he'd seen me come in less than half an hour ago, I was screwed.

From where I was standing, it didn't look as if he was being any more forthcoming with Jeremy than he'd been with me. Jeremy's face spasmed with irritation, then he shoved his hands into his pockets and stalked away. I gazed at his retreating back, continuing to watch until long after he'd been swallowed up by the darkness. I'd have to contact him soon and do whatever I could to alleviate his worries, though I wasn't sure how I'd manage that.

My heart was like a dead weight in my chest and my soul felt even more leaden. Passing a hand over my eyes, I moved back into the room before realising where I was. It was an honest-to-goodness weapons room. I forgot all about Jeremy and gazed round in open-mouthed astonishment. The last thing I'd been expecting was something on this scale.

All four walls were covered with hanging weaponry. On one side there were crossbows, on another daggers. To my right, there was a mind-boggling collection of swords; in front of me were numerous throwing implements, from small axes to gleaming shuriken. Bloody *shuriken*. I stared. It was like nothing I'd ever seen before.

I walked over to the swords and touched the blade of an elaborately curved scimitar. It was coated in dust, but I still nicked myself on its lethal edge. I pulled away, sucking at the bead of blood. I wondered if the likes of Lucinda Barnes had any knowledge of this room. The idea that all this weaponry was simply lying around for the taking was barely credible.

Something itched at the back of my mind and I looked at the wall of daggers. Huh. I stepped closer. Every spot was filled. If I'd needed further confirmation that Tony hadn't slit my throat, this full complement of weaponry provided it. The dust proved that none of these blades had been touched in years. I didn't need a forensic team to tell me that none of them had been used in my murder.

'Tony,' I whispered.

The chilling reminder of why I was there galvanised me. Shaking off my guilt, I marched to the crossbows. I didn't like the thought of waving a dagger or a sword around, especially given my recent up-close-and-personal experience with sharp blades, but I could get behind a crossbow. Surely it would be like a gun, point and shoot? Right?

I scanned the various shapes and sizes and picked one that was a useful matte black colour and looked reasonably simple to use. I ignored the bows that had scopes; I wasn't planning to shoot anyone from a distance. This was for self-defence and close calls only.

The crossbow was far heavier than I'd expected as I hefted it from one hand to the other. I wouldn't be able to hold it upright for more than a few seconds. I grimaced and replaced it, then chose another one which proved to be considerably lighter.

I closed one eye and practised aiming at a random spot on the wall before examining the bow's spring mechanism. It didn't look complicated. Spotting a chest in the far corner, I opened it. It contained silver-tipped bolts, designed to take out werewolves, vampires and anything in between. I licked my lips nervously and picked one up.

Loading the crossbow was difficult. I fiddled for ages before realising that there was a foot stirrup. I slid in the bolt and tugged on the strings until they latched it into place, raised the crossbow up, aimed for the wooden door and fired.

Nothing happened. There wasn't even a faint jolt. I frowned and looked over the crossbow again until I finally spotted the safety button. Ah-ha. Using my thumb, I flicked it. A moment later, I tried shooting again.

I missed the door by a good metre and the bolt thudded into the wall, embedding itself in the plaster between two daggers. I hissed. Hitting a target would take far more time and practice. Then again, I didn't actually want to kill anyone; the purpose of taking the crossbow was to ensure that no one killed me. It was a deterrent. By carrying it, at least I'd look like I meant business even if nothing was further from the truth.

I reloaded, this time double checking that the safety was on rather than off. I could do without shooting myself in the foot. Then, because this was all about appearances, I grabbed a black-lined quiver and filled it with more bolts before looping it over my shoulder. Glancing at my own dark reflection in the window, I smiled grimly. I was ready.

Chapter Twelve

Max's replacement didn't look at me when I walked outside. I ignored the bellman rather than asking him what Jeremy had said and risking giving myself away to someone who seemed to hate my guts.

I marched in the direction of St James's Road and the DeVane Hotel. I'd try and find Tallulah before breaching the expensive hotel. If the car was anywhere in the vicinity, she wouldn't be hard to spot. I held the crossbow loosely at my side, doing my best to appear casual about it, because nothing proclaims confidence more than relaxed insouciance.

It still wasn't late and there were quite a few people out on the streets. I passed three young men who I was certain were werewolves. They goggled at me, stared at the crossbow in my hand then darted off, no doubt to tattle to their wolfy superiors. Let them. I meant business and I didn't care who knew it. The more supes who were wary of me, the better.

I nodded at the tourists who stopped to check me out, and frowned in warning at the woman who was approaching to ask for a selfie. She pulled back and I kept walking, maintaining a good pace but not hurrying. I didn't want to appear panicked to anyone watching me.

I made a point of avoiding St Erbin's Church. Regardless of my weapon and my bravado, I had limits – and the dark streets were making me jumpy, no matter how much I acted to the contrary.

I skirted round St James's Park, taking care to stay out of the deepest shadows. The traffic was reasonably light but there were still plenty of cars passing. More than one driver beeped their horn at me, though I wasn't sure why. *Hello, I can see you and I've noted that you're carrying a lethal weapon in your hand?* Or something to that effect.

I didn't react, but I was glad to be noticed. Their attention made it less likely that I'd be grabbed from the bushes on my right. I did cut across into a side street when I spotted two police officers out on patrol, though; The last thing I wanted was to explain myself to them, even if we were on the same side.

St James's Road was wide and stretched for about a mile. I turned and walked northwards towards the Thames river, which lay not far beyond. I kept my eyes peeled for any sign of Tallulah. There wasn't much on-street parking here, but that wouldn't have stopped Tony.

I walked past a sports field and a church and passed beneath the boughs of several large trees before emerging at a crossroads. The road continued; I was just about to cross over when I noted a Tesco Express and a leather-clad woman standing outside it. She had long black hair tied into a plait. From her tightly bound corset to her knee-high stiletto boots, her clothes screamed 'look at me'. But it wasn't her showy attire that gave me pause, it was her red-lipsticked smile and the glimpse of pearly-white fangs.

I walked towards her. When she saw me coming, she licked her lips in predatory anticipation. Then her eyes dropped to my crossbow and her expression changed.

'Good evening,' I called as I approached.

'Why are you carrying that thing?' she asked, dispensing with any niceties and getting straight to the point. She spoke with a rough London accent that was at odds with her immaculate appearance. 'Only Supe Squad are allowed shit like that.' She paused. 'Unless you're looking for trouble.'

Her last comment was more for herself than me. She was trying to convince herself that she wasn't scared. Two days earlier, I wouldn't have been able to recognise that.

'Well,' I answered with a smile, 'as it turns out I *am* with Supe Squad.'

'No, you ain't.'

I raised an eyebrow. 'So you know DC Brown?'

''Course I know him. Everyone knows him.'

I kept my eyes on her face and adjusted my grip on the crossbow so she didn't forget I was holding it – and that it was loaded. Go me. I could be intimidating, after all.

'When was the last time you saw him?' I asked.

She didn't answer. Instead, she curled her lips into a sneer. 'He don't carry that shit with him. Not ever.'

I didn't flinch. 'That's his choice.'

The vamp looked me up and down, her confidence growing until a thought occurred to her and she took a step back. 'Wait,' she said. 'Are you D'Artagnan?'

I froze. How in hell had she heard that name? 'How do you know that?' I demanded.

She paled. 'I'm sorry,' she whispered. She lifted her chin. 'You were asking about Brown. The last time I saw him was Thursday.'

Thursday was a lifetime ago, long before the thought of Supe Squad had occurred to me, but I wasn't about to ignore her sudden willingness to answer my questions. 'You're sure?'

She nodded. 'He was on Brewer Street. He hangs out there quite a lot.'

My eyes narrowed. 'Anywhere in particular?'

'Usually the Pulteney.'

'That's a pub?'

'Yeah.' The vamp sucked her bottom lip; it made her fangs protrude more than normal. It wasn't an alluring look. 'I helped you, right? I answered your questions?'

'I have one more. How did you know I was called D'Artagnan? Where did you hear that name?' If she hadn't seen Tony since Thursday, it certainly hadn't been from him.

Her eyes flicked nervously from side to side. 'Everyone knows.'

'Everyone?'

The vamp stared at me, then her muscles tensed and she sprang away. I blinked. She moved so fast that I didn't even see where she'd gone. I glowered at the spot where she'd been standing. I had a strong suspicion I knew who'd told *everyone* my nickname. I also had a strong suspicion that he'd appear out of nowhere again very soon.

***

With no sign of Tallulah on St James's Street – and not a flicker of a shadow from any other vampires – I wheeled round and headed for the DeVane. It was so close that Tony could conceivably have driven there without getting picked up again by ANPR. If he'd parked there and was now sitting at the bar sipping a champagne cocktail, I'd kill him myself. My fingers tightened around the crossbow. Oh God. I hoped against hope that was exactly what he was doing.

There was something about the façade of the hotel that always made me think of Paris. Not that I'd ever been to Paris, but I'd seen enough of the French capital on television to know that the glitzy DeVane was designed with that intention. I'd never set foot inside it – why would I have? It was the sort of place that's very existence made someone on my salary feel inadequate.

I didn't allow that to show on my face; when I approached the steps, I straightened my back and sauntered up them as if I belonged there. It didn't do me any good. Before I could get within touching distance of the door, I was stopped by the bellman.

Max and his grumpy colleague were well-dressed, but this guy was on another level. I swear I could see my reflection in the gold buttons adorning his long coat. 'Good evening, ma'am,' he said, doffing his hat. He didn't drop his gaze to my crossbow, but I knew he'd clocked it. 'Are you residing in the hotel?'

Obviously not. I was still dressed in the death garments Laura had given to me, and I definitely didn't look like I could afford to stay there. I doubted that all the money in my bank account would pay for a cup of tea here.

I flashed him a tight, professional smile. 'I'm here on police business. I'd like to speak to the hotel manager as soon as possible.'

The bellman didn't miss a beat and his expression didn't alter. Man, this guy was good. 'Do you have an appointment?'

'No, but it's a matter of extreme urgency.'

His training had clearly prepared him for every challenge. The last thing the hotel wanted was an armed woman hanging around the opulent lobby, but neither did they want to antagonise the police. They knew their business – and so did the bellman.

'Please take the side entrance.' He gave me brief directions. 'I'll ensure that someone meets you there.' He turned away to greet the next guests in exactly the same manner he'd spoken to me, despite their considerably more expensive clothes and their high-born demeanour. I was impressed.

I murmured my thanks, although I wasn't sure he heard me, and walked round to the trade entrance. It suited me; now that I was within the relative safety of the hotel, the fewer curious eyes I encountered the better.

I'd just gone inside when a woman wearing a neat suit approached me. Her name tag proclaimed as one of the assistant managers. I gave her a perfunctory smile and she returned the favour. 'My name is Wilma Kennard,' she said. 'May I see some identification, please?'

I pulled out my trainee's warrant card and passed it over, aware that this was where things might get dicey. 'I'm with Supe Squad,' I said quietly. 'I'm not yet properly qualified as a detective, but I am a certified member of the Metropolitan police force. My mentor, Detective Constable Brown, has gone missing and his trail leads here. I need to locate him before his disappearance creates a bigger incident.'

Wilma Kennard winced. If there was one thing worse than having a crossbow-bearing police officer wandering through your hotel

and scaring your guests, it was having an entire troop of police officers searching your hallways for a missing colleague. Trainee or not,
she wanted to deal with me with the least amount of possible fuss; if
that meant giving me access, that was what she was prepared to do.

She passed my warrant card back to me. 'Follow me, Miss Bellamy.'

We tracked through the narrow staff corridor to a small office
not far from the door marked 'Lobby'. Kennard motioned me to a
chair, sat behind the desk and started to tap at her computer keyboard.

A frown creased her forehead as she scanned the screen. 'We
have an Anthony Brown who checked in last night,' she told me. 'He
walked in off the street and paid up front for two nights.'

I sucked in a breath. So Tony *was* here. A wave of relief – followed immediately by a flash of anger – rippled through me. He was
holed up in a swanky room ordering room service and enjoying himself.

Kennard tapped a few more keys, the furrow in brow deepening.
'He has a *Do Not Disturb* sign on his door, so his room wasn't cleaned
this morning.'

My stomach muscles tensed again. 'No one has seen him since
last night?' I leaned forward. 'Has he ordered any food? Been to the
bar? Used the phone?'

Kennard raised her eyes to mine. 'No, none of that.'

I swallowed. Tony didn't strike me as the kind of bloke who
would empty an expensive minibar; neither was he a man who would
skip meals.

'I have one thing here,' she said. 'I doubt it's helpful. He phoned
in a complaint not long after he checked in. He called housekeeping
and said that his fridge wasn't working properly. We offered to check
it over and fix it in the morning. He said that he'd manage without it,

and that he'd rather not be disturbed.' She shrugged. 'That's all I've got.'

'When did he make that call?'

She frowned at the computer. 'Just before 1am.'

Tony was as much of a night owl as the vamps. I sucked on my bottom lip and tried to think of where to go next. 'Do you have any camera footage from when he checked in?' I asked finally. 'Or from outside his room?'

'I can't show you any of that if you haven't got a warrant. I'm not being obstructive, it's merely procedure.'

I cursed inwardly and thought some more. A hotel like this would have a state-of-the-art keycard system that must have electronic records. 'How about his door?' I could feel a prickle of urgency between my shoulder blades. 'Can you tell me when it was opened?'

Kennard shook her head. 'Again, Miss Bellamy, without a warrant that's not possible.' She paused. 'But if you're genuinely concerned for his well-being—'

'I am.'

'Then I can take you up to his room and we can check on him.'

I immediately stood up. 'Let's go.'

If I'd had my way, I'd have sprinted to Tony's room. At least the assistant manager had a brisk gait; no doubt she was keen to confirm Tony's presence and get rid of me as quickly as possible.

We took the service lift then marched along the fourth-floor corridor to Tony's room. There was indeed a *Do Not Disturb* sign hanging from the doorknob.

I glanced at Wilma and knocked. 'Tony!' I called. 'It's Emma. Are you in there?'

There was no answer. Kennard took over and rapped on the door. 'DC Brown? This is Wilma Kennard. I apologise for disturbing you, but we need to confirm that you're alright.'

Again, no answer. Kennard waited for a few seconds then reached into her suit pocket, took out a keycard and unlocked the door. She nudged it open slightly and called again, 'Hello? DC Brown?'

I'd had enough. I pushed past her and walked inside, noting the sour smell in the air. The television in the corner was turned on but the sound was muted. The bed was rumpled, although it looked like it hadn't been slept in. An open magazine lay on one of the small bedside tables next to several opened miniatures of vodka. I glanced at it and pursed my lips. Unpleasant-looking porn.

I scratched my head while Kennard checked the bathroom. My eyes drifted towards the wardrobe. The door was open, blocking my view. I sidled over and checked inside. A split second later, I desperately wished I hadn't.

'Anything?' Kennard enquired.

I stared at Tony's naked body hanging inside the wardrobe, a blue tie looped around his neck.

My crossbow fell to the floor.

Chapter Thirteen

'It happens more often than you'd think,' Kennard said kindly, pushing a cup of hot, sweetened tea into my hands. 'It doesn't get spoken about because I don't think the authorities want to give people ideas, but we usually get a case of auto-erotic asphyxiation every couple of years. And we're not alone. Lots of hotels have to deal with this.'

'Uh-huh.' I couldn't get the image of Tony's corpse out of my head. His glassy, bulging eyes were burned into my own retinas. I wasn't sure I'd ever forget what I'd seen.

'We'll keep his room sealed until the police get here.' She coughed. 'I mean, I know *you're* already here and you're with the police, but...'

'I know what you mean,' I said distantly.

I had the impression that Kennard was relieved that Tony's passing hadn't been more bloody and that nobody else was involved. It made things easier for both her and the hotel. Despite Tony's rank and profession, the fact that he'd done this to himself meant the ensuing investigation would be minimal. Once the police had made their initial examination of the scene and Tony's body was removed, the coroner's assessment would no doubt edge towards death by misadventure. Nobody would want to advertise the fact that a Metropolitan police detective had died by strangling himself in some bizarre sexual game, even if that detective had been hidden away in Supe Squad.

I lowered my cup. It was the ideal way to kill someone if you wanted to make sure that nobody looked into their death too closely. If two police officers in the same department both had their throats slit on the same night in different locations, all hell would break loose and the fallout would be unprecedented – especially given what had happened to Tony's flat.

I sprang to my feet. 'You wouldn't show me the CCTV or the room records before. Surely you can now.'

Kennard looked vaguely alarmed. 'We should wait for—'

I hardened my voice. 'Show me.'

She muttered something under her breath, then her jawline tightened. 'Very well.'

She brought up the files on her computer screen and swung it round it to me. 'The front desk has already isolated the footage of his entry into the hotel.' She clicked on an icon. 'Here.'

We watched as Tony strolled through the hotel lobby to the front desk. He was wearing the same clothes he'd been in earlier that day. There was a brief exchange of words as he passed over his credit card and received the room key card. He sauntered over to the lifts, his body language displaying no hint of what was to come.

'The security system is computerised,' Kennard told me. 'He entered his room at 12.32am last night. His door hasn't been opened since, we're certain of that.'

I passed a hand over my face. I didn't believe I was wrong about this. 'Where's Tallulah?' I asked.

Kennard blinked. 'Pardon?'

'His car. He had a car. He must have parked it here.'

She checked his details. 'Yes,' she said finally. 'He registered it when he checked in. It's in the underground car park.'

I didn't say another word. I grabbed my crossbow, nodded at her and walked out. This wasn't over – not by a long shot.

***

Even at that time of night, the DeVane car park was well lit. Unfortunately, that didn't help me find Tallulah any quicker. All the other cars were large, luxurious beasts so, although the scrappy purple Mini was certainly unique, she was hidden from view by the towering vehicles that surrounded her.

I marched down one side of the car park and came up short before swivelling and preparing to return in the opposite direction. That was when I caught the flickering shadow out of the corner of my eye about fifty metres to my right

It could have been anyone. This was obviously a well-used car park, so the chances were that it was merely one of the hotel valets. All the same, I slowed my steps, glad that my scruffy shoes had soft soles. Then I heard a rattle, followed by the sound of tearing plastic. The shadow in question was trying to break into one of the cars – and there was only one car down here that had plastic on it. I'd bet my soul on it.

I raised myself onto the balls of my feet and controlled my breathing as I

uncocked the safety on the crossbow. I edged closer until I confirmed that I was right; someone was indeed rummaging around Tallulah's interior. Whoever it was, they must have squeezed in through the broken rear window before shimmying through to the front seat.

I stopped and waited for the sneaky bastard to either emerge or drive away. I was neither shaking nor afraid; my only feeling was cold, grim determination.

There was a faint click as the car was unlocked from the inside. A moment later, I spied a dark head appearing from the open door. This was no car thief: the fucker was searching Tony's car. For what, I didn't know – but I was definitely going to find out.

'Police!' I yelled. My voice echoed round the car park. 'Stop right there!'

'Should I put my hands up, D'Artagnan?' Lukas's now-familiar voice drawled. 'Or should I freeze?'

I hissed. Of course it was him. 'Put your hands up, turn around and freeze. In that order.'

He did as I asked. I expected to see a smug smirk on his face, but his expression was serious. He glanced at the crossbow and raised his eyes to mine. 'I'm glad to see you took my advice and armed yourself properly. Do you know how to use that thing?'

I ignored his question. I was the one in charge, not him. 'What are you doing here?'

His response was mild. 'The same thing you are, I imagine.'

I glared at him, silently demanding an answer.

'I'm looking for Tony Brown,' he said. 'I tracked his car to this location.'

'How?' I demanded. 'How did you track it here?'

'It might surprise you to learn there are vampire eyes all over this city. And Tallulah,' he patted her bonnet, 'tends to get herself noticed.'

I didn't react when he gave the car's name. I doubted it was a secret. 'Keep talking.'

Lukas sighed. 'Sometimes we entertain clients from a particular subset, the sort of subset who like to stay here at the DeVane.'

'People who are wealthy?'

He inclined his head. 'Yes. Consequently, we keep some of the staff on a retainer so they can inform us when certain clients are visiting. It helps us to prepare should they wish to travel a few streets over and come to see us.'

'You mean you bribe the staff.'

Lukas shrugged. 'That's a crude way of putting it, but essentially yes. The valets are particularly useful.'

'So one of these valets contacted you about Tallulah?'

He gazed at me. 'Is this questioning going to take all night, D'Artagnan?' He deepened his voice by a mere note, but it made it sound altogether more provocative. 'I'm sure there are more productive things we could do with our time.'

I ignored his brief attempt at flirtation. Boy, was I not interested. 'Which valet?'

'Lily Twist.'

I made a mental note of the name and pressed on. 'Why are you looking for DC Brown?'

'Because, D'Artagnan, I find it curious that even without your death and subsequent re-birth, he is allowing you to wander the streets on your own. You're a babe in the woods and,' he opened his mouth an inch, before running his tongue over his sharp fangs, 'there are monsters lurking around every corner.'

Too much had happened for his suggestive action to intimidate me. 'Why do you care? I thought vampires only concerned themselves with hedonistic fun.'

He smiled. 'Our PR team is very effective. The façade we present to the world doesn't match the reality.'

I filed that titbit away for a later date. 'Where were you last night?'

'You already know the answer to that. I was investigating your death.'

'Did you come anywhere near this hotel?'

Lukas's eyes narrowed slightly. 'No.' He tilted his head. 'Tell me, did you find Brown in one of the rooms just now? There's nothing in the car to help pin down his location. If you tell me where he is, you'll save me a whole lot of bother.'

'Is there anyone who can vouch for your whereabouts last night?' I persisted.

'Are you going to answer every question with another question, D'Artagnan?'

All of a sudden, his phone rang, a high-pitched sound that startled me so much that I jumped – and involuntarily squeezed the trigger on the crossbow.

The silver-tipped bolt flew in his direction, whistling through the air with lethal force. Lukas leapt to the side with a lightning reaction that was too fast for my eyes to follow, and the bolt embedded itself into the concrete pillar behind him with a thud. A cloud of grey dust belched out. Oh God.

Lukas touched the tip of his ear and frowned. I stared in horror at the dab of blood on his fingers. 'You caught me,' he said drily. 'Maybe you do know how to use that thing after all.' He took out a pristine white handkerchief and wiped off the blood. Then, with chilling calm, he answered his phone which had continued to ring throughout. 'Yes.'

He listened to the other speaker while I looked from the crossbow to the bolt to Lukas and back again. I could well imagine that a vampire might take it personally that I'd almost shot them in the head. Under any other circumstances, this would have been the ideal time to leave.

As soon as Lukas hung up, I started to apologise. 'I'm sorry,' I said. 'I didn't intend to...'

Lukas sprang forward and grabbed me by the shoulders. The convivial light in his eyes had gone, replaced by complete darkness. He loomed over me and, for the first time, he genuinely scared me. 'When?' he bit out. 'When were you planning to tell me that Tony Brown is dead?'

I stared up at him, suddenly mute. I'd thought that vampires were all about cold emotions and even colder grips, but Lukas was the complete opposite. Even through the bulk of my borrowed clothes, I could feel the heat of his skin. And I was certainly aware of the furious fire in his face. The familiar terror uncoiled in the pit of my stomach and an involuntary tremor ran through my body from head to toe.

'Fuck!' He released his hold on me and stepped back. He didn't take his eyes away from me, but I felt some of the tension leave my body. I could breathe again. That helped.

'Was that Lily Twist again?' I asked shakily.

Lukas shook his head. 'Housekeeping.'

I watched him warily in case he made another move. Even if I could have reacted quickly enough, the crossbow was all but useless without a bolt loaded in it. 'Bad news travels fast,' I whispered. 'It's been less than an hour since I found his body.'

Lukas began to stalk up and down, five paces one way, five paces the other way. I flicked my gaze to the right. The exit from the car park into the hotel was fifty metres away. I'd never get there fast enough; I'd already seen enough of Lukas's reaction times to know that.

'Cause of death?'

'I'm no pathologist.'

Lukas stopped pacing and glowered at me. 'Your throat was cut. Did that happen to Brown too?'

'No.'

'Were there any similarities between your death and his?'

'No.' I paused. Other than the fact that we were both killed within hours of each other, of course.

He curled his fingers into fists. 'I am not the enemy, D'Artagnan. It might not feel like it, but I am on your side. I can help. What happened to Brown?'

I knew that I shouldn't believe him. I knew I should turn tail and run away as fast as I could. But I had few friends and even fewer answers. If Lukas was going to keep appearing out of the blue, maybe I should make use of him. I no longer seemed to have much to lose.

I sighed. He'd hear it from the housekeeper anyway. 'On the face of it, Tony died as a result of auto-erotic asphyxiation that went too far.'

Lukas blinked. 'Interesting kink,' he murmured. 'You don't believe it?'

'No.' I watched him, expecting him to tell me that I was being naïve and people got up to all sorts of things behind closed doors. He didn't; he simply waited. 'I went to his flat,' I said. 'It's been trashed. It's like someone was looking for something but I have no idea what.'

Lukas absorbed that. 'And your home?' he inquired. 'Has it been ransacked too?'

'No.' Then I amended my reply. 'Actually, I don't know for sure. I've not been back since last night. But I don't live alone – my boyfriend is there.' I thought of Jeremy and the worry on his face when he'd knocked on the Supe Squad door. Had someone broken into our flat too?

Lukas gazed at me with a strange expression on his face that I tried – and failed – to decipher. 'Have you told this boyfriend of yours what's happening?'

'I'm trying to keep him out of it. He's not with the police. It's safer for him if he stays out of it.'

'Not to mention the fact that you died and came back to life again,' Lukas murmured. 'That isn't the sort of thing that happens to normal people.'

I wanted to argue that I was perfectly normal, but I knew I wouldn't win that debate. Truth be told, I'd been doing my best to forget my impossible resurrection. One problem at a time. Unless... Hope flared in my chest. 'Maybe Tony will wake up just like I did.'

'Maybe,' Lukas said. He didn't sound convinced. His eyes grew distant as he mulled over something.

'He used a tie,' I blurted out.

'Pardon?'

'Tony used a tie. Round his neck. He used it to...' I swallowed '...to hang himself.'

'Is that important?'

'I can't pretend that I knew him well, but one of the first things he told me was that he didn't own any ties.'

Lukas rubbed his chin. 'Take me to him. I want to see him for myself.'

The last place I wanted to go was back to that room, but Lukas was a vampire. He might notice things that I couldn't. I didn't believe Tony's death was an accident or suicide – and I realised that, deep down, I needed someone else to believe that too.

Chapter Fourteen

Kennard had posted a security guard outside Tony's room. I couldn't imagine why anyone not on official business would want to go in there, but I guessed that whoever she'd spoken to when she'd called the police had insisted upon it. I was prepared to argue my way back in and insist that I had every right to be there, trainee or not, but Lukas already had the matter in hand.

'You will open the door and step aside,' he intoned. I caught an odd rasp in his voice. Whatever strange vampire magic he employed, it worked: the guard, who I'd been certain was about to deny us entry, did exactly as instructed.

'Jedi mind tricks again?'

Lukas glanced at me. 'I don't have a light sabre, but I'd take on Luke Skywalker any day. He wouldn't stand a chance.'

Did that mean the vampire belonged to the dark side? It wouldn't have surprised me.

The odd sour odour clinging to the air seemed stronger. Lukas paused inside the door, his nostrils flaring. 'The smell of fear?' I asked.

He shook his head. 'Death.'

Was that what I'd smelled like? I pushed away the unbidden thought. Focus, Emma.

I straightened my shoulders and followed Lukas into the room. I was on the verge of becoming a fully qualified police detective; I couldn't let a dead body get to me. I knew it was the fact that it was Tony's dead body that bothered me, but a corpse's identity shouldn't matter. It should simply make me more determined to find out what had happened.

'Be careful not to touch anything,' I said, in a bid to re-assert my authority. 'Assuming this is a crime scene, we don't want to contaminate any evidence.'

'Not my first rodeo,' Lukas replied mildly. 'But thank you for the tip.'

He walked round the room, glancing at the porn magazine and the rumpled quilt on the bed. When he reached the wardrobe, he gazed at Tony's body for a long moment. I thought his manner was detached and clinical until he looked at me and I saw the anger in his dark eyes. 'Check the window,' he said. 'Can it be opened?'

I stared at him. 'We're on the fourth floor.'

'We're not in your world any longer, D'Artagnan,' he retorted. 'Humour me.'

Supe or not, I failed to see how anyone could clamber in from the outside; even so, I did as he asked. I pulled my cuffs over my hands so I could tug the catch without leaving fingerprints. It slid upwards without so much as a whisper.

'Unfortunately for Brown,' Lukas said, glancing at the open window, 'this is an old building that's not sealed its windows to guard against jumpers. Unfortunately for all of us, jumpers aren't the only thing we need to guard against.'

I peered out. 'I still don't—' My voice faltered as I stared at the marks etched into grey stone wall beneath the window frame. If I hadn't been looking, I wouldn't have seen them. Without Lukas, it wouldn't have occurred to me to look.

He joined me, his body brushing against mine as he leaned out. He stiffened when he saw the gouges in the stone.

I measured the distance between us and the pavement below. It seemed an impossible height to scale. 'You don't mean that a werewolf climbed all this way up?'

'Do you believe that Brown was murdered?'

I didn't hesitate. 'Yes.'

'Then,' Lukas said simply, 'this is the only way they could have got in.' He pulled back. 'Although the question remains, why go to the bother of making Brown's death look like misadventure then leave your murdered body out in the open so ostentatiously?'

'And why kill either of us in the first place?'

Lukas nodded abruptly. 'You've spent less than two days with Supe Squad. Did you have any interaction with wolves when you were with Brown? Did any of them visit the office?'

Before I could answer, the door opened. I whirled round. When I saw who it was, my mouth dropped open.

'Ah,' Lukas said, 'I was wondering when you'd get here.'

Detective Superintendent Lucinda Barnes frowned. 'The pair of you are disturbing my scene.'

'DC Brown doesn't mind,' Lukas answered.

I just stared.

Barnes strode in, gazed at Tony's corpse and sighed. 'Such a shame.' She tutted and glanced at us. 'The hotel has given us the room opposite to use as a base. Come on, you two. It's time we had a little chat.'

***

Wilma Kennard knew what she was about; she'd already sent coffee and sandwiches to the hotel room. I grabbed a cup and gulped it down, then sat awkwardly on the edge of one of the twin beds. DSI Barnes and Lukas took the chairs.

'So,' Barnes said, looking at me, 'obviously these are far from ideal circumstances. Explain briefly what has happened up to this point.'

I drew in a breath. 'Tony didn't show up for work today. I went round to his flat, found it turned upside down and tracked him here.'

'Yes.' She sniffed. 'I saw your logins on the system and your request to track his phone. You're not supposed to do that on your own, you know. You're not qualified yet.'

The last thing I was going to do was apologise for investigating Tony's disappearance. I met her eyes and shrugged. 'I don't think this was an accident. I think Tony was killed deliberately.'

DSI Barnes glanced at Lukas. 'What do you think?'

'I concur with D'Artagnan's assessment.'

Her eyebrows shot up. 'D'Artagnan?'

I looked away. 'It's what Tony called me.'

A tiny smile lifted the corners of her mouth. 'Did he, indeed?'

'I'm sure you know by now what us supes are like with names,' Lukas said. 'At least when it comes to people we don't know very well. But in any case, D'Artagnan here has left out the most important information.'

I stiffened. Wait a minute.

'What's that?' Barnes asked.

'DC Brown is not the only police officer who died recently.'

'We don't need to cover this!' I snapped.

'Actually,' Lukas said firmly, 'we do. DSI Barnes, I take it that you heard about the woman killed at St Erbin's Church?'

'Yes.' Her lip curled. 'I also heard that we are no further forward identifying her, and the pathology team are delaying the post-mortem.'

Lukas pointed at me. 'Meet Jane Doe.'

I folded my arms and looked away. Great: the fanged freak had just told my boss that I was the walking dead. Whatever happened to me now, there was no chance that it would be good.

'Pardon?'

'Your cute little trainee had her throat cut and her skull fractured,' Lukas said. 'I saw her corpse myself. Twelve hours later, she woke up very much alive and without a single wound on her.'

Barnes stared at me.

'Did you know this was going to happen?' the vampire asked.

She flinched. 'No,' she whispered. 'I had no clue. Have you tasted her?'

He smiled, clearly amused. 'I don't think we've reached that stage in our relationship yet.'

I flicked my eyes from one to the other. 'What the fuck is going on here? Are you discussing drinking my blood? And why on earth would DSI Barnes have known what was going to happen?' I got to my feet, raising my voice. 'What the hell is this?'

'Sit down.' Barnes sighed. 'There's no great conspiracy here.'

'That's not what it sounds like to me!'

'Sit down,' she repeated, her expression returning to its usual hard-nosed professional facade, 'and I'll explain.'

I did as I was told like a recalcitrant child. I'd hear her out – but I wanted some fucking answers.

She unbuttoned her jacket and leaned back in her chair. 'I'm sure it didn't take you long to work out what things are really like in Supe Squad. The government has been decreasing funding for decades, but if we lose the last control we have over the supes then that will be it. We'll never gain it back – not without a fight.'

Lukas didn't look happy. 'Control is not the word I'd have used.'

She waved a hand at him dismissively. 'You know what I mean.' She sighed. 'DC Brown has been negotiating on our behalf with both the vampires and the werewolves. We want to keep a hand in their affairs – after all, nobody knows what's around the corner. Our involvement makes the public at large feel better about the supes' existence, and helps us to maintain peace.'

'From what I understand,' I said, 'a police presence is neither required nor desired.'

'That's what we keep saying,' Lukas said. 'However, we also wish to expand. We find the current limits placed on our kind constricting. For example, we can only turn one in every thousand applicants. We are virtually ghetto-ised and prohibited from trading outside our area. All supes are seeking to ease some of those unfair restrictions placed on our kind.'

'Unfair restrictions? We can't let you turn every Tom, Dick or Harry who shows up at your door into a vampire,' Barnes returned. Despite her obvious irritation at vamp methods, I had the sense that she was holding herself back out of some strange deference to Lukas. Perhaps DSI Barnes was actually afraid of vampires.

'It is not a process we take lightly,' he growled at her. 'You know that. Neither is it a case of biting someone and suddenly they're a vampire. It takes weeks. The vampires we turn become part of our family. Even without the restrictions, very few would make the cut.'

'It's not just about that. We can't allow you to grow your wealth to such a point that you have a stranglehold over the country. You take enough blood from us as it is!'

'All our blood comes from willing participants,' Lukas said. 'And you know very well that we only need to sup once a month to survive.'

'You live twice as long as the average human. That's a lot of months.'

Lukas looked calm, but I sensed that inside he was seething. 'Vampires are not the only ones seeking concessions. The wolves want to expand into another pack, turn more humans and make better use of the countryside.'

'Which is all very well,' Barnes snapped, 'until the next full moon when they lose control and end up killing innocent farmers! Regardless of its failings in recent years, Supe Squad exists for a reason!'

'Supe Squad is all but superfluous,' he shot back. 'As you know.'

I held up my hands. 'This is all very well and good,' I said. It looked like this argument could go on for hours. 'But what exactly does it have to do with me?'

Barnes calmed down slightly. 'DC Brown would have acknowledged that he had a somewhat laissez-faire approach to his job. But he was approaching retirement and he wasn't ... enthusiastic about giving it up. His wife died not too long ago, and he feared losing himself to the loneliness of old age. We had agreed that he would insinuate himself more into the supes' day-to-day lives. In return, we'd delay his retirement and try to find a second Supe Squad detective to continue the process alongside him. One new detective to begin with, then the plan is to introduce more.'

She glanced at Lucas. 'It has to be someone who both the vampires and werewolves can accept. I acknowledge that many of the police officers who've worked out of Supe Squad have been less than ... effective. We've been searching for a detective who is willing to learn, and has the potential to grow into the job, but who won't let their head be turned by what the supes have to offer. Someone who won't take any shit.'

I met her eyes. 'Me,' I said flatly.

'You are our opening gambit. You meet our skill requirements and, as a trainee, you haven't got the baggage that other detectives might carry.' She leaned forward. 'Please understand that you'd never be *forced* into taking a position at Supe Squad. The plan was that we would discuss it with you at the end of your rotation. If you found the notion distasteful, we would never mention it again. There are plenty more trainees where you came from.'

I frowned. 'You should have explained this to me at the start.'

'If we had, your attitude would have been different. We need someone who is completely unbiased.'

'Well,' I remarked, 'you won't find a much more unbiased police officer than a dead one. Good work.'

DSI Barnes winced. Lukas was unmoved, however. 'Very few vampires, werewolves or humans know what's been going on, or that the Metropolitan Police are seeking a more active role. If Brown was murdered because some supe is unhappy about the police wanting to involve themselves more in our lives, the killer wouldn't have tried to mask his death as an accident. They would have made it as bloody as possible in order to make a point.'

'*My* death was pretty damned bloody,' I said. 'And I think that killing two Supe Squad police officers in one night would be more than enough to scare off any others from wanting to work there.'

'I don't believe that's why you were murdered,' Lukas said, grinding his teeth. 'Either of you. It might be hard for you to understand what it's like to be a supernatural, but I've been doing this for a long time. We don't care about subtleties. We don't send coded messages. We don't have to. The motive for the killings is something completely separate.'

I think that he believed that but, until I had proof to the contrary, I was withholding my judgment.

'But you do think it was a supe who did this?' Barnes asked.

His answer was terse. 'Yes.'

'Which brings us back to the need for Supe Squad's existence. And you, D'Artagnan.' She smiled slightly. 'DC Brown wouldn't have given you a nickname if he didn't think you were good enough to stay. He was giving you his blessing as his successor.' She linked her fingers together. 'So let's get down to it. If you died last night, why are you alive now? Are you a vampire?'

Lukas rolled his eyes. 'Obviously she's not.'

'There's no *obviously* about anything. Not any more.'

These two were giving me a headache. 'I don't know what I am,' I said aloud. 'And frankly, right now I don't care.' I pointed at the door. 'My mentor is hanging in his wardrobe across that hallway. He is *dead*. And whoever killed him has tried to make it look like he committed suicide. Whatever their motives, I will find the bastard that did that to him and who also murdered me. The rest of this is bollocks.'

There was a knock at the door and a uniformed police officer put his head round. 'DSI Barnes,' he said. 'Can I have a word?'

She nodded and walked out, leaving Lukas and I alone.

'I wish you hadn't told her about me,' I complained.

'She needed to know. And DSI Barnes, for all her designs on Supe Squad, isn't a bad sort. She'll keep your secret to herself.' He ran a hand through his hair. 'I want you to be aware that my dislike of Supe Squad is not personal to you,' he said quietly.

'Ditto.' I met his dark gaze. 'And I want *you* to be aware that I don't care what you think, and I don't care what's gone on in the past. I'm going to find the bastard responsible for this and bring them down.'

'So am I.' He smiled humourlessly. 'Finding whoever murdered you and Brown is the only way I can keep your lot from sticking your noses in where they don't belong. It's why I involved myself in your death. We both have a vested interest in locating the killer. You don't want to be in Supe Squad any more than I want Supe Squad to continue. We might as well join forces since our interests align. And perhaps,' he added, 'we can find out what you really are along the way.'

It made a sort of warped sense, but I wasn't prepared to shake hands on it yet. 'Why did DSI Barnes want to know if you'd tasted me?'

His eyes shifted. 'In the past, there've been a few detectives in Supe Squad who've become ... close to vampires.'

'They allowed themselves to be bitten?' I was incredulous.

'They didn't just allow it, they wanted it. They *asked* for it.'

I felt sick.

Lukas continued. 'And to taste someone's blood is to understand their essence. If I drank you from you, it might help me to understand what you are and why you cheated death so successfully.'

'That,' I said, 'is never going to happen.'

'It wasn't an invitation.' He said it almost primly. 'And I'd never drink from someone without their permission first. No vampire would be so uncouth.'

I snorted. 'That's a pretty sweeping statement. You can't speak for all of your kind.'

'Yes, I can,' he said.

Barnes re-entered the room, her expression troubled. 'I sent two uniforms round to Tony's flat. You said it had been ransacked?'

I nodded.

'They broke down the door. The place is pristine. There's not so much as a speck of dust out of place.'

I started. 'But—'

'The killer is covering his tracks,' Lukas said. 'He still wants us to believe that Brown died by his own hand.'

I sucked in a breath. 'I only went to Tony's place because of what had happened to me. I wouldn't have gone there to search for him so quickly otherwise. I wanted to confront him because I thought he was responsible.' My voice dropped to a whisper. 'I thought he was the one who'd killed me.'

'That's understandable. And this is a good thing.' Lukas sounded satisfied. 'The real killer doesn't know that you've returned to life, otherwise he'd have cleaned up the mess at Tony's flat sooner. He wouldn't have risked anyone seeing the devastation there and becoming suspicious.'

'So you think our perp attacked Tony in his own home? Then Tony escaped and came here, thinking he'd be safe?'

Lukas nodded. 'But he was followed. The killer broke in through the window and finished what he'd started. He took his time tidying up because you'd not been identified, and no one suspected that Brown's disappearance was anything but innocuous.'

'Well,' DSI Barnes marvelled, with a definite hint of sarcasm, 'look at the two of you. It's like watching Cagney and Lacey.'

Making a decision, I stood up. 'We'll work together for now. We'll find the supe responsible for this and bring them to justice.'

'*Supe* justice,' Lukas said.

Barnes' mouth tightened. 'Very well.' She began to re-fasten the buttons on her jacket. 'I won't advertise any suspicions about the manner of DC Brown's death until we have proof. The two of you have the freedom to investigate further – but I don't want word getting out either about DC Brown, or that I'm permitting a trainee to remain in place without adequate supervision. These are extraordinary circumstances. It will harm all of us if anyone gets wind of what might have really happened. The last thing we need is to sour relations between the police and the supes even further, or to create any more public ill-will.'

She glanced at me. 'And that silence covers your ... resurrection, too. I don't understand what happened to you, or what you are, but I strongly suggest you keep it to yourself for now.'

'Agreed.' I jerked my thumb towards Tony's room. 'Send him to Dr Hawes at the Fitzwilliam Manor. She'll know what to do. We can trust her.' I checked my watch. 'We don't know how long he's been dead but, if he's going to wake up like I did, it won't be long until he does.'

'Noted.' She raised her chin. 'Tony Brown was one of us. Find the bastard who did this.'

Lukas nodded. 'Count on it.'

Chapter Fifteen

Lukas and I headed down to the DeVane carpark. 'Here,' he said, tossing something at me.

I caught it and looked down. A car key. My head snapped up again. 'What's this?'

'It's for Tallulah.' He ambled over to the pillar where my crossbow bolt was still embedded, reached up and yanked it out as if he were sliding a knife out of butter.

'Where did you—' I frowned at the key. 'You took this from Tony's hotel room?'

He shrugged. 'He doesn't need it any more.'

'I told you not to touch anything. I thought we were coming down here because you had a car of your own parked here.'

'I do,' he answered smoothly. 'But Tallulah is better.'

'Tallulah smells funny,' I muttered.

Lukas stilled and gave me a long look.

'What?' I asked.

'What is it exactly that you smell?'

'Tony told me it was a blend of verbena and wolfsbane, but I get patchouli too.'

Lukas absorbed my words for a moment then passed me the silver bolt. 'Careful with that,' he said. He continued walking.

'Wait.' I caught up to him. 'What's the big deal with the smell?'

He put his hands in his pockets. 'Did Tony tell you why it smells like that?'

'Not exactly. It's the same as inside the Supe Squad building, though.'

'Indeed it is.'

Becoming frustrated, I nudged him. 'So?'

'So what?'

'The smell. Why is it a big deal?'

'I'm not sure that you really want to know the answer to that, D'Artagnan.'

I ground my teeth. 'Tell me.'

'The quantity of herbs burned to release the smell is miniscule. Far less than a human nose could detect.'

'Bullshit. It was so strong the first time I walked into the Supe Squad building that it made my eyes water.'

He gave me a sidelong look. 'I told you that you wouldn't like the answer.'

'You're saying that because I can smell it, I'm a supe,' I said flatly.

'Pretty much. You're not a vampire or a werewolf. You're clearly no gremlin or pixie, either. You, D'Artagnan, are something new.'

The back of my neck prickled uncomfortably. I couldn't pretend that this was news; it wasn't as if normal people had their throats slit and woke up twelve hours later in a burst of flames. And I'd not even mentioned the flames to Lukas.

'In theory,' he continued, 'Brown used the herbs to root out any supes who are hiding their identity. It's a technique Supe Squad have used for decades.'

'And in practice?'

'Could be habit. But it's probably for the tourists.'

I frowned. 'To impress them?'

Lukas laughed. 'No. To ward off all those idiots who appear at the door convinced that they themselves are supes. People who pass by a vampire in the street and think that they've been turned because they've breathed the same air. Or the people who think that they're werewolves because they enjoy their steak rare.' He grinned. 'Humans are far crazier than supes will ever be. And if they can't smell the herbs then they ain't supe, no matter how much bloody meat they consume.'

'I'm vegetarian,' I informed him snippily, as if that meant I couldn't possibly be supernatural.

He glanced at me, still amused. 'Good for you.'

We reached Tallulah. I did my best to repair the black plastic sheeting then got into the driver's seat. Lukas had to all but fold himself in to fit inside next to me. I snickered slightly at his discomfort. 'I thought Tallulah was better than your car. What do you drive? A Little Tikes Cozy Coupé?'

'I'm not an entirely selfish bastard,' he said, shifting himself around. 'Driving Tallulah makes you instantly recognisable to any supes. It means you won't be treated as a tourist and you'll be taken more seriously.'

'Like Tony was?'

Lukas didn't answer.

I clipped in my seatbelt and turned on the engine. I was briefly tempted to head back to Tony's flat and see its now unblemished state, but that was pointless and would only waste time. I already knew what it looked like, and there was no chance there would be any new evidence lying around that would help us.

'You said only a few people know about the plans for Supe Squad to become more active,' I said to Lukas. 'Do you happen to have a handy list of these people? Specifically werewolves?'

He sighed. 'It's a fool's errand. This is not why either you or Tony was killed.'

I waited.

Lukas clicked his tongue. 'I don't have a definitive list. But I assume all four werewolf clan heads and their immediate deputies are aware of the plans.'

I glanced at my watch. It was already one in the morning. 'Will they still be up and about?'

'Probably.' He crossed his arms over his chest, indicating that it was a pointless effort. I ignored him and released the handbrake. Werewolves, here we come.

***

Taking a leaf out of Tony's old playbook, I parked Tallulah smack bang in the centre of the wolves' quarter, ignoring the fact that there were no others cars and the streets were teeming with people.

Lukas sniffed. 'It's always so much quieter here at this time of night than in Soho.'

I stared at the crowds and wondered just how busy the vampires' quarter got. 'Four clans. Sullivan, McGuigan, Carr and who?'

'Fairfax.'

'Anything important I need to know about them?'

'They're werewolves.'

I rolled my eyes. 'You know what I mean.'

'I wasn't being facetious. No matter how friendly – or human – they might appear when they're in human form, werewolves still possess an inherent wildness that can make them wholly unpredictable and incredibly dangerous.'

'Unlike vampires, who are warm and cuddly?'

'Werewolves are governed by the moon,' he responded without rancour. 'They are less in control of themselves than we are. And full moon is only a few nights away.' He waved a hand. 'The closer it is, the longer the wolves stay out for. They sleep less. From tomorrow, they'll start fasting in preparation. A tired, hungry animal should always be approached with caution.'

Point taken. 'Is that why Tony and I were killed?' I asked. 'Because a werewolf gave in to their inner animal?'

'No.' Lukas was silent for a moment. 'Those murders were planned. Nobody walks the streets at night with a sharp dagger like the one used to cut your throat unless they intend to use it. And everything we've seen so far suggests that Tony was stalked before he was killed.'

A shiver rippled through me and I rubbed my arms. 'Where to first?'

Lukas nodded towards the line of people queuing up outside some sort of club. 'Lord Fairfax will be holding court in there.'

It was as good a place to start as any. I nodded and began to get out of the car. Before I could, Lukas leaned across and placed a hand on my arm. The touch of his skin seared into me.

'Tread carefully,' he warned. 'And leave the crossbow in the car. You won't be in any immediate danger in this place, but these are still powerful people. If you start flinging around accusations, it won't go down well. Especially when there is no chance that these were alpha-sanctioned kills. You don't want to start a war, D'Artagnan.'

It was on the tip of my tongue to snap that I wasn't stupid even though I was a trainee, but I knew that he was genuinely trying to help. 'I will be careful,' I promised. 'But don't you do anything stupid either, like telling them that I was killed too.'

'I give you my word that they won't hear it from me,' he promised.

Good.

I stepped onto the street, very aware of the wide eyes staring in our direction. He'd been right about Tallulah.

The last thing I was prepared to do was join the back of the club's queue. I strode to the front with my head held high, ignoring the well-dressed people waiting behind me. The heavyset bouncer didn't hesitate; he simply unclipped the rope and allowed both Lukas and I access. I could get used to this.

As soon as we entered, I realised this wasn't a head-pounding nightclub filled with sweaty bodies and thumping tunes. On the contrary, despite the long queue of people waiting hopefully outside, it was more like a sedate gentleman's club. Round tables dotted the main room, each one lit with a small lamp, the green glass shades giving off an intimate, warm hue.

A group of classical musicians were performing on a small stage. I recognised the music as Wagner and glanced at Lukas. 'I suppose these tunes are from your era?'

He snorted. 'I'm not that old, D'Artagnan.'

I smiled and continued to look around. 'Can you tell who's wolf and who's human?'

'Here everyone is wolf,' he told me.

A young woman walked towards us. She was wearing the uniform of service staff the world over: a plain black skirt and starched white shirt. Both were immaculate and, even from a distance, I could tell the material was expensive. I supposed it paid to be a supe.

'Good evening.' She inclined her head and flicked me a look of unashamed curiosity, even though most of her attention was on Lukas. 'May I get you a drink?'

'No,' I said, at the exact same time as Lukas answered, 'Whisky on the rocks.'

'Very well. Please follow me.'

She led us towards an unmarked door at the rear on the opposite side to the musicians. I felt a tug of anxiety that we were leaving the safety of the crowded room and snuck a look at Lukas. His expression was bland, his smile disinterested. At least it was until a wiry man at one of the tables nearby got to his feet and swaggered over to us, his arms swinging by his sides like he was preparing for a fight. At that point, Lukas bared his teeth and displayed his fangs for all to see. The other man immediately thought better of his approach and faltered. Neither Lukas nor the woman missed a step.

We passed through the door and walked down a short hallway into another room that boasted even greater splendour. There were only three tables but the decor, from the lavish oil painting depicting a naval battle to the lit fireplace and the huge Chinese vases flanking it, suggested the owner had incredible wealth. Either that, I mused, or it was designed to advertise wealth and intimidate guests.

The waitress, if that's what she was, gestured at the nearest table and left. I remained standing. 'What's this about, Lukas?' I asked. 'Nobody has asked us who we are or what we're doing here. Why are we in this room?'

'Just relax,' he advised. 'Everything will be fine. Although, if I can ask a favour, don't call me that while we're here.'

I blinked. 'Don't call you Lukas?' Surely that was just his nickname? I stared at him. Had he given me his true name?

'If you wouldn't mind.' He offered me a gentle smile. Taken aback, I nodded agreement.

He pulled out one of the chairs for me, an action that made me surprisingly uncomfortable. I sat down gingerly, my back straight and my feet flat on the carpeted floor. Lukas sat opposite, leaned back and rested his feet on one of the other spare seats. He stretched out his arms, linked his hands behind his head and yawned. Any second now, I thought, the man would be taking forty winks.

The door opened again. A man in his mid-thirties appeared with two others behind him. I stood up to greet him. Lukas remained exactly where he was.

'Good evening. I am Lord Fairfax.'

He was so finely dressed that I almost curtseyed. Instead, I stuck out my hand. Habit told me to give him my real name; instinct told me otherwise. 'You may call me D'Artagnan,' I said. 'I'm on temporary assignment with Supernatural Squad.'

Fairfax smiled. 'What a lovely coat you're wearing,' he murmured, even though the puffy jacket swamped me and would have looked more appropriate on a mountain hiker than a city copper.

'Thank you. What a lovely ... cravat you're wearing,' I said, returning the compliment. Two could play at that game.

I waited for Lukas to introduce himself, or for Fairfax to speak to him. When that didn't happen, I sat down again. Enough fannying around. I had questions that needed answers. 'I appreciate you taking the time to meet with us,' I said. 'I'm afraid that I'm here on official business. A serious crime has taken place.'

Fairfax sat down, leaving his two colleagues standing. They took up positions on either side of the room, poised for action. I couldn't imagine what they were expecting would happen.

'A crime involving Supernatural Squad?' Fairfax enquired with a disbelieving tilt of his head.

'Unfortunately, yes.' I watched his expression closely. 'DC Anthony Brown has been murdered.'

Lord Fairfax didn't flinch, but I was certain that I briefly registered shock in his eyes. Alas, I didn't get chance to confirm it. There was a knock at the door and the woman entered again carrying a tray of drinks. She handed them round and moved to back of the room. We were now effectively surrounded by werewolves.

Fairfax sipped his drink. 'I won't pretend to be devastated by this news,' he said. 'Brown and I were never great friends and he owed me several favours, which he was in no hurry to pay back. However,' he glanced at Lukas, 'I'm not pleased either. This will have consequences for us all.'

'Happy consequences?' Lukas drawled, speaking for the first time since Fairfax had entered the room.

'Certainly not. As you well know.' Fairfax swirled the clear liquid in his glass and placed it on the table. 'Have you apprehended a suspect?'

'No.'

'Do you have a suspect?'

I chose my words carefully. 'There is no specific suspect as yet. However, there's evidence to suggest DC Brown's killer was a werewolf.'

Fairfax's reaction was instantaneous: he stiffened, his entire body went rigid and his cheeks suffused with red. 'That is not possible.'

'It is perfectly possible,' Lukas said. 'As *you* well know.'

I stared at Fairfax. The flesh on his hands was twisting, his fingers curling and growing long claws in front of my eyes. Wiry dark hairs were springing out along his jawline. I'd assumed that someone of his stature and bearing would be in full control of his wolf, but I'd assumed wrongly.

The door opened yet again. This time, it wasn't a member of staff on the threshold, it was Lady Sullivan. Her icy gaze swept over all of us. 'Well, well, well,' she murmured. 'Isn't this cosy?'

I was confused. If this was a Fairfax club, what was she doing here? I watched as she glided in and stopped in front of an empty chair. Then she waited. Lord Fairfax rolled his eyes and nodded at the wolf standing nearby who sprang forward and pulled out the chair. Lady Sullivan didn't acknowledge the gesture; she merely shook out her long heavy skirt and sat down. 'Tea,' she said to no one in particular. 'Darjeeling.'

The waitress looked at Fairfax. He sighed. 'Fetch Lady Sullivan a cup of tea,' he said. 'And you might as well arrange for an Appletini and a beer while you're at it. I don't expect the others will be far behind.'

Sullivan examined her fingernails. 'It was a rather conspicuous entry.'

I glanced at Lukas. He hadn't moved an inch. My eyes narrowed at him; it was our entry that Lady Sullivan was referring to. He must have known this would happen: four birds with one stone. That wasn't necessarily a bad thing – although I'd have appreciated a warning first.

I realised that Lady Sullivan had looked up from her manicure and was staring at me with an openly speculative and rather suspicious expression. I folded my arms across my chest and stared back at her. She allowed herself a tiny smile then blinked, and broke contact.

We didn't have long to wait. Within minutes, the door opened and another couple appeared – a burly male with heavy jowls and a broad chest, and a slender woman who was his complete opposite. She looked like she might snap in a strong breeze. She gulped at the beer that was placed in front of her, while the man curled his squat fingers round the delicate Appletini glass and lapped at the drink with his tongue like a cat. I goggled at them both.

'Lady Carr,' Fairfax said by way of introduction. 'And Lord McGuigan. This is ... D'Artagnan, the latest addition to Supernatural Squad.'

Neither of them raised an eyebrow; either the two clan heads already knew of my arrival or they didn't care.

Lord Fairfax drained his glass, smacked his lips and looked at me. 'Perhaps you should start from the beginning.'

An unbidden image of my own corpse engulfed in flames rose up in my mind, but I quashed it. Not that beginning. 'I am here,' I said baldly, 'because I believe my mentor, Detective Constable Anthony Brown, has been murdered. His body was discovered a few hours ago at the DeVane Hotel. There is evidence outside his room that a werewolf was involved.'

All four werewolf leaders looked at Lukas. He leaned forward, picked up his whisky and took a drink.

'What evidence exactly?' Sullivan inquired.

'His fourth-floor room was accessed via the window,' Lukas said. 'There are claw marks in the stone work outside. Wolf claw marks.'

McGuigan started to splutter. 'Preposterous! This is obviously some ploy on the vampires' part to make us look bad. None of us wanted Brown dead. Quite the opposite, in fact!'

Lukas finally removed his feet from the chair and sat up straight. 'I can assure you that no vampire wished for anything other than for Brown to continue in his position. If you doubt that it was a werewolf who killed him, then you're more than welcome to visit the crime scene yourselves.'

Lady Carr wiped her mouth with the back of her hand. 'How did Brown die?'

'The cause of death has not yet been determined,' I said. 'His body is only just being transported to the morgue.'

Her nose wrinkled. 'Yes, yes, but you must have some indication about what happened. Was his throat torn out? Was it a head wound? Blood loss? What?'

'His body,' Lukas said, 'was made to appear as if he'd hanged himself.'

I breathed out. I was both surprised and grateful that Lukas had chosen not to reveal all the salient details. I might not have known Tony well but the least he deserved was some scrap of dignity in his death.

'Made to appear?' Fairfax inquired. 'Or did he actually hang himself? He lost his wife recently, remember.'

I cleared my throat. 'The pathologist will be able to confirm what actually happened, but there is other evidence to suggest foul play.' I outlined what I'd seen at Tony's flat and its subsequent clean-up.

I expected further dissent from the wolves; instead, they gazed at each other. The atmosphere in the room changed from suspicion to worry.

'What does this mean for us?' McGuigan asked. 'Are we to expect a sudden influx of police?'

'Bound to.' Carr's mouth turned down. 'They might have no legal authority, but they could easily use Brown's death as a way to force their position. We need to be prepared for a fight. We should put out a statement to the press straight away. Then we need to find the fucker responsible for this, and rip their heart from their body.' She licked her lips and I suddenly understood that she wasn't speaking metaphorically.

Fairfax nodded. 'I'll contact the Prime Minister's office and reiterate our loyalty.'

'Right now, the police are keeping the matter quiet,' Lukas interjected,

Lady Sullivan's eyes narrowed. 'Why? Is Barnes going to use this as an opportunity to send in more troops? More than this girl here? Whoever she really is?' She hissed. 'All that money we spent trying to keep Brown in place. We might as well have pissed it up that damned wall.'

I blinked, surprised at both her vehemence and her language. 'What money is that?' I asked.

The four werewolves, who I sensed didn't necessarily like each other but who were in agreement, didn't answer. Realisation hit me; now I got it. 'The police wanted him to retire,' I said. 'They wanted him out of the way so that different detectives with different agendas could be moved in. You wanted him to stay. His attitude was exactly what you wanted. You were all bribing him.'

Sullivan's lip curled. 'It was not bribery. He was free to act however he wished. We simply enhanced his earnings. He performed a difficult job, and we were happy to help him.'

The worst thing was that I believed her. And I believed that Tony would have argued that he wasn't in any way compromised, and that he was still doing his job. But even he would have known that he couldn't continue as the sole Supe Squad detective indefinitely.

DSI Barnes seemed to think Tony had sanctioned me as his replacement. Was that because Tony had thought I'd be happy to take the same kind of backhanders? Or was it because he knew I wouldn't? I shook my head; either way, it didn't matter. The four clan heads were desperate for damage control. They hadn't wanted Tony out of the way, they'd wanted him to stay exactly where he was.

Lukas had been right; whichever wolf had killed Tony, their motive wasn't anything to do with police politics, or to prevent humans from taking a greater interest in supe affairs. This was something entirely different.

I stood up. 'I'm only in Supe Squad for the next twelve days. After that, I don't know what will happen. Frankly, I don't care. What I'm going to do, however, is find out who killed DC Brown. I will do that with or without your help. I suspect that your cooperation will make whatever comes next easier on all of you – but that's up to you.'

A deep grumble sounded in McGuigan's chest. 'We can't be seen to be helping the police. Most of my wolves have no idea what's going on behind the scenes, and it's better if it stays that way. I have too many hotheads to deal with as it is.'

Fairfax agreed. 'I have the same issues.' He met my eyes. 'We will not stand in your way, however. We need the killer found – assuming, of course, that it really was a werewolf who did this.'

Lukas who spoke up. 'It was.'

'The last thing we need is for others to find out that a werewolf might have killed a police officer. Even if turns out not to be true, the rumour could be our undoing and the tiniest leak could spell disaster,' Sullivan said.

I lifted my chin. 'I have reasons of my own for keeping this as quiet as possible. I will find out who did this.'

'And I,' Lukas smiled, 'will help.'

Carr gave him a hard look, but Lukas pretended not to notice. He got to his feet and extended his hand to me. I ignored it; I was perfectly capable of walking out of here without his assistance. Fairfax snickered but Lukas looked more amused than offended.

'When we find the culprit,' he said to the clan leaders, 'I'll let you know so that you can deal with them in your own way.'

Like hell. I'd sort out the bastard on my own terms. Wisely, I kept my mouth shut. Nobody had bought *my* soul – and nobody would.

Chapter Sixteen

'I trust you're satisfied now it's been confirmed that DSI Barnes' plans for Supe Squad had nothing to do with Brown's death,' Lukas asked, as we returned to Tallulah.

My response was grudging. 'I am, but I still need proof positive that a werewolf killed him. I'm quite sure you vampires can also scale walls.' I eyed him. 'Right?'

He splayed his fingers towards me. 'No claws here.'

I noticed he hadn't answered my question. 'A definitive cause of death will make a massive difference.'

'I'm sure your pathologist friend can help you with that.'

I hoped so. I'd visit Laura first thing in the morning and keep my fingers tightly crossed that there was real evidence of foul play.

'You should get some rest,' Lukas advised. 'It's been a long traumatic day and you look tired. We have some vampire guest houses where you can sleep if you still don't want to go home to your boyfriend.'

Guilt twinged at me. I'd barely given Jeremy a thought since he'd walked away from Supe Squad's door. 'I appreciate the thought, but there's a sofa at Supe Squad that will do me just fine. I can drive there and park outside.' I paused. 'Would you like a lift back to Soho first?'

Lukas stretched out his arms and grinned at me with an edge of wicked delight. 'D'Artagnan, this is *my* time. We vampires might be able to go out during the day, but at heart we're creatures of the night. I'll walk. And I'll enjoy every breath of the sweet, dark air.'

Okay then. 'That's not creepy at all,' I muttered. I fiddled with Tallulah's door, eventually wrenching it open so I could clamber inside. 'You don't have to keep helping me, you know. I can take care of the rest of the investigation from here.'

His dark eyes danced. 'I wouldn't dream of abandoning you.' He winked at me then took off.

Lukas strolled down towards the elaborate wooden archway leading out of Lisson Grove. The werewolves that were still milling around gave him a wide berth. I didn't suppose they were very happy about having a vampire in their midst. His presence, and the nonchalant way he strolled towards the archway, laid waste to the theory that it was a deterrent for vampires.

He glanced over his shoulder and saw me watching him. I coughed and hastily looked away, then shoved the key into Tallulah. It was time to get a move on. Regardless of what Lukas might think, my work wasn't done.

I put Tallulah into gear and drove off. In theory, I could easily park at Supe Squad and walk the remainder of the way, and I'd probably get there faster if I did so. Navigating London's one-way system, especially this close to the centre of the city, could be a minefield. But I still wasn't prepared to wander round the streets on my own.

As far as I was concerned, the night air was far more bitter than sweet. The memory of my death was very fresh – and very traumatic. It was nibbling away at the edges of my psyche; if I thought about it too hard, my mind felt like it would explode. The safest thing would be to do exactly what I'd told Lukas and curl up on Supe Squad's sofa for some sleep.

I'd confronted the werewolf alphas, however. It was only right that I did the same with the vampires and located their leader, Lord Horvath, so I could question him. Lukas might indeed be a vampire – and a helpful one at that – but for all I knew he was at the bottom of the pecking order. And his opinion of the vampires was obviously biased.

I was determined to keep an open mind regarding all the supes and their potential involvement in Tony's death. Seeing the whites of Horvath's eyes, and registering his reaction when I informed him about Tony, would be priceless investigatory material. Assuming that

Lukas and his contacts at the DeVane hotel hadn't beaten me to the punch. I mentally crossed my fingers that wasn't the case.

I found a parking spot on the edge of Soho and the vampires' quarter. Lukas had been right about one thing, I thought, peering out of the window. It certainly was a lot busier here than in Lisson Grove. The groups of people wandering around were comforting, but I still glanced down at the crossbow and debated whether to take it with me. But I doubted its presence would endear me to the vampire Lord, assuming I could get close to him. And I'd almost taken Lukas's head off with it by accident. I left it where it was.

The one obvious stumbling block about this little venture without Lukas in tow was that I had no clue about Lord Horvath's whereabouts. Soho wasn't massive, but I could search it all night before I stumbled across him. I considered – and discarded – the idea of asking someone for directions. I wanted to catch Horvath unawares so that he couldn't prepare glib answers to my questions. In order to locate the vampire Lord, I'd have to be sneaky.

From the relative safety of Tallulah, I watched a group of women cross the road. A few of them looked the worse for wear, no doubt having imbibed a lot of alcohol. To a woman, they were wearing short skirts and pretty tops that were entirely at odds with the cold weather. I glanced down: I'd have to do better than an oversized coat and sweater if I wanted to blend in.

I removed them both, then tied the bottom of the large T-shirt into a knot so my midriff was exposed. My get-up was hardly the stuff of high fashion, and it made me feel more vulnerable, but it would have to do. I ran a hand through my hair to muss it up. A moment later, I left Tallulah and slid in behind the women so anyone watching would think I was a part of their group.

A pretty blonde, with tanned skin and long false eyelashes, staggered into me. 'Sorry.'

I smiled at her. 'That's fine.' I hooked my arm into hers.

She frowned, obviously trying to place me, then she shrugged and giggled. 'I've had way too much to drink,' she confided.

I laughed lightly. 'That makes two of us.' I leaned my head in towards hers. 'But I heard that the vamps like it when we're drunk. It makes our blood taste better and gives them more of a rush.'

'Have you been bitten before?' she asked in a loud whisper.

I winked. 'I'm a vampire virgin.'

The woman beamed. 'Me too!'

'I want tonight to be my first time.'

'Me too!'

'But I want it to be a good vampire.'

'Me too!'

I was beginning to think I'd chosen the wrong person to attach myself to. I'd need more than agreement to get the information I needed. 'You know,' I said, 'I want to find the sort of vampire who's quite high up. One with a lot of power. Someone,' I lowered my voice, 'who's in the inner circle.'

'Me too!'

Damn it. 'Where are we heading to now?' I persisted. 'Is it somewhere with the right kind of vamp?'

'We're going to Heart, silly.' She rolled her eyes. 'Didn't you know?'

I was about to mumble a reply, but she continued speaking. 'All the best vamps hang out there.' Her eyes widened. 'And that often includes Lord Horvath.'

I exhaled. Praise be.

One of the other women turned round. She jigged up and down, although I wasn't sure whether it was from excitement or the cold. 'Word's come down that Horvath has just shown up. He's inside Heart right now.'

'Do you think he'll bite one of us?' my companion asked eagerly.

I grinned at her. 'Why wouldn't he? We're a tasty bunch.'

'We have to get into Heart first. They don't let just anyone through the door.'

All the more reason to stick close to these ladies and slide in with them.

'Piece of cake,' I told her, exuding all the confidence I could muster. If there was one thing I'd already learned, the vampires' quarter wasn't for the shy and retiring.

We rounded the corner. High above the street was a flashing, heart-shaped neon sign. Not a love heart: this was an anatomically-correct heart. I swallowed and looked at the long queue snaking outside. Maybe sneaking in was a mistake. Perhaps I should mimic what had worked at the Fairfax's place, march to the front and demand admittance. The last thing I wanted was to wait around for hours and then be turned away.

I needn't have worried. My group of women were glitzy enough and loud enough to attract the attention of one of the bouncers. He was more slender than a wolf, but he had even more of a dangerous edge as he sauntered over and looked us up and down.

The blonde next to me pressed the palms of her hands together in mock prayer while one of her friends offered him a saucy wink.

'Go on, then,' he said. 'You guys can get in.'

There were several squeals from the group – and several groans from the other people waiting. I exhaled with relief and made sure that I kept close as we tripped past the queue and headed inside.

'All phones and cameras have to be checked in,' intoned a second vamp. He pointed to a desk, behind which lay a mind-boggling number of stacked lockers. It was just as well I'd not brought my crossbow; if they were this pernickety about phones, they certainly wouldn't look kindly on lethal weapons.

I indicated to the vamp that I had nothing on me. He looked at me suspiciously, as if he were sure I was lying. Unwilling to lose ground now that I'd come this far, I gestured towards my body with what I hoped was a sexy smirk. 'You can search me if you want.'

He grunted. 'I'm on the job. Maybe another night.'

Trying not to look relieved, I winked at him. Then I ducked past my new women friends and pushed open the swing doors leading to the club's interior.

Lukas had mentioned that the vampires had great PR to advertise to the world that they were nothing more than hedonistic fun-lovers. From my vantage point, it looked like a hell of a lot more than PR. The sight that greeted my eyes was like nothing I'd ever seen before. No wonder people were queuing to get in.

The place was vast, and everyone was having a good time. Servers dressed in blood-red clothing wove between tables and skirted the edge of the huge, packed dance floor. Most of them had their arms in the air and were swaying to the music which, while not earsplittingly loud, was definitely upbeat.

It felt like I'd wandered into an adults' version of Disneyland. I noticed that my foot was tapping and frowned. I wasn't here to have a good time; I had serious business to attend to. But there was an oddly joyous sensation zipping through my body, and I wondered whether the vamps pumped some sort of happy chemical into the air. It wouldn't have surprised me.

I shook myself and focused. There was a roped-off area to the left and a raised mezzanine area. If Lord Horvath was here, that was where he'd be.

I plunged in, pushing my way through the crowds. A server approached me, her eyebrows raised questioningly. I didn't want a drink, so I shook my head and continued moving. I'd work out the lay of the land then approach Horvath directly. This wasn't the best place for an interrogation, but it would have to suffice. I could adapt.

I sidled past a crowd of blokes in their twenties who were gathered round one of their friends; from the look of the L-plates round his neck, he was here on his stag night. I tried not to stare at the female vampire, whose fangs were buried deep in his neck. From the glazed look of ecstasy in his eyes, he didn't mind.

I licked my dry lips and pushed myself up onto my tiptoes to get a better glimpse of the VIP area. I took in the assembled vampires on the balcony. Some had their heads bowed in conversation and some were gazing outwards, thoughtful expressions on their face. I shivered as I wondered if they were looking for conquests.

On a raised dais in the centre of the area was a gilt throne. I could just make out the top of the head of the person sitting there: Horvath himself, no doubt. His face and body were obscured by the two scantily-clad women in front of him, one of whom was caressing his face with long, scarlet-painted talons. The other was dancing, her hands travelling up and down her body suggestively. I hopped to the right to get a better look, just as the dancing woman also moved.

I gasped aloud. That had to be Lord Horvath – his body language certainly exuded authority and power. He was leaning back, one leg draped loosely over the arm of the throne. Despite the attentions of the women, he looked mildly bored. But it wasn't that which shocked me; it was the fact that Lord Horvath's face belonged to Lukas.

I moved behind a pillar in case he glanced over the sea of bobbing heads and noticed me. I could have slapped myself for not working it out earlier. Suddenly everything was starting to make sense, from DSI Barnes' odd deference, despite her obvious anti-vampire beliefs, to the way the werewolves had acted when we'd entered Fairfax's club. When everyone stared it wasn't because of Tallulah, it was because I was wandering the streets with the vampire Lord himself. No wonder the female vamp at the front of Tesco's had suddenly decided to play nice with me. He must have put the word out – and his word was no doubt sacrosanct.

I clenched my teeth. His involvement in both my murder and Tony's death was also making sense. He was the vampire leader, so any brutalities on his doorstep were ultimately his responsibility. I shook my head in dismay at my own stupidity. Had he been laughing at me all this time? So much for confronting him to gauge his reaction about Tony's death; he knew as much as I did – if not more.

I ducked my head and moved away from the pillar. I had to get out of there. My shame at not working out what had been right in front of my face was too much to bear. Some detective I was.

Then anger began to seep in. This might all be a joke to him, but it was real life to me. And real death.

A figure stepped in front of me, blocking my path. I muttered an apology and moved to the side. He reached out and grabbed my arm. My head jerked up.

'Emma, where have you been?'

I stared at Jeremy. His eyes were roving over me like he couldn't quite believe I was real. He pulled me in close, wrapping his arms around me tightly. He smelled warm and familiar and I couldn't stop myself from hugging him back.

'What are you doing here?' I asked, my words muffled into his chest.

'Looking for you, of course! I get a cryptic message from you and you don't come home. Nobody at the Met seems to know what's going on and, when I went to Supe Squad, the building was empty.'

I leaned back my head and looked into his eyes. He gazed back at me. I had the strong sensation that there was something he desperately wanted to ask but he was afraid of the answer.

'I'm sorry, Jeremy. I'm so sorry. Everything's been crazy lately.' I linked my fingers with his. 'Can we get out of here and talk?'

He nodded. Gripping my hand tightly, as if he were scared to let go, he led me out.

Chapter Seventeen

Unsure of where else to go, and desperate for some peace and quiet, I took him to Supe Squad. He looked disapprovingly at Tallulah but he didn't say anything, even when I had to move the crossbow so he could sit in the passenger seat.

'This is my mentor's car,' I said, by way of feeble explanation.

'Doesn't your mentor need it?'

I couldn't answer that, so I didn't. Instead I focused on the road and not driving over the drunken pedestrians tripping out of the other vamp clubs and bars. Jeremy didn't repeat his question, and for that I was grateful.

We didn't speak again until I'd used my key to get us into the Supe Squad building. I led him into the main office and flicked on the kettle. I was going to need a damn sight more than caffeine to get through this conversation but, unless Fred had a secret stash of vodka underneath the sofa, tea was the best I could do.

'Emma,' Jeremy sighed. He ran a shaky hand through his hair. 'What's going on? What are you wearing? None of this is like you at all.'

I handed him a mug of tea with three sugars, just as he liked it, and sat down next to him. I knew I could still be in danger – and that meant he was also at risk. He might have forced my hand by appearing at Heart out of the blue, but I couldn't change my current course.

I had to come up with something. Telling him that I'd been murdered and come back to life wasn't likely to arouse his sympathy. Knowing Jeremy, it was more likely he'd run in the opposite direction while calling for the men in white coats to take me away. He didn't even like it when I discussed my own parents' death and they'd not been resurrected. My heart wrenched at that thought and I quickly shoved it away.

'You shouldn't be here, Jeremy. It's incredibly dangerous.'

'If it's dangerous,' he snapped, 'then you shouldn't be here either.'

I grimaced. 'It's my job.'

'You're not qualified yet. And I thought we agreed that you were going to take a desk-based position at Cyber Crimes. That's where you're supposed to be working, not here.' He looked round, unimpressed.

'We've been through this. I didn't have a choice,' I said quietly. Then I started improvising. 'The thing is, I'm anonymous here. The vampires don't know me and neither do the werewolves. I'm working undercover to get as much information about them as I can. It's not what I'd have chosen to do, but it's what I've been asked to do.'

I smiled humourlessly. The more truth I could weave in, the more plausible I'd sound. 'I have my own code name. I'm not Emma any more, I'm D'Artagnan.'

'You realise how crazy all that sounds, right?'

Not as crazy as the truth. 'Yes,' I said. 'But it's why I have to stay away from home and stay away from you.' I reached for him. 'I don't want to, but I don't have a choice. It's not for long – maybe a week then everything will be back to normal. Maybe even sooner.'

'It doesn't seem right, Emma. You're a trainee.' His eyes searched my face. 'Are you okay? You've not been ... hit on the head or anything?'

I tried to laugh. 'No, of course not.'

'Can't you tell the Academy no? Can't you just come home?'

'If I want to graduate and have my pick of jobs afterwards, this is what I've got to do.'

Jeremy reached out and cupped my face. He seemed puzzled and there was an edge of genuine alarm to his expression. I wasn't surprised; not only was I acting out of character, but my tale didn't add up. Nobody was sent undercover without proper training, and no trainee would ever be tasked with such a potentially dangerous job.

'I've been so worried about you, Emma. This is mad! It's four o'clock in the morning and I'm running around the streets of London looking for my crazy girlfriend!'

'I'm really sorry.' I wasn't sure how to make it up to him, so I tried putting a positive spin on things. 'Look on the bright side,' I said. 'You'll have some time to yourself for a change. You can kick back, play video games, see your friends...'

Jeremy's mouth flattened. 'Speaking of friends, Becky and Tom were very disappointed that you couldn't make it out for drinks. We missed you. *I* missed you. If you'd been there, it would have been so different.'

I bit my lip. He had no idea how different things would have been if I'd gone with him.

I could keep apologising, but I wasn't sure what good it would do. Part of me was happy to see Jeremy, but another part of me was desperate for him to leave. I brushed my mouth against his. 'You should go,' I whispered. 'You've got work in a few hours.'

'Won't you come home with me?'

I shook my head. 'I have to stay here and see this through. By the end of next week, it will all be over.'

He kissed me again, more deeply this time. His hand snaked round the back of my head, pulling me in closer. His mouth pressed harder, almost bruising mine.

I yanked away with more force than I intended. 'Jeremy...'

He reached for his inside pocket. 'I have something for you, Emma,' he breathed, his eyes fixed on mine.

I had a horrible feeling that he was about to slide out a ring. That was the last thing either of us needed. 'Um...'

There was a sudden loud banging on the door. Jeremy dropped his hand.

I jumped, then scrambled to my feet. 'I have to get that,' I said. 'It might be important and I'm the only member of Supe Squad here right now.'

'Leave it, Emma. You can't be on duty twenty-four hours a day.'

I was already moving to the door. 'Someone might need help!' Either that, or it was my killer, who'd finally worked out that I wasn't dead yet. I yearned forlornly for the crossbow that was sitting inside Tallulah. Then I peered through the spyhole to see who was out there.

Lukas.

My stomach dropped. Why now?

I opened the door warily. He gazed at me with glittering dark eyes. 'D'Artagnan,' he said. 'I saw you in the club as you were leaving. I wanted to check on you and make sure you were alright.'

I heard Jeremy behind me as Lukas's eyes clocked him. His expression closed off. 'You're not alone.'

'No, Lord Horvath. I'm not.'

There was a faint tightening around Lukas's mouth.

Jeremy cleared his throat. 'I'm her boyfriend,' he said loudly.

'I see.' Lukas spoke coolly. 'It's nice to put a face to the name. D'Artagnan here has told me about you.'

I glanced at Jeremy. The fact that Lukas had called me by my nickname was a mark in my favour.

Jeremy relaxed visibly and smiled at me. 'All good things, I hope.' He paused. 'Did I hear that properly? Are you Lord Horvath?'

I jumped in before Lukas could answer. 'He is. He knows I'm working undercover. He asked Supe Squad to get involved because we're investigating matters which the vampires can't deal with themselves.' I knew it was a lie that would irritate Lukas, but I couldn't resist it. 'You can't tell anyone you've seen him with me, Jeremy.'

'My lips are sealed.' He looked at Lukas. 'Undercover or not, this is a strange time to come calling.'

'Well,' Lukas answered smoothly, 'I *am* a vampire. Night time is when I do my best work.'

I coughed. 'Indeed. You'd better go home, Jeremy. Get some rest. I'll call you as soon as I can. I just need to sort out a replacement phone first.'

He stood next to me. 'Yes, you should do that. You didn't tell me what happened to your own phone.'

'I lost it.' I raised my shoulders in a self-deprecating shrug. 'What can I say? I should take more care.'

'Well,' Jeremy said, with a teasing twinkle, 'I hope you reported its loss to the police.'

I managed a laugh. 'Not yet, but I will. Thanks for dropping by. I'll see you at home.'

He nodded and dropped his head for another kiss. Jeremy wasn't usually prone to public displays of affection, and I suspected that Lukas's brooding darkness was the catalyst. At least this time he was more gentle.

I kissed him back and gave him a little nudge. 'I'll be home by this time next week. Come hell or high water.'

A shadow of sadness crossed his eyes. 'Don't make promises you can't keep. Bye, love.' He strolled out, whistling a desperately melancholy tune.

Lukas and I watched him go. At the end of the street, Jeremy raised his hand and a black cab pulled up. He got in without looking back. A moment later, he was gone.

Lukas looked at me. 'Interesting,' he murmured. 'I wouldn't have put the two of you together.'

I ignored that and glared at him. 'Why didn't you tell me who you really were?'

'I didn't lie, D'Artagnan. You didn't ask.'

'Don't play the fool, Lukas, it doesn't suit you. You knew I had no clue about your identity. Do I call you Lukas? Or should I call you "Lord" and curtsey?'

He made a face. 'Lukas is my real name,' he said, surprising me.

'Really?' My voice was flat. 'Aren't you afraid that I'll use it against you?'

'I'm too powerful for my name to be used against me.' He wasn't boasting, he was simply stating a fact.

He sighed and put his hands in his pockets. 'Besides, there are very few supes who have the power to dominate through their voice, even with the use of a given name. You're right. I could have told you who I am, but it would have altered how you acted around me. Bear in mind that while you were wondering whether you could trust me or not, I was wondering the same thing about you.'

I frowned. He'd used the past tense. 'And now?'

'I've seen into your heart,' he said quietly. 'I no longer have any fears on that score.'

I folded my arms across my chest. I wasn't about to yield just yet. 'Do you know what I am?' I demanded. 'Do you know what sort of ... being is killed and then rises again?'

Lukas didn't look away. 'No, I don't,' he said. 'D'Artagnan, while I might have managed the truth by omission, I haven't actually lied. Lying isn't in my nature.'

I wished that I didn't want to believe him so desperately. 'Fine,' I said. I stepped back. 'Dawn is only a few hours away. I should get some sleep.'

Lukas didn't move. 'Is he going to be a problem? Your boyfriend?'

'No. Jeremy doesn't like the fact that I'm training to be a detective, but he understands that I'm doing it regardless. Now that he's spoken to me in person, I'm sure he'll stay away.'

Lukas didn't blink. 'We are often blinded where matters of the heart are concerned.'

'Jeremy won't be a problem,' I stated firmly. 'Goodbye, Lukas.'

I closed the door, double checked the lock and turned away.

Chapter Eighteen

The sofa was lumpy and I was in such turmoil that I was convinced I wouldn't sleep, despite my exhaustion. I should have had more faith in my body. When I woke up, Liza and Fred were murmuring to each other in low voices and sunlight was filtering in through the large windows and landing on my face. I must have been out for the count.

I rubbed my eyes, groaned and sat up. 'What time is it?'

'Almost eleven,' Liza answered. She raised her eyebrows. 'Did you have sweet dreams?'

I'd been too far out of it to have any dreams – unless she counted the nightmare I was currently living in. 'I was working late last night,' I mumbled. 'It made sense to crash here instead of going home.'

'Uh-huh.'

Fred handed me a cup of coffee. I had the odd sensation that my near-total collapse on his sofa of choice had made him decide that we were now kindred spirits.

'Thank you.'

He nodded, glanced at Liza and took a deep breath. 'We still haven't heard from Tony. This isn't like him. We might not do much around here, but Tony puts in his hours. He doesn't go AWOL like this – and he's still not answering his phone. I'm about to head round to his flat and check on him.'

I pushed the hair out of my eyes. They didn't know. Of course they didn't.

Regardless of what salient details Lucinda Barnes wanted to keep quiet, I knew that the news would zip round the entire Metropolitan Police Force before the morning was out. I had to tell them before they heard it on the grapevine. And they deserved was the truth; they'd known Tony far better than anyone else.

'What is it?' Liza asked, reading my expression. 'What's going on?'

I took a deep breath. 'You'd better sit down.'

Fred did as I suggested but Liza remained standing. I respected that. I could tell from the paleness of her skin that she knew what was coming. I wouldn't do them the discourtesy of prevaricating or hedging the facts. 'Tony is dead,' I said baldly.

Fred gasped. Liza wavered, but she stayed where she was.

'After you left yesterday, I tried to track him down. I went to his flat first and found it trashed, then I used ANPR to locate Tallulah at the DeVane Hotel. I finally found Tony hanging naked in the wardrobe of a room there.'

I paused to allow them to absorb what I'd said. 'During that time,' I continued, 'someone returned to his flat and tidied up. On the surface of it, his death appears to be a result of auto-erotic asphyxiation. My belief is that he was murdered but, until further notice, that news is not being broadcast. Whoever killed Tony wanted to make it look like an accident or suicide. We don't want them to know that we suspect otherwise.'

Fred blinked furiously before giving in and allowing tears to flow freely down his cheeks. 'Shit,' he whispered. 'Oh, shit.'

Liza turned on her heel and walked to her desk. She gazed at it for a moment, then raised her hand and swept everything onto the floor – computer, photo frame, magazine. I winced at the violent crash but didn't say anything. She straightened her back and looked at me. 'What do we do now?' she asked calmly.

'If either of you want to take time off...'

'Fuck off.' She said it quietly and without rancour, but her meaning was clear.

'Yeah,' Fred agreed. 'Fuck off.'

I smiled slightly, not with humour but with the recognition of two kindred spirits. 'Okay, then. Nobody can know that we think Tony's death involved foul play, so we have to proceed very carefully. I've been trying to get onto his computer to find out what he was working on. Now that he's confirmed as,' I swallowed, 'deceased, IT support can help us bypass his password.'

'We don't need them. I know his password,' Liza said. 'His favourite sandwich filling.'

'Roast beef?' I blurted out.

A tiny crease marred her forehead. 'Egg mayo.'

'I don't think it's really his favourite,' Fred said. 'I think he just likes stinking out the office.' He dropped his head. 'He *liked* stinking out the office. He won't be doing it any more.'

I swallowed the lump in my throat. So much for the dedicated carnivore; Tony's extravagant disgust of my vegetarianism had all been for show.

'Egg mayo, it is. Get onto it and see what's in his files.'

'He didn't use the computer very often,' Liza warned. 'There might not be much.'

'We'll take what we can get. Check his emails, his calendar, any notes he made, and look through his internet history.' I glanced at Fred. 'I need you to investigate Tony's neighbour. I met him yesterday and, for reasons that make no sense to me, he had a spare key to Tony's place. Without making a song and dance about it, can you find out more about him? He's probably not aware that Tony is dead, but he knows that his flat was turned over.'

'I'll get right on it.' He jumped up to his feet, grim focus in his eyes.

I gazed at them both. I wasn't qualified yet, but this was what we did. It was what we'd signed up for. We did this to catch the bad guys and stop them hurting other people. This was what would keep us going. One for all.

The phone rang and we all jumped. Liza looked at it like it was a snake about to strike, then she walked over and picked it up.

'Good morning.' I'd never heard her sound so professional. 'You have reached Supernatural Squad. How may we help you?' She listened for a moment and held it out to me. 'It's for you.'

Suddenly nervous, I took it from her. 'Hello?'

'Emma, it's Laura. I'm here in the morgue with your colleague, Anthony Brown. You should get down here.'

My mouth went dry. Was he...? Could he be...?

'He's not woken up. I estimate his time of death about thirty hours ago, give or take. He doesn't have what you have.' She hesitated. 'Whatever that is.'

The momentary flash of hope died away. 'Have you found something on his body? Is there any indication that he was murdered?'

Laura's answer was brisk. 'I wouldn't have seen it if I'd not been warned to look. Whoever did this knew what they were about.'

'What is it?'

'It's easiest if I show you in person.'

Cold rippled through me; that meant confronting Tony's corpse yet again. 'I'll be there within the hour.'

I hung up the phone. 'That was the pathologist,' I said, in answer to Liza and Fred's desperate, questioning glances. 'I think she has something.' I grabbed my coat. 'I'm going to find out what.'

Fred cleared his throat pointedly.

'What is it?'

'I don't mean to be rude, Emma, but—'

'Go on.'

He waved a hand. 'Is this it? I mean, you're not a real detective yet. Tony is dead. Are we not going to get someone more qualified to help?'

It was a good question. 'I don't think so. Not yet, anyway. The politics between humans and supes are complicated, and there's not enough proof that Tony was murdered, regardless of what I believe.' I met his eyes. 'We're not entirely alone. Lord Horvath has been help-ing.'

Both their jaws dropped. 'Yeah,' I said. 'Make of that what you will.'

***

The young bespectacled man at the hospital morgue's front desk, who I assumed was Dean, sat bolt upright when he saw me approach. He didn't smile, but his expression was friendly and empathetic. I could only imagine that he'd been working here for some time and he'd perfected the look. I was surprisingly grateful for it.

'Hi. I'm Emma Bellamy. I'm looking for Dr Hawes.'

'She's expecting you. Right this way.'

I followed him down the same corridor I'd been in just a couple of days earlier. Somehow it seemed different, and I wondered if that was because I was coming to terms with the fact of my own death. Fortunately, I didn't have too long to dwell on that thought.

Dean took me into the room where I'd woken up. Laura was waiting in front of a gurney occupied by a sheet-covered body. She looked up from her clipboard and smiled. 'Thank you, Dean.' She walked over and hugged me.

At first the action surprised me then I began to appreciate it. I hugged her back, as if we were old friends who'd known each other for years.

'How are you doing?' she asked softly. 'Everything the same?'

'Yeah.' I shrugged. 'I feel the same as always. Apart from up here, of course.' I tapped my temple.

'That's only natural, Emma. This isn't something you just get over.'

No, I supposed not. I rubbed the back of my neck awkwardly and gestured at the gurney. 'Is that him?'

'Anthony Brown? Yes. His identity was confirmed by a DSI Lucinda Barnes earlier this morning.' Laura gave me a sidelong look. 'She has put us under strict orders not to reveal anything about his death to anyone except you. Is this related to your murder?'

I wrapped my arms around my waist. Being in this room where I'd lain dead was incredibly discomfiting. 'It would be too much of a coincidence to assume otherwise.'

Laura grimaced in sympathy. 'That's what I thought.' She leaned down and carefully lifted the sheet.

It took me a moment to look directly at Tony's corpse. When I did, I breathed out in relief. He didn't look like he had in the hotel room. Now, with his eyes taped shut, he seemed at peace. This was his shell, not the man himself. Not any longer.

I gazed at him. He wasn't coming back to life. I couldn't have explained how I knew that for certain. It was simply what my gut told me.

Laura pulled the sheet further away. 'You can see the ligature marks and bruising around his neck.'

I forced myself to look.

'On the face of it, this is an open-and-shut case of auto-erotic asphyxiation. There's no history of depression, and initial bloodwork shows no traces of anti-depressants in his body. Actual cause of death is almost definitely strangulation. However, there's no evidence of either ejaculate or sexual arousal. On its own, that's not necessarily proof of anything but, after I spoke to DSI Barnes and took a closer look, I found this.' Laura carefully brushed back a section of hair from Tony's neck.

I peered more closely. There was a tiny mark, barely visible.

'I wasn't sure at first,' Laura admitted, 'but when I examined it more closely with a portable microscope, it became very clear. Anthony Brown was injected with something shortly before his death. At this angle, it would have hit his bloodstream directly.'

'Tony,' I murmured. 'He preferred to be called Tony.' I stared at the little blemish. 'Is there any chance he did it to himself?'

Laura shook her head. 'The angle means that it was administered by someone else. When more blood test results come back, I think we'll find evidence of a paralytic. He was rendered immobile so that his assailant could position him for strangulation and make it appear self-inflicted.'

A deep, dark, yawning chasm of emptiness opened up inside me. 'How long will it be until you know for sure?'

Laura grimaced. 'A few days. And it's entirely possible that the drug has already broken down in his bloodstream and is already undetectable.'

'So there might never be proof that he was murdered?'

'Yes. I'm sorry.'

'It's not your fault,' I said distantly, damning to hell and back the bastard who'd done this.

'That's not the only thing,' Laura said, more cheerfully this time. 'There's something else.'

I glanced at her.

'I found a hair. Just one hair, mind, and I'm not sure how useful it will be. After I found the injection mark, I went back to look at the tie that was used round his neck. The hair was caught in the knot. It's too long and too light to belong to Anthony Brown. To Tony,' she amended. 'I've examined it and there's no doubt in my mind that it's lupine.'

I sucked in a breath. 'Werewolf?'

'Yep.' Laura looked pleased with herself. She had good reason to be. 'You won't find a match for it on any system. We're not permitted to keep records of supes' DNA or fingerprints. But it definitely came from a wolf.'

'Can you show me?'

She nodded and pointed at a microscope. The hair in question was trapped beneath its glass slide. Russet coloured, and with a definite curl. I stared at it. Gotcha.

'I don't need to tell you that, because Tony Brown worked in Supernatural Squad, he'll have come into contact with supes all the time. A single werewolf hair isn't proof of anything. It could have come from anywhere.'

I smiled. It was proof enough for me. 'Thank you, Laura.'

'Any time.' Her smile vanished. 'I should tell you that someone called last night asking about you.'

I stiffened. 'About me?'

'It wasn't my shift,' she said apologetically, 'so I didn't speak to them, and the caller didn't mention you by name. The phone call was logged – I heard about it when I came in this morning. They wanted to know about your body, if it had been brought in to this morgue, that sort of thing.'

'Police?'

'I doubt it.' Her voice was grim. 'They didn't leave a name.'

I drew in a sharp breath. I hadn't been sure I could feel much worse after re-visiting the scene of my rebirth and seeing Tony's body again, but I did. 'Male?'

She nodded.

My killer. It had to be. He'd gotten wind that I was wandering around the streets and wanted to know what had gone wrong. 'Are the phone calls recorded?' I asked, desperation uncoiling and manifesting itself in the tremble in my voice.

Laura made a face. 'Sorry, they're not. It was decided by the powers that be that recording grieving families when they enquire about their loved ones was an intrusion too far.'

As much as I could understand the sentiment, it didn't help me.

'Maybe you should lie low for a few days,' Laura advised. 'We didn't give out any information about your body, not even confirmation that you'd been brought in. We're not allowed to without ID validation. But that doesn't mean you're not in danger.'

I thought about Tony's body lying on the cold gurney. 'I can't do that.'

'Somehow I knew you'd say that.' She reached out and squeezed my hands. 'Be bloody careful, Emma.'

Easier said than done.

Chapter Nineteen

Putting my worries about the mysterious caller to one side because there was nothing I could do about him, I walked outside with my head held high. Despite the lack of proof, I was beyond convinced that Tony had been murdered. I didn't know why his death had been made to look like an accident while mine had been the complete opposite, and there was no apparent motive for either of our murders, but I felt like I was getting somewhere. The answers were within my grasp if I looked hard enough.

I smiled to myself – then I saw Lukas leaning against Tallulah and my smile vanished.

He raised a hand to me as I approached. 'There's no need to look quite so glum when you see me, D'Artagnan.'

'Are you stalking me now?'

'In a sense,' he replied. 'I came looking for you and I suspected you might be here.'

'You mean you don't have hospital workers on the payroll?'

'Actually, I do.' He offered me an easy grin. 'But none of them work in the morgue. It wasn't rocket science to work out that you'd be here. You told me yourself that you'd be visiting.'

I had – but I didn't like the idea that he was going to continually show up without warning. I had enough metaphorical shadows as it was; I didn't need real ones too.

'Are you alright?' he asked.

'Fine.' I paused. 'Why do you ask?'

'I thought it might be difficult for you to come back here after what happened to you.' His expression was serious.

His show of empathy flustered me more than I wanted it to. 'I coped,' I said.

'I knew you'd *cope* but that doesn't make it any easier.'

For a moment I didn't speak, then I glanced at him. 'Thank you for asking.'

Lukas inclined his head. 'If you ever need to talk, I'm more than willing to listen. While my experience was nothing like yours, I do know a little about rebirth.'

'When were you turned?' It wasn't curiosity that made me ask but the opportunity to turn the conversation away from myself.

'Close to fifty years ago.' He rubbed his chin. 'I might look like a young, sprightly specimen of masculinity, but I'm close to eighty years old.' His gaze suddenly sharpened. 'Does that bother you, D'Artagnan?'

'Should it?'

He didn't look away. 'Different people react in different ways.'

His age didn't make any difference to me and I couldn't imagine why it would. I had other questions, however. I jerked my chin up to the sky. 'It's not long past midday. Are you sure the sun doesn't bother you?'

'I'm sure. I prefer the night. All vampires do, because our vitality increases as the sky darkens, but I don't shrivel up at the sign of a sunbeam. Much as you might wish that were so.'

'I don't wish that.'

'Good.' He gazed at me, then he shook himself. 'So did you find out anything useful in there?'

I exhaled. 'You were right about the werewolf.' I outlined what Laura had discovered. Lukas listened to what I had to say, and his expression darkened.

'If news of this gets out,' he muttered once I'd finished, 'it could spell chaos. Whoever did this knows that, otherwise they wouldn't have tried to conceal Brown's death as a suicide and yours as a knife-based mugging gone wrong. It appears that Brown was killed because he was a danger and he needed to be shut up. We can assume that the same is true for you.' He gazed at me thoughtfully. 'So, D'Artagnan,

what have you seen and what do you know that might tempt someone to kill you?'

I'd been thinking about this. 'I was only in Supe Squad for a day,
so there's not much to sift through. There is one thing, though.'

Lukas raised his eyebrows. 'Go on.'

'There was a woman,' I said. 'A female werewolf. I saw her running down the street in the middle of the day covered in blood.'

'Stranger things have happened where the wolves are concerned.'

'I wouldn't know about that, but it's not something I see on a
daily basis,' I admitted. 'I went after her to make sure she was okay.
When I found her, by the sound of things she was one who'd been
attacking rather than the other way around. She was screaming at
a male werewolf about her sister who was missing. She seemed to
think he had something to do with it.'

'And?'

'And nothing. Tony appeared with Lady Sullivan in tow and
bawled me out for getting involved. And that,' I said flatly, 'was the
last time I saw him.'

Lukas smiled sympathetically. 'Well, at least I know where I
should go first.'

'We,' I corrected. 'Where *we* should go first.'

'It might be wise if you kept out of sight,' he said. 'If our killer still
thinks you're dead, it might be better – and safer – not to disillusion
him.'

As I'd already told Laura, there was absolutely no chance I'd simply cower away. This was my mentor's murder we were talking about
– and mine. 'For all we know,' I argued, without mentioning the
phone call to the morgue, 'that ship has already sailed. I've been up
and down both Lisson Grove and Soho. Besides, if I appear alive and
well in front of the bastard who killed me, their reaction might tell
us everything we need. And this is *my* investigation.'

'If they tried to kill you once, they'll try again. It's not safe.'

'I'll have big bad Lord Horvath by my side,' I taunted. 'I'm sure I'll be fine.'

Lukas's eyes gleamed and he suddenly relaxed. 'True. I suppose I'd better stick by your side at all times.' He opened Tallulah's door and got into the passenger seat without another word.

My eyes narrowed. He'd given in very suddenly. I couldn't help thinking that he'd been manipulating the conversation all along so that we could reach this very point and he could glue himself to me. Bloody vampire.

***

I parked Tallulah smack bang in Lisson Grove, metres away from the spot where Tony had said his last words to me. I'd barely climbed out of the car when a young woman – whose long hair was not only remarkably thick but also russet coloured –strode towards me. 'You can't leave that thing there!'

I patted Tallulah's bonnet. 'You must recognise her.' And then, because I couldn't help myself and I'd always wanted to say it, 'Don't you know who I am?'

She glared at me and opened her mouth to argue but Lukas interrupted. 'Good afternoon. Is there a problem?'

'Yes, there's a problem,' she began. 'In fact—' She glanced at him and stopped abruptly.

Lukas winked at me. 'She knows who *I* am.'

'Sorry. I'm sorry.' She dropped her shoulders and her head. If she'd been in wolf form and had a tail, it would no doubt have been between her legs. Either that, or she'd have presented him with her belly.

'This woman,' Lukas said, pointing at me, 'is from Supe Squad. You have heard of Supe Squad, haven't you?'

Her head was now so low that her chin was pressing against her collarbone. 'Yes, sir.'

'Well then, you'll know that Supe Squad is permitted free access to this area. That includes parking.'

'Yes, sir.'

'You will remain here and look after Tallulah until we return.'

'Yes, sir.'

I sincerely doubted that was necessary; only a madman would try and steal the little purple Mini, and no amount of vandalism could make her look any worse than she already did. But this little show of power was about far more than the car. There was a great deal about this world that I didn't understand.

'Your hair,' I said softly. 'Do many werewolves have hair that colour?'

She mumbled something.

'Speak up!' Lukas ordered.

'Yes, sir. Yes, ma'am. Many werewolves are this colour.'

It was my first time being ma'am-ed. I wasn't sure I liked it. 'Thank you.'

'Predominantly Sullivans,' she continued. 'But not exclusively.'

Huh. I nodded and walked towards the sandwich shop. Lukas adjusted his long stride to match mine. When I glanced back, the woman was standing directly in front of Tallulah with her arms folded. She really was going to stay there and guard the car, then.

'Was that completely necessary?' I asked under my breath.

'It's how the werewolves work,' Lukas said. 'To them, hierarchy and power are everything. Everyone knows their place. Sometimes they just need to be reminded of it.' He gave me a sidelong look. 'Tony knew *his* place.'

I took that to mean that I didn't know mine. 'And the vampires?' I enquired. 'Are you all about hierarchy, too?'

'When you're a vampire,' Lukas said, briefly displaying his white fangs, 'there's only one thing you need to know when it comes to power and leadership.' He paused and waited for me to ask.

I sighed. I'd bite. 'Go on then. What's the one thing?'

He grinned. 'That I'm in charge.'

I rolled my eyes.

Lukas's expression grew serious. 'By now, everyone knows that Brown is gone. That young wolf back there knew exactly who you were. Even if she hadn't, Tallulah's presence was more than enough to tell her. If you want to gain respect and set the foundations for a successful role in Supe Squad, you need to assert your authority from the beginning. If you don't, in six months' time every supe in the city will be walking all over you.'

'I won't be anywhere near here in six months' time,' I said baldly. 'And in any case, I thought you despised the very existence of Supe Squad.'

Lukas took his time before answering. 'There are many grey areas in life, D'Artagnan. I do indeed dislike Supe Squad. However, I do not dislike you. And it could be argued that Supe Squad's continued existence is a necessary evil that must be borne. What I definitely do *not* want to happen is its expansion into something different.'

'So you want us to remain toothless.'

'I didn't say that,' he said mildly. 'I want us,' he gestured towards himself, 'to remain independent.'

'I won't be bribed into staying away from real investigations.'

The corners of his mouth lifted. 'But D'Artagnan,' he murmured, 'you already said you won't be staying here.'

I cursed him silently. This entire conversation was a waste of time. I came to a halt, turning so that my back was to the sandwich shop, and pointed to the street in front of us. 'There,' I said. 'That was where I saw the woman. She appeared there, covered in blood, and ran in that direction.'

Lukas's gaze followed my pointing finger. 'Well then,' he said, 'let's go and find her.'

'We should talk to Lady Sullivan first. She was very unimpressed that I was snooping around.'

'Let me guess,' he said drily, 'you backed off immediately. That's exactly the sort of thing that I've been talking about. Where the wolves are concerned, you never back off.'

'Tony said—'

'D'Artagnan.' His voice was quiet. 'If you do things the way that Brown did, you've already failed.'

'So you believe he was a failure?'

'Brown? Not entirely. He inherited a shitty situation from the previous Supe Squad detectives, and he did the best that he could with it. His approach was to work from underneath and weasel his way in, while appearing unthreatening. You might think badly of him for taking bribes, as you call it, but I think there was a purpose to that. I think he was paving the way for better things to come. However,' Lukas's eyes hardened, 'he was also murdered.'

'So was I.'

He wagged his finger at me. 'Indeed. You should make sure that doesn't happen again.'

'Noted,' I said sarcastically. I started to cross the street, making a show of leading the way. 'Come on then, Lord Horvath. Giddy up.'

'Yes, ma'am.'

Chapter Twenty

The bloody trail left on the cobbles by the werewolf was long gone, even to a vampire's finely tuned senses. Lukas scanned the road and his nostrils flared, but I knew from his studied focus that there was nothing left to detect. I also knew from the glimpses of wide-eyed faces appearing at the windows above us that his presence here was causing a stir. I wasn't sure whether that was a good or bad thing, but I had to admit that I felt safer having him around. I wasn't planning to tell him that, though.

'There,' I said finally, after we'd rounded the corner and I recognised the door. 'That was the house where I found them arguing.' I straightened my shoulders. 'It's time to see if anyone's home.'

I walked up and rapped sharply on the door. Lukas hung back. I knew that he was trying to give me the lead so that I could assert my authority as he'd suggested. I wasn't sure whether that knowledge troubled me or warmed me. The idea that he might want me to stick around in Supe Squad was not one I wanted to think about too closely.

Fortunately, someone was indeed home. We didn't have long to wait before there were heavy footsteps inside and the sound of the door being unlocked. It opened and a man peered out – the same man who'd transformed from a wolf in front of my very eyes just a couple of days earlier. His clothes were unkempt, and he had a scraggy beard that hadn't been there last time I'd seen him. I glanced over his grubby T-shirt, the blue tag pinned to his left arm and his bare feet caked in dirt. This was not someone who'd been taking care of himself.

When he saw me, he stumbled backwards. 'It wasn't me!' he blurted out. 'I know it might look that way, but I didn't do anything to her!'

I glanced at Lukas, whose expression was dark and forbidding. 'Perhaps it's better if we come inside to discuss it,' I said,

He shook his head and moved further back. Given that he hadn't actually denied me access and the door remained open, I stepped across the threshold. Lukas followed. The man noticed him belatedly, his eyes widening as he recognised the vampire Lord.

The wide hallway still bore traces of the fight. The wallpaper was ripped in several places and had tattered scraps hanging down, and there were scars gouged into the carpet where the wolves' claws had dug into it. I could still smell the faint tang of spilled blood clinging to the air. The evidence outside might have been washed away but, as far as the house was concerned, the fight had only just occurred. I took it all in. He'd obviously made no effort to tidy up.

'Do you have somewhere we can sit?' I asked kindly. Despite Lukas's advice, I didn't think this was the time for a show of aggression. From the looks of him, this werewolf was already well and truly cowed.

He sighed heavily and gestured to the door on his right. I walked into a small living room. Crumpled tissues littered the floor, and there was a bottle of vodka with less than inch of liquid in it on the table next to the sofa.

'I'm not drunk,' the werewolf said defensively. 'I had that yesterday. And anyway, it was already almost empty.'

'We're not here to judge,' I told him. I sat down gingerly and waited for Lukas and the wolf to do the same.

'Why is he here?' the wolf demanded, sitting as far away from Lukas as possible. 'I already spoke to Lady Sullivan yesterday.'

'Yesterday?' I prompted. The fight I'd witnessed had been days ago.

'Yeah. She came to question me about Becca.'

'Becca is the woman who's gone missing?'

He gave me a blank look. 'No. Her sister. The one who attacked me.'

I frowned. Hang on a minute. Something about that didn't compute.

'What's your name?' Lukas asked.

The werewolf didn't answer immediately.

'We're not going to use it against you,' Lukas said gently. 'We just want to get to the bottom of all this.'

The werewolf's head fell further. A bulbous drop of green snot slid from his left nostril, but he made no move to wipe it away. 'I don't care any more,' he whispered. 'I don't care what you do.' He lifted his head. 'My name is Gregory. And, yes, that's my real name. Do with it what you will.'

I watched him carefully. So this name business really was about far more than tradition. 'Why don't you start at the beginning, Gregory? Tell us what happened, and don't leave anything out.'

He sniffed loudly and the snot droplet disappeared into his nose again. 'I bumped into Anna, Becca's sister, inside Crystal on Saturday night. She was out with Becca and a few of her mates. One thing led to another and we ended up here. Anna didn't want to go to her place because she lives with Becca and she's a real ball-breaker.' He looked at me. 'Anna's words. Not mine.'

'Are those their real names?' I asked. 'Anna and Becca?'

'Yeah.' He gave me a defiant glare. 'But even if I was strong enough to use someone's name to dominate them, I couldn't have. I didn't find out either of their real names until after all this shit happened.'

I glanced over at Lukas to see if that rang true. He nodded.

'Who's more dominant?' Lukas inquired. 'You or Anna?'

'Me.' He sniffed again. It was hard to imagine Gregory being more dominant than anyone. I supposed it was a wolf thing. 'But if you're going to ask whose more dominant between me and Becca, then it's definitely Becca.'

Given what I'd witnessed of their fight, I could attest to that. 'So you had sex with Anna?'

'Didn't I just say that?' His eyes flashed. That was good to see; maybe he wasn't completely cowed after all. 'And it was good sex, too. Nothing kinky. No ropes or handcuffs or smacking or anything. It was vanilla.'

I leaned forward. 'Do you prefer it kinky, Gregory?'

He met my eyes. 'Sometimes. Not always. I don't go into for waterplay or cross-action, but I don't mind a bit of role play or furry handcuffs from time to time.'

My brow furrowed slightly. Lukas glanced my way and murmured, 'Cross-play is when one partner is in their normal form while the other is wolf.'

I blinked.

'Water play is when—'

'That one I know,' I said drily. 'But thanks.'

Lukas raised his eyebrows at Gregory. 'What about Anna? Was she inclined towards those sorts of sexual games?'

'I don't know. We only had sex once, and we were both pretty drunk. It was vanilla, like I said. When I woke up in the morning, she'd already gone.'

'And this was Sunday morning?' I asked.

He nodded. 'That's the last time anyone saw her,' he whispered. 'But no matter what you think, I didn't hurt her. I don't know what happened to her. I didn't realise anything was wrong until later that day when her sister came at me.'

He ran a hand through his hair. 'Becca wouldn't believe that I had nothing to do with Anna's disappearance. She kept on and on at me, then she attacked me in the middle of the street. I was passing her house and she came bounding out and threw herself at me. I got away, ran back here and she followed.' He nodded at me. 'That's when you showed up.'

'There's been no sign of Anna since then?'

'No.'

'So what happened to Becca? What did Lady Sullivan tell you yesterday?'

'Whatever Becca did,' he said, without listening to my question, 'she did to herself. It wasn't me. It wasn't my fault.' He started to wring his hands, turning them over and over in his lap. From where I was sitting, it appeared that he was rocking. That didn't bode well.

I put as much steel into my voice as I could. 'Gregory,' I said, 'what has happened to Becca?'

His head snapped up. 'She killed herself. Yesterday morning.' He sank into himself. 'Becca committed suicide.'

***

I was seething. Once Lukas and I were back outside Gregory's house, I let rip. 'Why didn't Lady Sullivan tell us about Becca? Or Anna? You can't seriously tell me that it's normal for werewolves to vanish, or for young women to kill themselves! In the context of what happened to Tony, she was being incredibly reckless by not revealing that information!'

'I doubt she thought it was relevant,' Lukas said.

'Could a more dominant supe with a lot of power have used Becca's name and compelled her to commit suicide?' I asked, horrified at the thought.

Lukas shook his head. 'Not a chance. Compulsion will go a long way but, regardless of how much power you might have, you can't use it to fight against another person's inner soul and true nature. Think of it like hypnosis: you couldn't hypnotise some to kill themselves. It doesn't work when someone is wholly set on a different path.'

I was only slightly mollified. 'That's good to know, but Lady Sullivan should have informed us about both women.'

'I'm not disagreeing with you,' he said gently. 'It would have been better if she'd told us, especially considering that Brown's last movements involved breaking up the fight between Becca and Gregory.'

'He didn't break up the fight,' I said, curling my fingers into fists and damning Lady Sullivan to hell. 'I did.'

'Mm.' Lukas's black eyes seared into me. 'That's not the only thing you've done. Did you feel it when you said his name?'

'What?'

'The thrum of power,' he said. 'Did you feel it?'

I gave him a blank look. 'I have no idea what you're talking about.'

'Gregory is a delta – or at least he *was* a delta. He doesn't look like he'll be retaining that position for much longer.'

'I'll repeat what I just said. I have no idea what you're talking about.'

Lukas's expression was patient. 'Lady Sullivan is the clan alpha.'

'Yep. Got that.'

'Beneath her are a dozen betas.'

'Okay.'

'Then there are selsas, who rank below the betas. Below the selsas are the deltas. Then the gammas, who are the betas of the deltas, followed by epsilons, zetas and iotas. Iotas are the pups. That's not including the omegas, those wolves who are on the periphery of the clan and outside the usual hierarchy for a variety of reasons.'

I stared at him. 'Are you even speaking English?'

Lukas let out a short laugh. 'I gave you the condensed version. It's not difficult. I thought everyone knew about the wolves' hierarchy.'

'I knew there was a hierarchy,' I muttered. 'I didn't know it was so complicated or that it was going to sound like an American college fraternity.'

He reached across and patted my arm. Again I felt my skin burn where he touched me. 'You're an innocent, D'Artagnan.'

I tried not to take offence. 'Getting back to the point,' I said, 'Gregory is a delta.'

'Yes. I'm assuming you didn't notice the blue tag on his shirt.'

'Actually, I did. But I didn't know what it was for.'

'Blue is for delta,'

'I get that now. So he's what? In the middle of the pack?'

Lukas pursed his lips. 'Essentially. You still have to be reasonably powerful to reach that point. Gregory was speaking the truth. He would never be strong enough to use another's name against them. I'm sure I've already told you that only a handful of supes can use given names to achieve dominance. In theory, the only people who can use a werewolf's name to such effect are those who rank far above them.'

'And in practice?' I inquired.

'In practice, a non-ranking trainee, with no power and no practical knowledge of anything supernatural, used Gregory's name to calm him down and ensure he answered her questions.' Lukas paused. 'It will be interesting to discover what rank Becca held, given that you also broke up their fight presumably without using her name to enhance your authority. You have more power within you than I'd realised.'

I wrinkled my nose. 'I might technically be a trainee, but I'm a mere smidge away from becoming a qualified police detective. There's authority and power in that.'

He snorted. 'That means nothing in the supernatural world. Brown certainly couldn't have done what you did.' He gazed into my eyes. 'So the question remains: what on earth are you, D'Artagnan?'

His scrutiny was making me uneasy – and so was his question. 'Lucky,' I shrugged, making light of the situation. 'Just lucky.'

'You don't believe that any more than I do. Who are your parents? What do they do?'

Discomfort tightened the muscles in my shoulders. 'They don't do anything. They're dead.'

Lukas drew in a breath. 'I'm sorry.'

I looked away. 'They died a long time ago.' I shook myself. Whatever I was, I couldn't see how it had any bearing on our investigation. I was convinced what had happened was nothing more than an unnatural by-product. I knew I was too afraid to delve deeper into myself – but I also knew that right now we had more important things to do. 'Lady Sullivan,' I said firmly. 'We need to talk to her.'

Lukas continued to watch me intently.

'Lukas!' I snapped. 'Lady Sullivan! We need to find out what the hell happened to Becca and why Lady Sullivan didn't tell us about it.'

He stepped away from me. 'Yes.' He pointed down the road. 'Her residence is this way.'

I began striding in that direction. Lukas followed. I didn't need to turn around to know that his eyes were burning into my back the entire way.

Chapter Twenty-One

The werewolf who opened the door to Lady Sullivan's imposing gothic house was considerably smarter than Gregory. He was wearing a well-tailored suit; unfortunately, the impact of his expensive attire was impaired by the way his face turned blotchy and tufts of fur sprang forth from his forehead when he saw Lukas.

My eyes drifted down to the tag on his arm. Yellow. Whatever that meant.

'Protocol dictates that I handle this,' Lukas murmured, before stepping up and giving the jittery wolf a dazzling, fanged smile. 'Inform Lady Sullivan that Lord Horvath is here to see her.'

More fur appeared; in fact, whiskers were now springing from the wolf's cheeks. He didn't utter a word, he simply bowed and turned away to pass along the message.

There was the sound of ripping fabric and I saw a long tail appear from the seat of his expensive trousers. It was very hard not to stare.

'We're getting closer and closer to the full moon,' Lukas said. 'It's not easy for the younger, less dominant wolves to control themselves.'

'His tag was yellow.'

'Zeta. He's a ranking wolf,' Lukas explained. 'But only just.'

Another man appeared, older with hints of grey at his temples. 'Lord Horvath. How lovely to see you at our door on this fine day.' He glanced at me. 'And the latest in a long line of Supernatural Squad detectives. I don't suppose you'd be willing to tell me your name?'

'That's incredibly rude, Robert,' Lukas said.

A lazy smile lit the older wolf's face. 'DC Brown never minded.'

'DC Brown didn't care.' There was an underlying tone of menace in Lukas's response. Interesting. And scary.

Robert, who was no doubt one of the higher-ranking betas given his lack of an arm tag and Lukas's knowledge of his name, continued smiling. 'Indeed.'

He raised his head, scenting the air. It wasn't the aroma of London city he was curious about, however, it was me. 'Alas, Lady Sullivan is very busy. She will grant you the boon of an audience as soon as she can. She is always enthusiastic about meeting with the police. There is an opening in her diary next week, after the full moon. Would 2.45pm next Thursday suit?'

Lukas growled. He appeared suddenly, genuinely angry and I had the distinct sensation that all hell was about to break loose. No doubt the fact that one of Lady Sullivan's underlings was treating me – and therefore, by extension, the Lord of all vampires – like a random passer-by was a punch in the face. And it was something that Lukas had to respond to.

If there was one thing I'd learnt in my detective training, it was that fighting fire with fire only ever led to a blazing inferno. Despite my own annoyance at Lady Sullivan's attempts to conceal the truth from us, I knew that we had to use water to fight effectively.

'Unfortunately,' I broke in smoothly, 'this is an urgent matter of the utmost importance. I'm afraid we need to see her straight away.'

'As I've already said, Lady Sullivan is very busy.' Robert paused. 'However, if you tell me your name, I will endeavour to slide you in before her next appointment.'

Lukas bristled. 'You will do nothing of the sort,' he said to me. Then he glared at the wolf. 'You may call her D'Artagnan.'

This show of machismo was rather exhausting to watch. 'It's a test,' I said.

'I don't care what it is,' Lukas replied. He didn't raise his voice, but there was no denying his mounting fury. 'It's disrespectful, discourteous and,' he bared his sharp teeth, 'downright dangerous.'

'Please be aware, Lord Horvath, that this is not intended as a slight to you in any way.' Robert bowed to add weight to his words. 'I don't wish to incur your displeasure. It is not you who concerns me. The young lady here is an unknown quantity. She has already met twice with Lady Sullivan without my knowledge. As head of Sullivan Security, I am merely performing the role I've been given and ensuring the absolute safety of my alpha.'

I couldn't be arsed with this. 'My name,' my voice rang out clearly, 'is Emma Bellamy.'

Lukas stiffened. Robert, however, smiled in triumph. 'In that case, Ms Bellamy, Lord Horvath, please follow me.' He turned on his heel and walked away.

'What the hell?' Lukas bit out. 'Why did you do that?'

'Because,' I answered simply, 'we need to speak to Lady Sullivan, and we need do it now.'

'You can't ever take back your real name! We're dealing with dominant werewolves here who will happily use your name against you.'

I shrugged. 'First of all, you've already suggested that I'm more powerful than anyone thinks.'

'You calmed down a delta werewolf. That's an entirely different matter to allowing betas and alphas know your real name! They could hold it over you for the rest of your tenure in Supe Squad. Look at what happened with Brown!'

'Second of all,' I continued as if he hadn't spoken, 'Lady Sullivan obviously wants to test the limits of whatever power I have. She already knows that I broke up the fight between Gregory and Becca. The fact that I'm trotting around with you while trying to investigate Tony's murder has probably piqued her interest even more.' I ticked off my fingers. 'Thirdly, I'm only in Supe Squad temporarily, so what anyone does or does not know about my name doesn't matter.'

Lukas glowered at me. 'Anything else?'

'Yeah.' I took a deep breath. This last part was a calculated gamble. 'You already knew my real name is Emma. You've already found it out.'

'Whether I have or not is beside the point,' he said, his face darkening further. 'I have done you the courtesy of not saying it aloud.'

I knew it. 'If the vampires know my name,' I said softly, 'then the werewolves can know it too.'

'I'm the only vampire who knows your name, I promise you that.' He gritted his teeth. 'Not that it will make any difference now. Do you realise how long it's been since I encountered a human as frustrating as you?'

I smiled. 'I'll take that as a compliment.'

Robert called from inside the Sullivan residence. 'I thought this was an urgent matter. Are the two of you coming in or not?'

I smiled more widely. 'Coming!' And then I stepped inside.

***

Lady Sullivan didn't quite have a throne like Lukas's, but she was seated on a grand chair on a raised dais. Various werewolves lolled around the room in front of her, some in full wolf form. I reminded myself that I wanted to be here and that I wasn't afraid. Not much, anyway. Even though I was in the wolves' lair, it was still daylight and that went a long way towards keeping my terrors at bay.

'Leave us,' Lady Sullivan said, barely raising her voice above a whisper. Every single warm body in the place rose up and left silently, until there was only Lukas, Robert and me. 'I do apologise for Robert's behaviour just now,' Lady Sullivan continued. 'His demands were made without my knowledge.'

Lukas rolled his eyes. 'As if.'

'I beg your pardon, Lord Horvath?'

'If you genuinely expect us to believe that he was acting on his own cognisance, then your opinion of us is even lower than I thought.'

'I can assure you that I hold a very high opinion of all vampires.' Her eyes narrowed slightly. 'I am not seeking any sort of argument with you, and I fully accept your recriminations.'

I realised suddenly that she was nervous. Regardless of what machinations she'd tried to employ to put me at a disadvantage, she genuinely didn't want to antagonise Lukas.

I filed away that information and spoke up. 'Let's move on,' I said. 'I have serious questions that I need you to answer, Lady Sullivan.'

'You are not a vampire, Emma Bellamy,' she responded, making a deliberate point of using my real name. 'You are merely a human.'

'Lady Sullivan,' Lukas began. 'This is completely—'

I held up a hand. Her test wasn't over, but that was fine by me. As long as I got the answers I needed, I didn't care.

Robert stepped forward. 'Lord Horvath is on par with Lady Sullivan,' he said. 'As such, he is exempt from the usual guest formalities. Ms Bellamy, whether you have met with Lady Sullivan before or not, you are now in her home. We ask that you show her the courtesy required and bow.'

It would have been a whole lot easier if I'd done as he requested and given my best impression of a low bow, but I knew that wasn't what he really wanted. It wasn't what Lady Sullivan really wanted, either. Maybe I was better at understanding supes than I'd given myself credit for.

'I'm honoured to be here and very grateful for your time,' I said. 'However, as a member of Supernatural Squad – whether my role is temporary or not – I am not obliged to bow to you, Lady Sullivan.'

'Bow, Emma,' Robert ordered.

I didn't move an inch.

Lady Sullivan's gaze slid momentarily to Lukas. If she was surprised that I'd not complied with the order, she didn't show it. Lukas didn't react; he merely watched me with expressionless black eyes.

'Emma Bellamy,' she said. 'Bow.'

This time I felt her power. A faint buzz zapped along my spine and itched at the base of my skull. I wanted to do as she'd commanded; the authority she'd exerted by using my real name made me desperate to obey. I resisted it and remained upright – but only just.

Lady Sullivan's expression flickered. 'I see.'

I swallowed. 'I trust you now have the answer you were looking for.'

'Not even close.' She leaned forward and examined me intently. 'Lord Horvath, is this why she was chosen? Is this why DSI Barnes sent her to Supe Squad?'

Lukas folded his arms. 'I have no reason to believe that any member of the Metropolitan Police Force is aware that Emma Bellamy has any special power or authority,' he said stiffly.

I hated being spoken about when I was standing right there. I pointed at him. 'What he said.' I tapped my foot, my impatience growing. 'Now, can we get to the reason why I'm here?'

Lady Sullivan waved at me dismissively. 'Carry on.'

Finally. 'Last night, I informed you about the murder of DC Tony Brown. You know that we suspect a werewolf is the perpetrator, and that his death was made to appear an accident gone wrong or a suicide. So why,' my voice hardened, 'did you not tell both us and the other werewolves present that one of your own died yesterday morning, too? And that her death was also apparently suicide?'

Although I searched every inch of her face, I saw no reaction on Lady Sullivan's part. 'I take it that you're referring to Becca,' she said smoothly. 'I fail to see any connection, remote or otherwise, between her death and DC Brown's.'

'Do your werewolves often commit suicide?' I asked.

Her mouth tightened. 'No,' she snapped, 'they do not. But Becca was under considerable pressure after the disappearance of her sister. You saw for yourself how close to the edge she was. She attacked another wolf without provocation! She was no pup – Becca was a delta.

She might not have been born a werewolf, but she chose to become one. She passed all of our threshold tests and was deemed strong enough and intelligent enough to be one of ours. As such, she was held to higher standards than street brawling. Unfortunately, despite her other qualities, her state of mind was obviously fragile.'

Lukas scratched his chin. 'If that were so,' he said, 'then why didn't you have someone watch over her? Why didn't you find her the help she so desperately needed?'

Lady Sullivan's face spasmed into something very ugly. 'As if hindsight hasn't suggested other avenues to you in the past, Lord Horvath! I should have acted faster, but I do not require further censure. Believe me, as Becca's alpha I feel the weight of guilt. And yet, however unfortunate her death was, she killed herself. She had nothing to do with DC Brown. I doubt she'd ever spoken to the man!'

Seeking to calm matters, I took another tack. 'You said she *chose* to become a wolf? When did that happen?'

'Six years ago. She recommended her sister for conversion three years after that.'

'Why would she recommend her sister if she was having trouble adapting to the change herself?'

Lady Sullivan looked away. 'We didn't know she was having trouble. You have to understand, Ms Bellamy, that there are strict limits placed on how many werewolves can exist at any one time. We do not turn humans without first being confident that they can adapt to an entirely new way of life. We receive thousands of applications. We can afford to be picky.'

Not picky enough if Becca really did commit suicide. 'How?' I asked quietly. 'How did Becca die?'

Lady Sullivan sighed. 'She didn't hang herself, if that's what you're asking. She slit her wrists in the bath and bled to death.'

My fingers went involuntarily to my throat, touching the spot where the knife had first slid in. 'What did she use to cut herself with?' My voice suddenly sounded weak.

She gave me a strange look. 'A knife. One of her own kitchen knives, in fact.'

Lukas glanced at me, concern in his gaze. 'You're sure?'

Lady Sullivan rose to her feet. 'What exactly are you trying to tell me? Are you suggesting that Becca didn't do this to herself?'

'I don't know.' I licked my lips. 'I need to see her body.'

'Is that completely necessary?' she enquired.

'Yes,' Lukas said.

Her lips tightened. 'No matter what dormant power this one might have within her, she is still part of the human police force. Are you prepared to pass on the reins of this investigation to her? I'm certain, Lord Horvath, that you are more than aware of the repercussions that might have.'

'I'm certain, Lady Sullivan, that you're also aware of the repercussions of a werewolf in your clan killing a member of the human police force. This is about damage limitation.'

'Their deaths are not related.'

'You don't know that,' I said, more loudly than I'd intended. 'Nobody does. To find out for sure, I need to see Becca's body.'

Lady Sullivan sighed, then she looked at Robert and gave him a tiny nod. I breathed out. I didn't thank her, however; she was only doing what she should have done in the first place.

'I will take you to her now,' Robert said, stepping forward. I had no idea whether he agreed with the order or not; his expression was inscrutable.

I didn't move. 'I'm not finished yet.'

Lady Sullivan clicked her tongue. 'What else do you want?'

I ignored her exasperated tone. 'Anna. Becca's sister. What information do you have on her disappearance?'

'She spent the night with Gregory. She left his house to return home and somewhere along the way she vanished.' She shrugged in a bored fashion. 'What else is there to know?'

'You don't seem very concerned about her disappearance.'

'I'm the girl's alpha, not her mother.' Lady Sullivan folded her arms; she was making a very obvious production of her apparent boredom. Far too obvious.

'What has been done so far to locate her?' I asked.

For a moment, I wasn't sure she would answer then she cleared her throat. 'Trackers have been out searching for her scent,' she said finally. 'They think they picked her up on the fringes of St James's Park. Becca was a rising star and progressed rapidly through the ranks. We had been hoping for the same from Anna, despite the fact that she lived in her sister's shadow. However, she only made zeta three full moons ago. Sometimes young wolves find the process of being ranked too much to handle and they snap. I suspect that is what happened to Anna.'

'Zeta is the lowest rank?' I asked, confirming what Lukas had told me.

'It is. But many wolves don't even achieve that.'

I sucked on my bottom lip. 'How?' I wanted to understand as much as I could. 'How do they achieve a rank?'

'It only happens during the full moon. Non-ranked werewolves may challenge ranked werewolves during the lunar change. If they win the fight, they take their opponent's rank.' Lady Sullivan regarded me coolly. 'You may think it's a barbaric process, but we need to ensure we have the strongest wolves in the best positions. Clan Sullivan is not a place for weaklings.'

'All the clans work like this?'

'Yes.' She raised an eyebrow. 'It's a far better system than written examinations and letters of reference and approval that you use for promotion.'

I wasn't in a position to argue with that. 'Fair enough. I want to see Anna and Becca's house as well.'

'We have already searched it, but very well. Do as you will. I can assure you, Ms Bellamy, that there is no evidence of foul play in either of their cases. And there is nothing to tie DC Brown to them. Equally, whether he's a convenient suspect or not, Gregory is not involved.'

'On that last part we are agreed,' I said equably. I smiled. 'Thank you for your time. I'm finished for now, but I may return with more questions later.'

She looked at Lukas. 'How about you, Lord Horvath? Do you wish to interrogate me further?'

'I do believe,' he said, with a tiny grin, 'that everything has been covered.'

'Good.' Her gaze hardened. 'Now the two of you can fuck off out of my house.' She raised a long finger and pointed it at my chest. 'But you should know that I've got my eye on you, Emma Bellamy. You are not normal.'

That was hardly news. I gave her an ambivalent shrug and turned away.

Chapter Twenty-Two

'As I'm certain Lord Horvath is already aware,' Robert intoned, 'all werewolves, regardless of their clan and whether they are dead or alive, are cared for within these walls.'

I gazed round the stark clinical décor of the building he'd led us into. It contrasted strongly to the other places in Lisson Grove that I'd visited so far. It had obviously been purpose built and was far more utilitarian than the grand buildings with their elegant stone facades and high-ceilinged interiors. I preferred it; somehow it seemed more honest. 'So this is a hospital for wolves, then?'

'Essentially,' he sniffed.

He could have said that at the beginning. 'Why don't you have your own separate clan facilities?'

'Whether there are ongoing clan animosities or not, at the end of the day we are all werewolves. Pooling medical resources makes fiscal sense. Besides, we all bleed the same and, deep down, we want the best for all of our species.' He allowed a flash of humour to light his pale eyes. 'We are not animals.'

'One for all and all for one,' I said drily.

Lukas flicked me a sideways look. 'Indeed, D'Artagnan. Although I should point out that vampires are not usually welcome within this facility.'

Robert tossed his head. 'Vampires are not werewolves.'

'And vice-versa,' he returned.

Okaaay. 'Well,' I said aloud, 'now we've cleared up that biological confusion, where is Becca?'

The wolf's expression shuttered. 'This way,' he muttered.

We followed him along the striplight-illuminated corridor and down a set of stairs. I was starting to realise that all morgues, regardless of who they were designed for, were located in basements. I supposed the dead didn't need a view and weren't claustrophobic, but it seemed a shame, especially given my recent experiences. I liked to imagine that any lingering souls would enjoy a few beams of sunlight through open windows before they finally faded away. I knew that I would.

The morgue staff had clearly been alerted to our visit: three white-coated figures were waiting for us by the entrance. My eyes automatically went to their arms, noting the yellow tags that indicated their zeta profile, although their bowed heads in front of Robert had already indicated their subservient status. The lupine hierarchy was embedded everywhere.

The werewolf on the left stepped forward. She was an older woman with same russet-coloured hair as whoever had left the single strand Laura had found on Tony's body. 'Good afternoon, sir,' she said to Robert. Then she inclined her head respectfully to Lukas. 'Lord Horvath.'

He nodded. She glanced at me, but apparently my human status didn't deserve a formal greeting.

I smiled brilliantly. 'Hello!'

She didn't smile back. 'If you'd like to follow me.'

Lukas nudged me. 'Don't take it personally.'

I was less bothered than he thought. I was the newbie here, and I'd done little to earn any respect beyond managing to avoid bowing to Lady Sullivan. Even if other people were aware of my rising-from-the dead experience, it was more likely to send them running away screaming rather than wanting to be my buddy.

A werewolf, a vampire and a zombie all strolled into a morgue... It had the beginnings of a fine joke. Unfortunately, I wasn't sure there would be much of a punchline.

Becca's body was laid out waiting for us. I was glad to see that she was in human form. I wasn't sure what happened to werewolves when they died; if they reverted to animal form, I'd have had considerable difficulty examining Becca. In fact, I didn't know squat about the physiology of werewolves.

I squared my shoulders and looked her over with a detached eye; at least this was easier than confronting Tony's corpse.

Becca's skin already possessed the pallor of the dead. 'How long has she been dead for?' I asked, gazing at the network of scars – both old and new – on her body.

The white-coated werewolf pursed her lips. 'Forty hours, give or take.'

I nodded, peering at the deep slashes on her wrists. 'And the murder weapon?'

'She committed suicide,' Robert answered instantly.

I waved my hand. 'Whatever. Where is the knife that was used to cut her wrists?'

There was a pause. I glanced up briefly and saw Robert indicating agreement to the morgue technician. She turned, opened a drawer and held up a sealed transparent bag. 'Here.'

The knife was surprisingly slender. I stared at it for a moment, trying to work out if it was the same one that had killed me. There was no way to be sure without testing it. 'It needs to be checked,' I said. 'We need to know whether there are traces of anyone else's blood on it besides Becca's.'

Robert's eyes narrowed. 'Why would someone else's blood be on it? Even if Becca's death is related to DC Brown's, you said that he hanged himself.'

I raised my head and regarded him coolly. 'I'm not required to explain every detail to you. However, it's important to leave no stone unturned. There is no excuse for shoddy detective work.'

'Are you implying that we are shoddy?'

'No.' My voice was flat. 'I'm saying that I want to make sure nothing is missed.'

He looked away and sighed. 'Very well.'

The technician handed the bag to Lukas. He broke the seal and began to draw out the blade.

'What are you doing?' I objected. 'You'll contaminate it! We have to send it to a lab!'

'D'Artagnan,' he said softly, 'I can find the answer to your question far quicker than any laboratory.' He raised the knife to his mouth and his tongue flicked against it. I watched him in horror.

'Well?' Robert demanded.

Lukas returned the knife to the bag and looked at me, apology in his black-eyed gaze. 'There is only one blood type on this blade, and it belongs to a werewolf.'

Fine. I turned away. It had been a long shot anyway.

I returned my focus to Becca. Crouching by her head, I brushed away the hair from her neck and gazed at her skin. I squinted and peered closer. Damn it: I couldn't see any evidence of any miniscule pinpricks that would tally with the one on Tony's body. I checked her other side. Nothing.

'If you tell me what you're looking for then I can help you,' the technician said irritably. 'I might be a werewolf, but I'm as good at my job as any human.'

I straightened up. 'Tony – Detective Constable Brown – had a tiny mark here.' I indicated the spot on my own neck. 'The pathologist who conducted his post-mortem believes he was injected with something prior to his death which might have incapacitated him.'

'I've found nothing of that sort here.'

I stood my ground. 'It was a very small mark. Have you tested her blood?'

The technician regarded me implacably. 'She slit her own wrists. There's nothing to test for.'

I waited. Robert sighed. 'Do the tests,' he said. 'We would hate for the Metropolitan Police to think that we weren't investigating the untimely demise of our own kind thoroughly enough.'

I knew that he was humouring me, but it didn't matter. As long as I got the results that I wanted, I'd put up with all manner of bull-shit.

'Why does she have all these scars?' I asked. 'Is this normal for werewolves of her age?'

He shrugged. 'Perfectly normal. You'd be hard pressed to find many wolves who don't possess battle scars.'

I raised an eyebrow. 'Battle scars?'

'From the full-moon challenges,' he explained. 'If a lower-ranking wolf is smart, they choose someone they know they can beat.' He grimaced slightly. 'Not every wolf is smart.'

The technician took pity on my ignorance. 'The day after the full moon is our busiest time.'

I blinked. 'With bodies? You mean you fight each other to the death for the chance to move up a rank?' Lady Sullivan hadn't mentioned that unsavoury titbit.

'I meant it's the *hospital's* busiest time.' She sniffed. 'Not the morgue's.'

'Accidental deaths do occur,' Robert explained. 'But not that frequently.'

I thought about what Tony had told me about the werewolves' reduced lifespan and wondered if that were actually true.

'I've yet to meet a human who understands our rituals.' The technician looked at me pointedly. 'Or who doesn't judge us by them.'

'Is that in much the same way that you've been judging me?' I asked.

She stiffened.

Robert cleared his throat. 'Shall we leave the morgue so they can conduct the tests you've requested and move on to her flat?'

I glanced at Becca's lifeless body. Finding a tiny pinprick amongst her many scars would be like looking for a needle in a haystack.

'That sounds good to me,' Lukas agreed. 'D'Artagnan?'

Despite my reluctance to leave off examining Becca's corpse, I nodded. 'Very well.'

***

Anna and Becca had shared a ground-floor flat. It was a few streets away from where I'd first seen Becca running and covered in blood. I paused outside the front door, trying to picture Gregory strolling past and Becca barrelling out in her underwear to confront him about her sister's disappearance. It seemed vaguely plausible.

'Did you speak to the neighbours after Gregory and Becca's fight?' Lukas asked Robert, taking the words right out of my mouth.

'We're not completely incompetent.' The werewolf gave him a sidelong look. 'Apologies, Lord Horvath – I didn't mean to sound so defensive. But it is hard to have our methods questioned in this manner. I'm unused to such interference.'

'We're not here to challenge you,' Lukas replied quietly. 'That's not what this is about. But I'd feel the same in your position. No apology is necessary.'

Robert licked his lips. 'May I ask why you have involved yourself? You haven't mentioned any evidence of vampire collusion, either in DC Brown's death or in these outlandish suspicions about Becca and her sister.'

Lukas didn't look at me. 'Let's call it professional curiosity, combined with a desire to continue to keep Supernatural Squad at bay.'

I rolled my eyes. Yeah, yeah.

I walked past them into the flat. I could take it from here.

Light filtered in through the large Georgian windows. Noting the indentation in a cushion on a chair nearby, I sat down in the same spot and gazed outside. I had a clear view of the whole street. If Becca had been here when Gregory walked past, no wonder she'd noticed him.

I stood up and looked around. There were a few glossy magazines on the streak-free, glass-topped table, together with a worn copy of Bram Stoker's *Dracula*. I smirked. Perhaps it was required reading for supes.

I picked it up, noting the small bookmark about halfway through. It was the stub of an entry ticket. I peered at it: it was for Crystal, the club where Gregory said he'd chatted up Anna. Hmm. I put the book down again.

In the narrow galley kitchen, I opened cupboards and peered inside at the neat stacks of plates and cups and cutlery. Nothing appeared out of the ordinary.

I frowned as Lukas appeared, his frame filling the doorway. 'Find anything useful?'

'Not yet,' I muttered.

He watched me for a moment as I continued searching. 'You're annoyed,' he said finally. 'Is it because of what I said to Robert? I haven't hidden my motives from you, D'Artagnan – I do want to keep Supe Squad from becoming too intrusive. Wrapping up this investigation quickly is the best way to do that. And, of course, I remain curious about you and your ... abilities.'

'Well,' I said, flipping open the bin lid and rifling gingerly through the contents, 'if you get any answers about that, be sure to let me know.'

I picked up a cellophane wrapper with a familiar sticker on it. That sandwich shop did good business. I dropped it back into the bin and turned to the fridge. Its metallic surface was covered with photos held in place by magnets and I gently pulled off one of two smiling young women beaming out at the camera. Anna and Becca. I stared at it for a moment. Not only did they look alike, they had the same shining optimism in their expressions. I sighed and returned the photo to its place.

'Perhaps,' Lukas said, 'it's time to consider that the deaths are un-related. It does appear that Becca committed suicide.'

'Mmm.' I moved towards him and gave him a pointed look to get the hell out of my way. 'Excuse me.'

He stepped back. I walked out of the kitchen and headed for the bathroom. It hadn't been cleaned. I gazed at the rim of blood round the bathtub and the splatters on the floor and swallowed. I wondered whether the blood traces bothered Lukas.

'What about Anna?' I asked. 'Where has she vanished to?'

'I don't know.' Lukas's expression remained calm. 'Robert is a professional and he knows what he's doing. Wherever Anna is, he and his team will find her sooner or later.'

It was the 'later' part which worried me.

'Emma.' His voice was low, and his eyes were warm with sympathy. 'I know you want to think that everything is connected, and that the attacks on you and Brown are related to what happened here. But there's no evidence to suggest a connection. Just because the deaths occurred within a similar time frame doesn't mean they're linked.'

'You don't think they are, do you?'

'There's no proof.' He reached out for me then seemed to think better of it and dropped his hand. 'You're too close to this investigation. And it's been a traumatic time for you.'

I didn't raise my voice. 'Don't patronise me, Lukas.'

'That was not my intention.'

I sighed and ran a hand through my hair. I was in desperate need of a shower and good scrub. 'I'm going back to Supe Squad,' I said. 'Then I'll think about where to go next and what to do.'

'I'm still on your side. I still want to help.'

'I know,' I said quietly. I managed a small smile. 'I'm sure I'll be seeing you soon.'

And then I walked out to have a quick word with Robert before leaving Lisson Grove.

Chapter Twenty-Three

I walked into the Supe Squad building, waving at Max on duty next door. The relief on Fred and Liza's faces when they saw me was unmistakable and gratifying. At least some people were pleased to see me.

'You must get a new phone sorted,' Liza scolded. 'We need to be able to contact you. Whoever killed Tony could be after you as well.' She shuddered. 'They could be after all of us.'

I couldn't meet her eyes. 'Yes. You should be very careful when you're out and about on the streets. Don't go anywhere on your own after dark.'

'Do you seriously think we could be in danger?' Fred asked.

'Yes,' I said quietly. 'I do.'

Fred straightened his back with a steely determination that was entirely at odds with the apathetic layabout I'd met on my first day. 'We'll keep a look out,' he promised.

'Good.' I scratched my neck. The oversized sweater was beginning to itch; I had to get my own clothes back. 'Have you managed to find out anything?'

They exchanged glances. 'I'll go first,' Liza said. 'I've been through Tony's computer. There's not much on there that's useful, but I did check his search history.'

I knew from her expression that she'd found something. 'And?'

'He was looking up poisons.' She paused. 'Specifically poisons that could incapacitate or weaken a person.'

I drew in a sharp breath. 'So he wasn't taken completely unaware. He had an inkling of what was going on and that he was possibly in danger.'

'That's what it looks like,' she said grimly.

I shook my head. 'Why didn't he report it? Why didn't he take measures to ensure his own safety?'

Liza's answer was quiet. 'I have no idea.'

'Was there anything else on his computer?'

She handed me a printout. 'There's this. It's what he was working on last. As far as I can tell, it's a list of all iotas – werewolves who are unranked.'

Rankings again. Why did that keep coming up? I frowned at the sheets of paper. There were a lot of names; the killer might well be one of them, but it would take a year to work through the list.

I sat down heavily. 'How about you, Fred? Did you get anything on Tony's neighbour?'

'Not much. Will Jones. Divorced. Forty-four years old. Pretty boring guy, if you ask me. He definitely doesn't like supes. He's signed a few petitions to try and get both Lisson Grove and Soho cleared of werewolves and vampires. A couple of years ago he had an altercation with a gremlin that got out of hand when she pranged his car. But he is exactly who he says he is – he works a lot, plays golf at weekends and generally keeps his nose clean. He's not the interesting part.'

I spotted a glimmer of excitement in Fred's eyes. 'Go on.'

'I went to see if I could talk to Mr Jones in person. He wasn't in, but I found something else.' He swung his laptop round so I could see it.

When I realised what the image was, I held my breath.

'There's an ATM not far from Tony's building,' Fred explained. 'And it has a camera installed. It's angled in the opposite direction so you can't see the entrance to the building, but you can clearly see who is walking nearby.' He pressed a key and the video footage began to play.

I hunkered down for a closer look. 'This is brilliant, Fred.'

His cheeks flamed red. 'I thought you'd like it.' He pointed at the screen. 'Look, there's Tony. From the time stamp, he left his flat just before eleven o'clock on the night he was killed.'

By that time, my throat had already been slit. Had Tony been lured out like me? Or had he been planning to meet me and merely been derailed?

I stared at his ghostly image as he strolled past the ATM camera. His expression was set, his eyebrows lowered, but he didn't look particularly upset or afraid.

'Obviously,' Fred continued, 'we don't know exactly what time Tony's flat was turned over. Between the time he left and the morning, only three more people walk by.'

He clicked on the laptop to show me. A bearded man, who was quite clearly drunk, staggered past just before midnight. He was followed by a late-night dog walker an hour later, and what appeared to be a homeless guy who was shuffling aimlessly.

'Unfortunately, we don't have a view of the other side and there are no cameras there. Whoever broke into Tony's place either did so earlier in the day or came from the opposite direction.'

'It makes sense that the perp gained access earlier, and Tony discovered the break-in when he returned home after work.' I frowned at the screen. 'That would explain why he went to spend the night in the DeVane.'

Fred's expression was earnest. 'That's what I thought. I've been through the earlier footage, too. There are a couple of suspicious-looking characters. This one looks the most likely.' He moved the mouse, clicking until he located the right part of the video. Liza and I peered more closely and watched a heavy-set man walk past. He glanced continually over his shoulder, as if he were afraid he was being followed.

'He does look suspicious,' I agreed. 'But he might not have anything to do with Tony. I don't suppose you've managed to ID him?'

He shook his head. 'No.' He brought the man's face into clearer focus.

As he did so, I spotted someone else and my blood immediately chilled. 'Wait,' I said. 'Zoom back out again.'

Fred glanced at me. 'You think you have something?'

'I don't know.' My voice was strained. 'See what you can get of that woman. The one walking behind our Mr Suspicious.'

Fred fumbled with the keyboard. It seemed to take an age, and I felt myself growing more antsy by the second.

I stared at the flittering image. There was no doubt.

'What is it?' Liz asked. 'Who's that woman?'

'Her name is Anna,' I whispered. 'She's a werewolf.' I wished I could reach into the computer and somehow yank her out. 'And two days before this video was recorded, she supposedly disappeared.'

***

I made Fred and Liza go home. Discovering Anna had lit a fire in all our bellies. I'd been right all along that Tony's death – and therefore mine also – was indeed linked to what had happened to Becca and Anna. But all three of us were feeling the strain of the day's events, and neither Fred nor Liza had had time to come to terms with Tony's loss. We all knew they needed a break.

For my part, I emptied my savings account and booked into Max's hotel next door. The Supe Squad sofa was all well and good, but I hadn't had a shower since before my first trip to the morgue. I desperately needed to scrub away the feeling of death and catch some sleep. A tired brain wouldn't help Tony – or Anna, assuming she was still alive.

Max was incredibly helpful. He spoke to some of the hotel staff and procured me a change of clothes after I muttered something vague about being forced to leave home in a hurry. I wasn't sure what conclusions he'd drawn from that, but he'd given me a brisk nod and patted my shoulder in sympathy. The man was a godsend.

When I walked out of the hotel a few hours later, refreshed and finally clean, I hoped he would still be on duty so I could thank him. Unfortunately, his glowering replacement was now standing outside. All I received was a dark look and a reluctantly muttered 'good evening'. I ignored him; I had more important things to worry about than a bad-tempered bellman.

Now that it was dark and I was alone, I could feel the familiar, unnamed terror itching at my shoulder blades. I went to Tallulah, retrieved my crossbow and reloaded it. No, I didn't know how to use it properly and, yes, I'd almost accidentally killed Lukas with it, but I needed something to fend off my fear of the night. Holding the weapon definitely helped. The closer I got to finding out what had happened to Tony and me, the more danger I was putting myself in. If the killer came for me again, at least I'd go down fighting.

I adjusted my grip until the crossbow felt comfortable, then took off down the street. I had one destination in mind and, while a part of me wished that Lukas was with me, I couldn't delay visiting it.

I wondered what Jeremy would make of me strolling along the street and jumping at shadows while hefting a lethal weapon. I couldn't dwell on him; he was safely out of the way, and that was what counted right now.

It was early for Crystal, the club where Gregory had picked up Anna, but its doors were open. I was hopeful that I'd get the chance to quiz some of the staff before they became too busy. There weren't any bouncers hovering outside, but there was a pair of young werewolves at the front desk just beyond the front door. Both their smiles flickered when they spotted the crossbow. That was a good start.

'You're the new one,' the blonde said. 'The one who's taking over from Tony Brown. We've heard about you.'

I wasn't sure if that was a good thing or a bad thing. It meant that whoever had slit my throat no doubt knew that I was back from the dead – and could well be planning another attempt. On the other hand, it also meant it would be easier to get answers to my questions.

'I'm not taking over from him. I'm only in Supe Squad temporarily.'

'Uh-huh.' She ran her tongue over her teeth in a predatory fashion. 'It's Emma, right?'

I glanced at the yellow zeta tag on her shoulder. 'Yeah,' I said. 'It is. Feel free to try and use my name to compel me to do your bidding – but I should tell you that Lady Sullivan has already tried that and failed. If you think you're bigger and better than her, then give it your best shot.'

Her wolfish expression immediately vanished. 'I wouldn't do something like that,' she declared in a slightly too loud voice.

'Of course you wouldn't.' I switched the crossbow to my other hand, and she swallowed.

The male werewolf cleared his throat. 'I have to inform you that we're closing early tonight.' He shifted his weight. 'You know, because it's almost the full moon.'

I supposed that free-flowing alcohol coupled with lunar effects wasn't a good mix. 'Very sensible,' I said aloud. 'I won't be staying long.' Then, without missing a beat, I asked, 'When was Tony last here?'

'Sunday,' he answered.

That was the night after Anna had gone missing, and the night before she'd popped up on the street outside his flat. Whether it was his job to do so or not, he'd been looking into her disappearance. Not only that, but he'd found her.

'He doesn't usually come in here,' the werewolf continued. 'But everyone knows who he is.' His gaze dropped. 'Who he *was*. I'm sorry that he's dead.'

Whether that was true or not, I appreciated the effort. 'Who did he talk to?'

They both shrugged. 'He wasn't here for very long,' the blonde told me. 'Maybe an hour at the most. He couldn't have spoken to many people.'

'Thanks.' I started to move past them towards the interior.

'It's twenty quid,' the female vamp said. 'The entrance fee is twenty quid.'

I stopped and looked at her.

'But you don't have to pay, of course,' she added hastily

'I'm not here to enjoy myself,' I said, in case they thought this was some sort of police shakedown. 'This is work. Tony – DC Brown – was here not long before he died. I want to know why.'

They exchanged glances. 'Kennedy,' the blonde blurted out. 'Talk to Kennedy. He's the satyr at the end of the bar.'

A satyr? In a werewolf club? I was already interested. I nodded my thanks and strolled through.

It was immediately apparent that this was a hangout for young people. I didn't think of myself as old but, in comparison to the handful of punters in Crystal, I felt ancient. I wondered how Tony had managed, then I gave a wry smile. From what little I knew of him, he'd have loved every minute. Sadness twinged at me. It would have been nice to get to know him better.

I sighed and glanced along the long oak-topped bar. At the far end there was a man wearing a leather biker's jacket. He looked as out of place as I felt. This, I decided, had to be Kennedy. When I drew closer and saw his long ears and snub nose, I knew I was right.

I walked up, motioning to the stool beside him. 'Is this seat taken?'

He didn't glance at me. 'It's a free country.'

I hopped up. 'I'm Emma.' I lifted the crossbow and placed it on the bar. This time his head turned, and he registered my weapon. 'Detective Emma, I presume.'

'Not quite yet,' I answered. 'But close.'

He reached for his drink and raised it. 'To Tony. He was a better man than he was allowed to be.' He drained the glass and motioned at the barman for another. 'What would you like?'

I deliberately misunderstood his question. 'To talk to you about Tony,' I said. 'You're Kennedy?'

'That's what Tony called me.' He swivelled to face me. 'My real name is Lee Oswald.' He smiled humourlessly. 'No middle name, though, and I don't tend to visit book depositories.'

Ah.

'You can try and compel me with it, if you wish. I don't care.'

'I'm not a supe,' I said. 'And I'm not powerful. I doubt it would work, even if I wanted it to.'

'That's not what I've been hearing.' The barman placed another drink in front of him and Kennedy raised his hand in thanks. 'Tell me, why is Lord Horvath so fascinated by you?'

I stared at him. Kennedy or Lee Oswald or whatever he wanted to be called might look like a well-worn barfly, but he didn't miss a trick. 'That I can't tell you.'

'Can't or won't?'

'Does it matter?'

He gazed down at his drink. 'I suppose not.' He took a sip and savoured it. 'Well, Detective Emma, what do you want to know?'

'When did you last see Tony?'

'Here,' he said. 'Sunday night. He was looking for a wolf. Girl from the Sullivan clan.'

'Did he find her?' I asked.

'Nope. I don't know why he was bothering. All he had to do was wait until this weekend.' He smiled sadly. 'Patience was never Tony's strong suit.'

'This weekend?'

He gave me a long look that suggested I was very dim. 'It's the full moon.'

'I know that. What difference does the full moon make?'

'Wolves are an honourable bunch and they follow the rules. They can't control the change during the full moon. It doesn't matter who they are or what state they're in, they all go to St James's Park. I've seen a werewolf riddled with cancer pull himself there. A grieving widow walked there from her husband's funeral just before sunset.' He snorted. 'Hell, there was one guy who'd been in a car crash and had his leg amputated in the morning. By the evening, he was with all the others. He was delirious with pain meds, but he was still there. Every wolf in the city gets to St James's on the night of the full moon. It's coded in their DNA.'

'Sometimes a werewolf must not be able get there. Or refuses to go.'

His response was gruff. 'It never happens.'

'If it did?'

'It doesn't.'

I leaned back. If what he was saying were true, then Anna would be at St James's in two nights' time. Assuming she was still alive. Maybe nobody had thought to tell me that because they believed I already knew. My lack of knowledge of the supernatural world was proving an insuperable barrier in this investigation.

'I'll never learn everything there is to know about supes,' I muttered, as much to myself as to Kennedy. 'We speak the same language, we live in the same city and we breathe the same air. And that's about as far as it goes.'

'The greatest enemy of knowledge isn't ignorance, it's the refusal to do anything about that ignorance. That's what we should really be afraid of. At least you're trying.'

I hadn't expected to find a philosopher in Crystal. 'Why are you here?' I asked curiously. 'Why come to a werewolf nightclub?'

'Our kinds are very different,' he told me simply. 'Everyone focuses on the vamps and wolves because they're the largest groups with all the power. The Others, like me, are often overlooked – but that doesn't mean there's not the potential for a lot to go wrong between us. Spending time with the clans helps me understand them better. And it's only through true understanding that we can have peace.' He met my eyes. 'I think Tony was just beginning to realise that for himself. Not many humans do.'

I gazed at him. And then, because it seemed the right thing do, I said, 'You know, I think I will have a drink with you after all.'

Chapter Twenty-Four

Kennedy aside, the rest of my evening at Crystal was a bust. It wasn't that the people I spoke to weren't friendly or forthcoming – quite the opposite, in fact. I got the impression that, after my little chat with the two out front, the other werewolves had been instructed to speak to me if I approached them. A few even approached me first, but I learned nothing that I didn't already know. Those who had witnessed the hook-up between Gregory and Anna confirmed it was just as he'd described; those who'd spoken to Tony had little to tell me except that he'd been looking for her.

When I asked why they thought he'd cared about Anna's disappearance, most of them shrugged and told me he was a good guy who would have cared even though it wasn't his job to investigate it. In fact, the likes of Lady Sullivan would have actively campaigned against his involvement. I couldn't help thinking that the pressure from Lucinda Barnes to do more had pushed Tony into it – and he'd been killed in the process.

The warmth of the booze and Kennedy's friendly company meant that I was far less on edge by the time I tripped back to the hotel. I still had the crossbow, but I wasn't jumping at every shadow. It wasn't night time that I had to be afraid of –although maybe that was the vodka talking.

Perhaps that was why, when the grumpy bellman barely managed to speak to me without spitting, I turned on him. 'What exactly is your problem?' I demanded. 'I'm a paying guest like everyone else. There's no need to be so rude to me. I can't believe you treat other hotel residents like this.'

'Paying guest?' he snorted. 'Sure, that's how it starts. I remember how it went with your boss. First, he was just like everyone else – the odd night here and there. Nothing too unusual. Then he started demanding special treatment – guaranteed anonymity, use of the rear staff entrance, breakfast delivered next door. He didn't want any member of staff to breathe a word of his existence. My taxes pay your wages, and you spend those wages getting all hoity-toity and licking supes' arses instead of getting them off the streets.'

I froze. 'Wait. What did you say?'

'What?' he sneered. 'Do you want me to repeat it so you can record me and write a shitty review on TripAdvisor?'

If he kept this up, I'd do more than that; I was tempted to punch him. 'About my boss. What did you say about my boss? Do you mean Tony? Detective Constable Anthony Brown?'

'Who else?' The bellman's lip curled.

'He stayed here? When? How often?'

'Whenever he couldn't be arsed to walk home to his flat.' He glared at me. 'Which I know for a fact isn't more than fifteen minutes away.'

I ignored his aggression and focused on what was important. 'And he demanded anonymity?'

'Yeah, like he was some sort of precious bigwig.' His features spasmed with distaste. 'Fucking pigs.'

Maybe the bellman was an ex-con, or he had an ex-wife in the force who'd left him to become a vamp. There had to be some underlying reason why he despised the police so much – and specifically Supe Squad. Whatever his beef, it wasn't my problem. What *was* important was the sudden knowledge that, if Tony stayed here from time to time and his identity and presence were kept secret, he had no reason to decamp to the DeVane Hotel. Unless he was staying there because he wanted to be in close proximity to another guest.

I spun round, damning myself for drinking alcohol and now being unable to drive legally. I needed to get back to the DeVane and I needed to get there now.

Lukas's dulcet tones drifted out of the shadows. 'Is everything alright, D'Artagnan?'

I all but jumped out of my skin. 'Are you still bloody following me?'

He stepped forward until he was bathed in the soft glow from a lamppost. His skin gleamed in the light, but darkness still glittered in his eyes. 'Yes. Until we find the killer, you are still in danger. It seemed prudent to ensure your safety. It won't go down well with the public if another Supe Squad detective is murdered.' He twisted his head towards the bellman. 'Although given the viciousness of the argument I just witnessed, I think we'd already have a prime suspect.'

'You ... you...' The bellman's skin turned from pure to white to violent puce. 'Lord Horvath.' He dipped his head. 'My apologies.'

'It's not me you need to apologise to.' Lukas's expression remained bland.

'I don't need you to stand up for me,' I snapped.

'I know that. But until your killer is caught, or you learn how to use that crossbow properly, you *do* need me to protect you.'

I really wished that he wasn't right.

'Her killer?' The bellman's eyes slid to me. 'What do you mean?' He almost said it like he cared.

I took Lukas's arm and propelled him out of earshot. 'I need to get to the DeVane Hotel. Can you drive me there?' I paused. '*Do* you drive?'

He grinned at me. 'Like a demon. But I also have a driver on standby who'll be ready at a moment's notice.' He registered my taut expression and his smile vanished. 'What's going on? Why the DeVane again?'

'I have a hunch, that's all.' I didn't want to say it aloud. Not yet. 'I don't need you to come into the hotel with me. In fact, it's probably better if you don't. I need a lift, that's all. I'd drive myself, but I've had too much to drink.'

'D'Artagnan...'

I looked away. 'Never mind. I can walk. It's not far.' I sniffed. 'And now you know where I'm going, it'll be easy for you to follow me.'

'It's always easy for me to follow you,' he murmured. 'Besides, I'm not refusing to drive. I'm just concerned.'

'It's something I need to check out.'

He gazed at me. 'And it can't wait until morning?'

I didn't answer.

Lukas sighed. 'Give me a minute.' He reached into his jacket, drew out a phone and muttered into it. Then he slid it out of sight again. 'The car won't be long.'

'It must be good to be a vampire Lord.'

'There are advantages,' he agreed. 'Though it doesn't seem to intimidate you. That is ... unusual.'

'I've far too much going on in my life to be intimidated by a vampire. Or a Lord.' Or by anyone who wasn't trying to kill me.

Lukas leaned towards my ear, his breath hot against my skin. 'Careful,' he murmured. 'I can still be dangerous.'

Of that, I had no doubt.

A sleek car, with paintwork as black and gleaming as Lukas's eyes, pulled up next to us. Lukas opened the rear door. 'After you.'

I felt the bellman's gaze burning into my back as I climbed in. I should have been wary of accepting a lift from a vampire, even though I'd asked for it. I hadn't stopped to think about it; that either made me a complete fool, or made Lukas my new best friend.

I double-checked the crossbow to be sure that the safety was on. The last thing I wanted was to shoot Lord Horvath in the back seat of his own car.

He gave me an amused look as he slid in next to me.

'I don't want to set it off by accident,' I explained.

'If you don't know how to use it, you shouldn't carry it around.'

'You're the one who suggested that I have a weapon. It's not like I have set of fangs to protect myself.'

'That's true,' Lukas conceded. 'Given what we already know of you, however, you might be more immortal than I am. It's even possible, D'Artagnan, that you can't die at all.'

I glanced nervously at the driver. There was a privacy screen but that didn't mean he couldn't hear us.

'Relax,' Lukas said. 'This section is soundproofed. And even if it weren't, my vampires are loyal to a fault.'

I imagined that if I questioned the clan alphas they'd say the same about their werewolves, even though there was evidence to prove that at least one of them was a stone-cold killer. 'Well,' I said, 'my immortality is not something I'd like to test again. It was probably a fluke.'

'Mmm.' He raised his eyebrows. 'You said your parents passed away. Are you sure they were your natural parents?'

I took a long time before answering. When I did, I was honest. 'I'm no longer sure of anything,' I whispered.

Lukas reached for my hand and squeezed it. For the rest of the short journey, neither us said another word.

***

'I meant what I said before,' I told Lukas when the car pulled up in front of the DeVane Hotel. 'It's better if I do this alone.'

'May I ask why?' he enquired.

I drew in a breath. 'Because if I'm right, the sight of you could scare her off for good.'

Lukas's eyes flew to mine and a gratifying jolt ran through me at the thought that I'd managed to surprise him. 'Are you going to tell me who you're talking about?'

'Nope. I might still be wrong – and then I'll be embarrassed.'

'*Are* you wrong?'

I shook my head. 'No.' This was the only thing that made any sense.

'I'll wait at the bar,' he told me. 'Come and find me when you're ready. But if I'm to be considered a threat, then at least leave the damned crossbow in the car. It's a lethal liability.'

I breathed out. 'I will. Thank you.'

I'd wondered if I should head for the unobtrusive side entrance again, but the sight of Lord Horvath by my side stopped any of the DeVane staff sending me off in that direction. They clearly recognised him. He nodded to me and turned left towards the bar, from which I could hear the strains of piano music filtering even though it was late at night.

I watched him go and then marched to the front desk and asked for Wilma Kennard.

It didn't take the assistant manager long to appear. She was dressed in the same professional attire as before. When she spotted me, her business-like smile didn't so much as flicker. 'Ms Bellamy. And here was I hoping that I'd never see you again.'

'It's lovely to see you too,' I murmured.

'I hear you're keeping some interesting company these days,' she said, her gaze drifting briefly towards the bar. 'Be careful with that one.'

I wondered whether she was aware that some of her staff had been bribed to keep Lukas and his vampires informed about the hotel's well-heeled guests and any unusual occurrences that took place. Then I wondered if *she* was on Lukas's payroll.

'I appreciate your concern.' I inclined my head. 'But let's move on – I don't want to take up more of your time than is necessary. I need to see your guest list.'

Kennard's eyebrows shot up. 'Do you indeed?'

'It's important.'

'No doubt it is. It always is. However, that simply won't be possible without a warrant. I have to safeguard my guests' privacy.'

I knew I could obtain a warrant via DSI Barnes, but it would take time. I was so close to the truth now that I didn't have the patience to wait. 'There's only one guest in particular I'm interested in. I need to know if she's here and, if so, what room she's in.'

Kennard sighed. 'One guest?'

I nodded.

'Under any other circumstances I'd be compelled to refuse, but I feel terrible about what happened to your colleague. I suppose I can bend the rules on this occasion.' She jerked her head. 'Come on, we can go to my office.' She smiled faintly. 'You already know where it is.'

I followed her through, wishing I didn't feel the disturbing sensation of déjà vu as I sat down in the same chair as last time and waited for Kennard to log in to her computer.

'What's the name?' she asked.

I cleared my throat. 'Sullivan. Anna Sullivan.'

She started. 'As in Clan Sullivan? Are we talking about a werewolf?'

'We are.'

Kennard tutted, then typed in the name and hit return. 'I'm sorry. There's no Sullivan staying with us.'

'How about an Anna?'

She frowned. 'No Anna, either.'

Damn it. I'd been so sure. Then I thought of something else. Anna was on the run so she wouldn't be using her own name. 'She might have checked in under a false name.'

Kennard looked up from the screen. 'Then I can't help you.'

'Dark hair? Early twenties? Pretty? She'll be keeping her head down.'

'I'm very sorry, Ms Bellamy...'

'She's in danger! If you want another fucking death on your hands, this is the ideal way to go about it! Show me the guest list and I might be able to spot her.'

'All you have to do is obtain a warrant.'

'I don't have time for a warrant. I'm not qualified yet.' Frustration was getting the better of me. 'I don't have judges waiting to take my call.'

Kennard rose to her feet. 'There are 246 guests in this hotel tonight. If your wolf is here under a false ID, I don't see how anything I do at this point will help you.'

I tried to think of some way round the bureaucracy. 'There might be something in the name she's using. Or you could show me CCTV footage of the lobby and I can identify her that way. I'm not sure when she checked in, but it would have been after Sunday morning.'

'I can't help you, Ms Bellamy. I'm sorry.' Kennard offered me another of her professional smiles. 'Why don't I fetch us some coffee? A hot drink might calm you down. You've obviously been drinking and—'

'I don't want any coffee.'

Her gaze hardened. 'Have a fucking coffee, Emma.' I blinked at her language. Then she smiled politely again. 'I'll go and fetch it.' She swept past me, patting the top of the computer as she passed. A moment later, I was alone.

For a few seconds I didn't move, then I leapt round Kennard's desk so that I could see her computer screen. All the guest names were there on an alphabetised spreadsheet. Thank you, Wilma Kennard.

I began at the top. I wasn't sure what I was searching for – I could only hope that I'd know it when I saw it. I scanned down the list, checking each name. There had to be a clue somewhere. If only there'd been photos attached, I could have found Anna easily. Instead, I'd have to rely on my intuition. It couldn't let me down now.

I ploughed past the Ds, Es and Fs. Nothing. There were very few surnames beginning with G, but lots starting with H. None with I. The words began to blur in front of my eyes; I was getting nowhere.

The further down the list I went, the more desperate I became. And it was because of this desperation that I almost missed it – or rather missed *her*. When I saw the name, however, it shone out at me like a beacon: Wilhelmina Murray.

She'd checked in on Sunday morning, walking in off the street just as Tony had done. She was staying on the same floor as him. It was her; I was sure of it.

The diminutive of Wilhemina is, of course, Mina. Anna Sullivan might be a werewolf, but she'd been reading the most famous vampire book of all time before she'd disappeared – and one of its main characters was Mina.

I stood up and made for the door. Kennard, whose hands were empty of any coffee cups, was standing in the corridor. 'I'm going to make a visit upstairs,' I announced. 'I want to see DC Brown's room again.'

'His body has been removed,' she told me. 'And the room has been emptied.'

I shrugged. 'All the same, I want to take another look. Do you have a keycard I can use?'

She hesitated before delving into her pocket and passing one over. 'Here. Use it wisely. It's a master keycard, which gives you access to every guest room. I'd hate to think you'd abuse that power. I expect to have it returned. However,' she added, 'if you do happen to run into any werewolves along the way, be sure to remind them that the full moon is approaching and we certainly don't want any of their kind rampaging around the hallways.'

Bless her DeVane-embossed cotton socks. 'I'll be sure to mention it if I see anyone furry. Thank you.' I marched off in the direction of the lifts, then I stopped and glanced back. 'Have you ever read *Dracula*?'

'I studied it at university.'

I tapped my fingernails along the edge of the keycard. 'I don't suppose you remember what Mina Harker's maiden name was?'

'Murray,' Kennard told me. 'It was Murray.'

Triumph spasmed through me. I had her.

Chapter Twenty-Five

I strode past Tony's old room without pausing. Wilhelmina Murray's room was only five doors away and I made a beeline for it. It was almost three o'clock in the morning; I could easily use Kennard's keycard to sneak in unannounced.

Anna wasn't a suspect, though; not yet. I weighed up my options before reminding myself that I was on the right side of the law, then I raised my fist and knocked.

'Who is it?' called a nervous female voice with such speed that I knew she'd not been sleeping. 'Who's there?'

I exhaled and chose my words carefully. 'My name is Emma Bellamy. I work with Tony Brown. Detective Constable Tony Brown. I'm with the police.' I steeled myself. 'Anna, I just want to talk to you.'

'You've got the wrong room.' She sounded even more anxious now. 'My name isn't Anna.'

'I'm not a threat. I promise.'

'Go away!'

'I only want to talk.'

'I said, go AWAY!'

I couldn't do that. I tensed then pressed the keycard against the lock. A second later, I burst through the door – but unfortunately Anna was ready for me.

There was a blur of movement. I caught a glimpse of smooth skin exploding into dark red fur before she was on me. Her jaws snapped open and grabbed hold of my arm. She sank in her teeth, and I cried out as hot pain flashed through me. I lashed out, not to hurt her but to free myself. I heard a brief whine, but she still wouldn't let go.

'Anna...' Involuntary tears sprang to my eyes. Fuck, that hurt. I tried to shake her off. It was only then, with sudden clarity, that I realised I already had the power to do what I needed to. I gritted my teeth. 'Anna, you will let go.'

Lukas had asked me if I'd felt a thrum when I'd used Gregory's name. I hadn't – but then I'd not been panicking. Neither had I been aware of what I was doing. This time the power flooded me, trembling through my body like an electric shock.

Anna's sharp wolf teeth immediately released me, my blood staining their white enamel.

'Back up,' I growled. When she didn't react, I repeated, 'Anna, back up.'

Every hackle along her spine was raised and she snarled at me, but her tail had already dropped between her legs. I was dominant – and she knew it.

I snagged a towel from the bathroom and wrapped it around my injured arm, hoping it would stem the blood even if it didn't do anything for the pain.

I pointed at the bed. 'I am going to sit down,' I said. 'Don't move, Anna.'

I sidled past her four-legged body and perched on the edge of the bed. I was still wary of her, but it was imperative that I got her on side as quickly as I could. I had no idea how long my hold over her would last.

'As I already told you,' I said, 'my name is Emma Bellamy. I'm a trainee detective. I was sent to Supe Squad on Monday to work with Tony, but he was murdered just along the corridor from here. I've been tracking down his killer ever since, and everything I've found suggests that you and your sister are involved. I need to get to the bottom of what's going on.' I tightened my makeshift bandage; blood was already seeping through the towel. 'I think you're in danger, Anna. I think we're both in danger.'

She stared at me with baleful yellow eyes. When she opened her mouth, I tensed and prepared for another attack. Instead her muzzle twisted, her fur yielding to smooth skin and human features. Even her eyes changed colour, darkening from pale yellow to cornflower blue.

She wrapped her arms around her body. 'What did he call you?'

I blinked. 'Pardon?'

'What did Tony call you?'

'Uh, D'Artagnan. He called me D'Artagnan.'

Anna's face crumpled. Then she sank to the floor and started to cry. 'Thank ... God...'

***

Anna dressed in a fresh set of clothes then sat down opposite to me, her hands turning over and over in her lap. The beaming young woman with sparkles in her eyes had completely gone; this Anna was a pale shadow, wracked with fear, guilt and more besides.

'He told me about you,' she said. 'I think he was worried that you'd interfere and get in the way, but he seemed to like you.'

'I liked Tony too,' I said quietly. 'I only knew him for a day, but he seemed like a good guy.'

'He was.' She wrapped her arms around herself and shivered. 'I only knew him for a day too, but he still came here to protect me. All that did was end up getting him killed.' Her head rose. 'He is dead, isn't he?'

I nodded.

'I thought so,' Anna said. 'I tried to go to his room on Tuesday to talk to him, and I saw that something terrible had happened.' She choked back a sob. 'It was my fault. He was only trying to help me.'

'It wasn't your fault. The blame for this lies solely at the door of his killer. This isn't on you, Anna.' I gazed at her and another terrible thought struck me. Oh no. 'Anna, have you been in touch with anyone in the last couple of days? Any werewolves?'

A single tear rolled down her cheek. 'I already know.' Her voice was barely audible. 'I know what happened to Becca. I tried to call her after I saw what had happened to Tony, and someone else answered.'

'I'm so sorry.'

Anna's eyes met mine, a sudden ferocity blazing in their blue depths. 'She didn't kill herself. She would never have done that.'

'I know.'

'Becca didn't do it!'

'I know,' I repeated. I reached for her hands. It was a pathetic reassurance, given what she was going through, but it was all I could do. 'This will be difficult for you,' I said, 'but I need to know everything. I need you tell me exactly what's happened from the very beginning.'

Anna closed her eyes for a beat. When she opened them again, she seemed calmer. 'That much I can do.' She didn't relax, but I knew she wanted to tell her story. She needed to get it off her chest.

'I went to a club called Crystal on Saturday night. I got chatting to a wolf there and we ended up at his place. Becca had been getting on my nerves. She hadn't wanted me to go out – she seemed to think that I should be meditating, or some kind of shit like that, so I could prepare for the full moon. All I wanted to do was blow off steam.'

I nodded understandingly. And then, because I had to be sure, 'Gregory, right? Did he hurt you? Or threaten you? Or do anything at all?'

Anna smiled faintly. 'No. The sex was kinda dull, but he was nice enough. The next morning, though, I felt guilty. I knew he'd want me to stick around, but I also knew I'd used him to piss off Becca. I left early and headed home to talk to her. I'd hardly drunk anything the night before but I felt terrible. It was like I had a bad hangover.'

She grimaced. 'I tried to walk it off and clear my head, but it kept getting worse. I had something to eat and ended up spewing all over the pavement in front of two tourists.' She shook her head. 'I knew if I went back to Becca, she'd tell me off even more for getting into that sort of state. She'd say I was irresponsible and stupid. I only made zeta last full moon, and new ranks often have to deal with challenges from other werewolves during the lunar change. I'm not stupid. I wouldn't risk my ranking after I'd worked so hard for it. But Becca took everything so seriously. She never allowed herself to have fun. It was all work, work, work.'

Her expression was downcast. 'She'll never have fun now,' she whispered sadly to herself.

My heart went out to her, but I had to keep her on track. 'So what happened?'

'I ended up at St James's Park. I was so woozy.' Her brow furrowed. 'I could hardly keep myself upright. I stumbled around for a bit and then ... and then...' She shook her head, unable to continue.

'What? What happened, Anna?'

'A wolf.' She flinched. 'A werewolf attacked me. She came out of nowhere and—'

'She?'

Anna nodded. 'It was definitely a female. I didn't recognise her, but everything was blurry by that point.' Her hand went to her throat. 'I thought she was going to kill me. She went for my throat. She would have ripped it out – I'm certain she wanted to. But then,' Anna swallowed, 'she spun me round and forced me down to the ground. She held me there while she changed.'

'Back to her human form?' I asked, surprised.

'Yes.' Anna tried and failed to smile. 'You have to be able to speak if you're going to make an effective threat.'

I leaned forward. 'What did she say?'

'That she'd see me on Friday night during the full moon at St James's Park. That she'd challenge me, and she'd win.' She wrung her hands. 'She laughed. It was like she knew she'd already won. She said that I'd better start saying my goodbyes to my family because she'd make sure I wouldn't see Saturday. Then she took off. She left me in the dirt and took off.'

Anna took another deep breath. 'I couldn't go home after that. I couldn't face Becca. I came here to the hotel instead. I thought that if I could recover from whatever was wrong with me, everything would be alright. But,' her voice dropped, 'it wasn't. It really wasn't.'

'What happened next, Anna?'

'I couldn't tell Becca I'd let myself get attacked, and I didn't know who else I could trust. I didn't know if it was someone from my own clan who'd hurt me or someone else. I didn't know what to do.' She hung her head. 'I went to see Tony. I thought that if he could find who'd attacked me, I'd be able to speak to Becca and we could confront them together. Tony was in Supe Squad and he wasn't a wolf – he wasn't even a supe. He seemed like the perfect person to help. He told me that everything would be alright and I should lay low for a couple of days until I felt better. He promised that he'd find out who'd hurt me.'

She licked her lips. I indicated that she should take her time. She nodded and continued. 'He came here on Monday night and said he thought he knew who was responsible, but I should stay here until he'd sorted it out. I was really scared. I didn't want to be left alone so I begged him to stay. I *begged* him. He got a room down the hall and then ... and then...' She gulped, her sobs preventing her from speaking further.

I thought about her story. All the pieces of the puzzle were starting to fall into place. Tony had found Anna's attacker. He'd probably told Becca what had happened, and that had set her off too. But whoever had attacked Anna had realised what Tony had discovered, followed him here then killed him to keep him quiet. She'd done the same to Becca, no doubt incapacitating her in the same way she'd incapacitated Tony – and Anna. She'd obviously thought I wasn't strong enough to need to be drugged first, and had slit my throat on the mere off-chance that Tony had also confided in me.

'I bet your drink was spiked in Crystal,' I murmured. 'Some sort of poison or drug to weaken you.'

Anna was pale. 'Whatever it was, it worked. I still don't feel well. I can't keep any food down. I still have to go to St James's Park tomorrow night, but I feel as weak as a kitten.' She met my eyes. 'I can't not go. We have to be there. I can't control my wolf at full moon. If I'm not in the park when I change, anything might happen – I could end up killing someone. It would be devastating for my clan if I did that.' She swallowed. 'It would be devastating for all werewolves.'

And vampires, too, I imagined. In the last few days I'd come across more than one human who was looking for an excuse to get rid of the supes. 'Let's not worry about that right now,' I said briskly. 'Let's focus on who your attacker was. We need to find them before the moon turns.'

'Tony didn't tell me who it was,' Anna said. 'I asked him, but he refused to say. I think he was afraid that I'd go and find her myself.'

Either that, I thought sourly, or Tony wanted to deal with the mystery woman so he could prove to DSI Barnes that he was keeping his end of the bargain. I ran a hand through my hair. What a fucking mess.

'Do you have anything to drink in here?' I asked. After all that alcohol, my mouth was dry and my tongue felt furry. I needed to rehydrate myself while I thought about what to do next.

'There's water and juice in the mini fridge,' Anna said.

I walked over and opened it. As I reached for a bottle of water, I spotted the sandwich on the bottom shelf. 'What's this? Where did this come from?'

'The sandwich?' Anna shrugged. 'Tony gave it to me. Not to eat but to store. He put it in there when he first arrived. He was planning to pick it up after he'd checked into his room, but then he called me and said there was a problem with his fridge. He made me promise not to touch it – but even when it was fresh there were no worries on that score. Just the thought of it turns my stomach. I've not been near it.'

I pulled it out gingerly. The sandwich was unwrapped, but it had been sealed inside an evidence bag. I held it to the light to examine it more closely. It looked like roast beef and sauerkraut.

'Oh,' I said faintly. I sank down onto the floor. *Oh.*

'What is it?'

'What did you eat after you left Gregory's place on Sunday morning?' I asked.

There was a beat of silence before Anna answered. 'A roast-beef sandwich,' she said in a small voice. 'From Sullivan's Sandwich Shop. It's my favourite. I grab a sandwich from there pretty much every day.'

'Did you tell Tony that?' I swung my head towards her. 'Did he know?'

Anna bit her lip and stared at me wide-eyed. 'Yes. He asked me about it.'

I stared at the sandwich in my hands. Bingo.

Chapter Twenty-Six

Other than the bartender, Lukas was the only person left in the De-Vane bar. I marched up to him, my arms swinging, grim determination propelling me forward.

'D'Artagnan. From the look on your face, you've found what you were looking for,' he murmured.

I raised my chin. 'I have.' My voice hardened. 'Butch Cassidy.'

'I'm pretty sure he died over a hundred years ago. I don't think he ever came to London, either.'

'Not that one.' I told him what Anna had revealed, together with my discovery of the sandwich.

He rubbed his chin. 'So Brown visited the sandwich shop to speak to this Butch Cassidy. When you went outside, he deliberately aroused her suspicions. He wanted to see if he could goad her into giving him a spiked sandwich.'

'That's what I think. She wanted to weaken Anna because the only way she could take Anna's rank from her is to openly challenge her during the full moon. She wouldn't beat Anna in a fair fight, so she thought she'd even up the odds. But she took it too far when she tested Anna in the park. Cassidy probably only wanted to check that the poison was doing its job. Unfortunately for everyone, the attack made Anna go to Tony, which then led Tony back to Cassidy. Deliberately or otherwise, he asked one too many questions and got himself a poisoned sandwich in return.'

'She broke into Brown's flat to kill him and retrieve the sandwich.'

'But he'd already gone to the DeVane Hotel with the sandwich. Maybe he meant to drop it off for testing afterwards, or maybe he had an inkling that Cassidy would go after him. Either way, she knew she'd been found out and she tracked him down to the DeVane. She injected him with the same poison she'd used in the sandwich and killed him. She wanted to avoid any further scrutiny, so she made his death look like auto-erotic asphyxiation.'

Lukas frowned. 'But before she did that, she dealt with you. She'd noted you in the store, and was worried that you knew what Brown did. She saw you running after Becca as well, and was concerned about Becca's involvement. Cassidy panicked and tried to cover her tracks. She wanted to make every death look different to avoid anyone connecting the dots. Becca suicide. Brown misadventure. You—'

'Murder,' I filled in flatly. 'And all because she wanted a leg up the werewolf ladder.'

Lukas's black eyes glittered. 'If you hadn't risen again, she might have gotten away with it.'

I shook my head. 'No. She's sloppy. She's made too many mistakes. Even the real Butch Cassidy got his comeuppance in the end.'

He smiled nastily. 'Let's make sure the same thing happens to this one.'

'Should we tell Lady Sullivan first?'

'She's not proved very adept at dealing with her werewolves thus far. We can take it from here, don't you think? At least until we get the confirmation of Cassidy's guilt.' He drew an inch closer. 'I always thought that three musketeers was over-kill. Two will more than suffice.' He raised a questioning eyebrow at me.

That kind of approach went against everything I'd trained for and every police regulation I'd come across. But I wasn't with the regular police; I was in Supe Squad. I grinned in response.

Lukas's eyes gleamed with satisfaction. 'Good.' He pointed at my arm. I'd wound a fresh towel round it so no blood was actually visible, but it was next to impossible to fool a vampire when it came to the hot, red, sticky stuff. 'Show me,' he commanded.

I sighed and carefully unwrapped the towel, wincing as it peeled away from the wound.

He examined it, frowning at the obvious bite marks. 'A werewolf bite is no laughing matter.'

'What?' I said lightly. 'Do you think I'm about to turn furry?'

'It would be the first time that happened as a result of a single bite.' He glanced up. 'You ought to take care that it doesn't happen again though. When we finally track down Cassidy, let me deal with her. Two bites in one day might cause problems. If you receive three – well,' he shrugged, 'it's a certainty.'

I blinked. 'It's that easy?'

'There's nothing easy about becoming a werewolf.' He clicked his tongue and lowered his head.

'Uh, Lukas?' I asked nervously. 'What exactly are you doing?'

'Relax,' he muttered. 'I'm not drinking your blood. I'll be careful.'

I hissed, feeling the edge of his sharps fangs brush against my skin. Then his tongue darted out and, with the delicacy of a cat, he licked around the edges of the wound. I stared at his dark head. 'I'm not comfortable...'

He glanced at me and pointed. I looked down. Instead of seeping blood, my skin had knit together. I gaped.

'Vampire saliva possesses many healing qualities' he said. 'Shall I continue, or would you like me to stop?'

'No,' I croaked. 'Keep going.'

He smiled and dipped his head once more. It was the strangest sensation, slightly itchy but also pleasantly warming. 'That's amazing,' I said, when he'd covered the entire area.

'The wonders of evolution,' Lukas murmured. 'After all, it would hardly do for humans to stumble out of Soho with blood spraying out of vampire-inflicted puncture wounds.' He offered me a crooked grin. 'We can't do much about serious injuries, but flesh wounds like this are a piece of cake.' He licked his lips. 'They're usually quite tasty, too.'

I recoiled. 'Ew.' Then I thought of something and peered at him. 'Do I ... do I taste different? From other humans, I mean?'

He paused. 'Yes.' He looked me in the eye. 'Your blood has a strange quality. There's an underlying taste I've never experienced before. Like,' he frowned, 'sulphur. Truthfully, it's not all that pleasant.'

I thought back to the smell in the small room at the morgue after I'd woken up. That had been similar to sulphur. I turned away. 'So I'm not human after all,' I whispered.

'It doesn't seem like it.' Lukas caught my wrist. 'Emma, it would be wise to keep that to yourself. We don't know what kind of supe you are. People tend to be afraid of unknown quantities, and you're beginning to grow on me. I wouldn't want to see you get hurt.'

'Yes,' I said with only the faintest hint of sarcasm. 'After all, we must maintain the illusion of Supe Squad, and preserve the vamps' and wolves' status quo.' I pulled my wrist away and ignored his expression. 'Come on. Let's catch ourselves a werewolf.'

***

The little sandwich shop was cloaked in darkness. I peered through the window and saw little more than shadows and the glowing green of the emergency exit sign. Lukas walked a few steps back and angled his head upwards, checking the floors above.

'It appears that there's a flat above the shop,' he said in a low voice. 'The curtains are closed, so it's likely that someone is there even though there's no light. Most werewolves don't tend to sleep well just before a full moon. We'll have to be quiet if we don't want to alert her to our presence before we break down her door.'

I glanced at him. 'Break down her door?'

'She's a wolf. As much as you might want to knock politely and walk her out in handcuffs, she doesn't come under human law. The best we can do is restrain her, extract a confession and hand her over to Clan Sullivan to deal with.'

'She killed Tony.' I folded my arms. 'She killed *me*.'

'Even more reason to proceed very carefully indeed,' Lukas returned.

'She deserves to feel the full weight of the law.'

'She will.' He glanced at me. 'But it will be werewolf law. If you want to back off now and let me—'

I interrupted him. 'No.' That was most definitely not an option. I wanted to look Butch Cassidy in the eye when she was brought to account. 'There must be another entrance round the back that leads to the flat. Let's try there first.'

Lukas inclined his head. 'As you wish.'

As the building was part of a terraced row, we skirted to the end of the street before doubling back. The rear of the property boasted a small garden, which was fenced off from passers-by. There weren't any more signs of life at the back than there had been at the front.

With my heart in my mouth, I reached round to unfasten the latch on the gate, wincing when it creaked open. Then Lukas and I sneaked in and headed for the back door.

There was only one button, positioned directly under the small intercom box. That was good; it meant that, assuming Cassidy did indeed live above the shop, hers was the only flat. The last thing we needed was to deal with a group of irate, sleep-deprived werewolves on the cusp of the full moon.

I sucked on my bottom lip and considered. We could break down the door as Lukas had suggested, but I was certain there was another way. I looked around and spotted an upturned plant pot by the side of the path. I scooped it up, holding it triumphantly in Lukas's direction.

'Nice work,' he said, seeing the key taped to the inside of the pot. 'But given your status as only an almost detective, why don't I do the necessary?'

I shrugged and passed it to him. He placed the key gently in the lock and turned it. There was a quiet click. He shot me a grin and pushed open the door. We were in.

Stairs led directly upwards. There was only one door on the ground floor, which presumably led into the shop. With his tread as silent as that of his shadow, Lukas inched up the steps. I followed at his heels. I was beginning to see why the recidivism rate for burglary was so high; there was something remarkably thrilling about sneaking into someone else's property.

Lukas paused at the top of the stairs. He cocked his head, listening hard. 'No-one's home,' he said, no longer attempting to stay quiet.

'Are you sure?' I whispered, unwilling to give up hope.

He raised his foot and kicked open the inner door. The sound was deafening as the wooden door split and then thudded against the wall. I tensed – but Lukas had been right. Nobody sprang forward to meet us. The place was empty.

I cursed and pushed past him to get a better look. 'Maybe this isn't her flat,' I said.

He picked up a photo frame from a side table and held it up. I squinted at it. 'Is this her?' he asked.

'Yes.' I grimaced. If Cassidy wasn't here, then where the hell was she? Perhaps she'd left a helpful clue. I wasn't defeated yet, not by a long shot.

Leaving the lights off so that we didn't alert a passer-by to our presence, I scoured the flat. It was very tidy – in fact, compulsively so. I trailed a finger along the bookshelf and glanced at the titles, then rummaged through the wastepaper basket for any useful notes or receipts that she might have discarded. I even lifted the sofa cushions in the vain hope that something might be wedged down the back. There was nothing.

'D'Artagnan,' Lukas called from the kitchen. 'Come and take a look at this.'

I gave up my search and joined him. 'What is it? What have you found?'

He held up a small vial of liquid. 'Check this out,' he said grimly. He pointed to an open cupboard. 'She's been stockpiling it.'

I took the little bottle from him and read the label. 'Xylazine.' I frowned. 'This must be what she used to poison the sandwich meat and to inject into Tony and probably Becca. It says it's for animal use only.'

Lukas's jaw was set into a tense line. 'We've got the proof. Now we need the wolf.'

I pursed my lips. 'This is her home and her place of work. It's her safe place. There's no reason for Cassidy to have gone anywhere else.'

'It's almost the full moon. She might be out enjoying herself.'

'Except all the werewolf haunts were shutting up early. It's only a couple of hours until dawn. None of them will be open now. She doesn't strike me as the type who'd slink over to Soho and hang around your vamp places.'

'No,' he agreed. 'But she doesn't seem the type who has friends or family to meet up with either. So where has she gone?'

I gazed at the rows of xylazine bottles. 'She's very well prepared,' I murmured. 'She got enough stock to last her into next century.'

'And she's quite methodical,' Lukas mused. 'Think about all the trouble she went to in order to hide her visit to Brown's flat, and to make both his and Becca's deaths appear anything but murder. Not to mention using enough poison to weaken Anna but not kill her. If she'd died before the full moon, there would have been no challenge for Cassidy to answer. Cassidy had to ensure Anna remained alive.' He checked his watch. 'There's only another twelve hours before the sun sets again and the werewolves converge for the change. Our girl isn't out partying. She's preparing.'

Of course. 'She's in St James's Park,' I breathed. 'Checking the lay of the land, calculating possible entry points, doing everything she can to make sure that she doesn't miss Anna and doesn't screw up the challenge.'

'The sensible thing would be to wait here until she returns,' Lukas said.

I was already heading for the door. 'She might not come back until she's taken care of business. Besides,' I threw out over my shoulder, 'I'm done with being sensible. This is for Tony and for Becca and for Anna – and for me.' Butch Cassidy wasn't going to get away. Not this time.

Chapter Twenty-Seven

For a park in the centre of London, St James's is surprisingly large. Bounded by Buckingham Palace to the north and Birdcage Walk to the south, it has a small lake in the centre and numerous monuments in the grounds. There were signs everywhere warning the public about the full moon and, to my surprise, barriers were already being erected around the park to prevent anyone who wasn't a werewolf from getting in.

A large group of people was waiting on the pavement. When we pulled up, they all turned in our direction. Vampires, I realised. Lukas had called in his own private cavalry.

I didn't care about any of that. I hopped out of Lukas's car, crossbow in hand. I was getting into that park and I was going to find Cassidy. The vamps could tag along if they wished, but for them this was merely work. For me, it was personal.

Every single one of the waiting vampires stared at me before turning to Lukas and bowing. A leather-clad vamp stepped forward. 'Lord Horvath. We might have a slight problem.'

Lukas raised an eyebrow. 'Go on.'

There was a loud cough from the side. I peered round the crowd of vampires and saw two uniformed police officers standing there. Both of them looked nervous but determined.

'Good morning, sir,' the older of the two said. 'We've been explaining to your, uh, your colleagues here, that we can't allow you to enter to the park. The area is being closed off for the werewolves.'

'Full moon doesn't begin for another twelve hours,' Lukas said. 'We won't be more than an hour, tops.'

'St James's Park is forbidden to the public for the next thirty-six hours.'

Lukas's black eyes narrowed dangerously. 'I am hardly the public.'

'All the more reason to keep you out. We don't need any brawls between vampires and werewolves, any more than we need dead tourists who think that they can take on four werewolf clans.'

Shit. I knew exactly what they were referring to. A couple of months earlier, a group of Australian students had sneaked into St James's Park before the full moon fell. Their plan had been to hide in the trees and film the wolves in their complete lunar abandon. It might even have worked. They'd scouted out the werewolf hiding places and checked the wind was blowing away from them in order to mask their scents. One of their number, however, couldn't resist clambering down from a tree to taunt a young wolf. The result hadn't been pretty. It wasn't the wolf's fault – even the Australian government had to concede that fact; the dangers were well documented and heavily advertised. But it did mean that legislation had changed, and now St James's Park was shut off for a longer period of time to discourage others from thinking they could do the same.

Lukas didn't bother arguing with the police officers. He drew out his phone. 'I'll speak to Lady Sullivan and the other alphas. They'll grant me temporary dispensation.'

I gazed at the two uniforms. I didn't envy them their job; it couldn't be easy to face up to a group of vampires, especially when it was still dark. It would be simple for the vamps to push past them and force admittance. The repercussions of such an action would be more than Lukas was willing to face, however. He still had to strike a balance between human law and supernatural desires. But I wasn't a supe like him.

I strode up to the officers. 'I'm with Supe Squad,' I declared, a fraction too loudly. 'I'm going into that park.'

They were implacable. 'We can't let you do that. Unless you turn furry, you're not getting in.'

I tried to move past them; they moved with me, barring my way. 'If you're really with Supe Squad,' the first police officer said, 'you'll understand we can't let you enter.'

I gritted my teeth. 'Look,' I began. 'It's vital that I get in there. There won't be any wolves for hours yet.' Apart from the one that I wanted to get hold of. 'Just let me in. I won't be long.'

'No can do.'

I reached for my ID and passed it over. The second officer took it and examined it. 'You're a trainee,' she said flatly. 'You're not qualified yet.'

'That doesn't matter! Call DSI Barnes. She'll tell you that—'

'You're not getting in.' The policewoman paused. 'I'm sorry. We have orders.'

I cursed and looked at Lukas. The phone was glued to his ear, but he didn't appear to be having any joy. 'Lady Sullivan isn't picking up,' he muttered.

I watched him for a moment. He was going about things the right way. There were strict procedures to be followed and damned good reasons for those procedures. But there were also damned good reasons for getting into that park and locating Cassidy as quickly as possible. If she spotted the congregating vamps, she'd know something was up. I wasn't willing to risk her going on the run and escaping.

I nodded to the officers and edged away. Just because this section was cordoned off didn't mean that all of the park was. There had to be a chink somewhere in the security where I could slip through.

Without looking back, I marched northwards. More police were stationed all the way along. As much as I wanted to yell that I was one of them, I knew it wouldn't do me any good.

Picking up speed I kept going, scanning for a spot where I could sneak through without being spotted. I rounded the corner, aware that I was now out of sight of Lukas and his vampires. I glanced into the park, my eyes straining through the shadowy trees in a bid to spot Cassidy. She was in there somewhere. I was sure of it.

'Emma?'

I jerked my head, alarm rippling through me. When I saw who'd called my name, however, I relaxed. I trotted over to Molly, pasting what I hoped looked like a genuine smile on my face.

'Oh my goodness!' she said. 'How the bloody hell are you? I heard what happened to DC Brown. Why are you still with Supe Squad? Barnes should have pulled you out.'

I muttered something non-committal. 'Good to see you, Moll. What are you doing here?'

She waved a hand behind her, indicating the familiar outline of Buckingham Palace. 'One of CID's duties is to make sure that the Palace is kept wolf free during the full moon. It's ceremonial, really, and it should be Special Branch who do this crap.' She shrugged. 'As I'm sure you know, the wolves don't leave the park, but apparently we've still got to be here just in case.'

'Ri-ight.' I nodded slowly.

She peered at me. 'I don't want to be mean, Em, but you look like shit. Supe Squad must be terrible.'

'It's not that bad.'

Molly wrinkled her nose. 'I heard it's really boring. And that the werewolves and the vampires are annoying.'

'Actually,' I said, surprising myself at my willingness to rise to their defence, 'they're more accommodating than you'd think.'

She nudged me. 'I'll believe it when I see it.' She paused. 'Is Lord Horvath actually down there trying to get into the park? What on earth is he trying to pull?'

I laughed awkwardly and avoided the question. 'Molly,' I said, 'I need your help.'

Her eyes widened a fraction. 'Anything. What can I do?'

'I need to get in.'

'In?'

'To the park,' I explained. 'I need to get into St James's Park.'

Her mouth dropped open. 'Why?'

'I'm tracking down a dangerous suspect. I think they're in here.'

'The park's been swept already. Nobody's in there. Apart from one wolf who entered an hour or so ago.'

I drew in a sharp breath. Cassidy. It had to be. 'It's a wolf that I'm after.'

She glanced down at the crossbow in my hand. 'Is that why you're carrying that thing?' she said, trying to make light of the situation. 'Do you know how to use it?'

'Of course,' I lied.

'Em,' she whispered, 'I thought we didn't have jurisdiction over the wolves.'

'Please, Molly. I wouldn't ask if it wasn't important. Trust me. I have to get into that park.'

She gave me a long look. 'If something happens to you...'

'It won't.'

'But—'

'Please.'

From the resigned expression on her face, I knew I had her. 'Fine,' she muttered. 'But if anyone asks, this wasn't me. Wait here and I'll distract the others. You can slip in when their backs are turned.'

I exhaled in relief. 'I owe you one.'

'And then some,' she said darkly. 'Does Jeremy know you're wandering around the streets of London chasing dodgy werewolves?' I grimaced. Molly sighed. 'I'd better not get into trouble for this,' she muttered. Then she turned away and wandered over to the other officers who were milling around.

I edged closer to the barrier, watching as she began to talk to them. She twisted away and pointed at the Palace. The uniforms and CID detectives followed her gaze and I didn't waste my chance. I leapt over the barrier and ran. A moment later, the trees swallowed me up.

I'd done it; I was in.

I flicked off the safety on the crossbow and slowed to a walk, my feet crunching the frost-covered grass. I had no doubt that Cassidy was well aware Anna had decamped to the DeVane. It made sense that she'd set up her trap close to the hotel. She'd want to challenge Anna as quickly as possible, and would aim to nab her as soon as she entered the park.

I swivelled on my toes, my head swinging from left to right as I searched through the darkness for any shadows that looked out of place. Given what Cassidy had already done to me, not to mention my ongoing trauma because of it, I should have been scared. Strangely, I felt the complete opposite; I no longer felt even remotely like prey. This time I was the predator – and I had the element of surprise on my side.

I crossed one of the pathways and skirted round the lake. The headlights of a few cars on the other side of the park's boundary lit up the area momentarily and I ducked down, but I didn't stop moving. I wove in and out of the trees, concealing myself as best as I could, and maintained my grip on the crossbow. I'd only get one shot. I wasn't nearly adept enough to reload it under pressure. I had to make the one bolt count.

I'd reached the halfway point when I heard something up ahead. It sounded like a twig snapping. I reacted instantly, crouching down and pointing the loaded crossbow. That was when a loud, derisive snort filled the air.

'You think you're some sort of smart-arsed, ninja, don't you?'

Ice hit my belly, but I schooled my expression into a mask.

'I'm a werewolf,' Cassidy said, from somewhere over to my left. 'I could smell you coming half a mile off.'

'Well, aren't you the clever one?'

'Yeah,' she said, 'I am.' She stepped out from behind a tree. Maybe it was the dark shadows, but she looked much more forbidding than when I'd seen her in the sandwich shop. Her hair was scraped back, and her face was devoid of make-up. It was devoid of anything, in fact, beyond curiosity.

'Remember me?' I taunted nastily.

She tapped her mouth thoughtfully. 'I think I do. You're Tony Brown's little trainee. The *late* Tony Brown.'

A low guttural growl that surprised even me rumbled from my chest. 'You killed him.'

Cassidy blinked. 'I believe he accidentally killed himself during a weird sex game he was having with himself.'

My eyes narrowed and she giggled. 'No, you're right,' she said. 'You found me out. I did kill him. I guess I wasn't quite as careful as I thought. It's not my fault, though. I had to improvise at short notice. It was his own fault for coming after me. I knew what he was about from the beginning.'

She smirked. 'He knew exactly what was happening, you know. Even after I injected him, he still knew. That's why the likes of Supe Squad shouldn't involve themselves with their betters. It only leads to upset.'

She waggled her finger. 'You're going to be quite upset soon, too. Fortunately, you chose to come here. It'll be easy to pass off your death as another unfortunate accident when this park is filled with werewolves. That is,' she added thoughtfully, 'if there's anything of your body to be found, once my friends are done with you.'

'You've already killed me once,' I bit out. 'I won't allow you to kill me again.'

Cassidy's brow creased. 'Did the death of your boss really affect you that badly?' she asked. 'Did it kill you when you found his body? You humans ought to toughen up.'

She tilted her head while I stared at her, a strange sensation flickering in the pit of my belly and a troublesome thought scratching at my skin.

'I never was human, you know,' Cassidy continued. 'I was born a wolf. I deserve to be treated better. Do you know what it's like to have your legacy torn away from you by some upstart who finagled their way into your family?'

I focused on her. 'You're talking about Anna.'

'Yeah,' Cassidy sneered. 'And her stupid, over-protective sister. They were bitten, not born. They don't deserve to be ranked wolves.'

I needed her to move closer because I wasn't confident enough to hit her with the crossbow from this distance. A few taunts ought to do the trick. 'But you do. You deserve the rank, even though you're not strong enough to achieve it without cheating.'

Her features twisted with fury. 'I'm not cheating! I'm just making sure I get what is mine!' She started to stride towards me. 'I deserve to make zeta. I deserve to go further. If Lady fucking Sullivan thinks I'm going to make sandwiches for the rest of my life, then—'

'Stop, Cassidy,' I said, raising my voice.

Her feet came to a halt.

'Get down on your knees.'

She looked momentarily confused.

'Cassidy,' I repeated, 'get onto your knees.'

She stared at me – and then she laughed. 'You ... you...' she spluttered. 'You're trying to compel me. You think you can make me do your bidding.' She laughed even harder. 'You're human. You couldn't make me open a door for you, no matter how hard you tried. And Cassidy isn't my real name.'

She shook her head in amusement. 'You're crazier than Tony Brown was. You deserve to be put down.'

I looked her in the eye. I'd tried to do this the easy way and it hadn't worked. I lifted the crossbow and aimed. 'You're under arrest,'

I said. 'I'm charging you with the murders of Detective Constable Anthony Brown and Becca Sullivan, and the poisoning of Anna Sullivan. Anything you say may be given in evidence against—'

Cassidy sighed. 'Oh, for goodness' sake,' she said. 'Do shut up.' Then she leapt towards me, her body transforming in mid-air into that of a wolf.

Time seemed to slow. I registered her outstretched claws reaching for me, and her vicious snarl as she bared her teeth. I pulled the crossbow trigger and the bolt flew out. Cassidy flung herself to the right – and the bolt thudded uselessly past her. She rolled and landed on all fours, the look on her lupine face one of unmistakable glee. Then she threw herself at me again.

I'd learned a lot from Anna's brief attack on me in the hotel room. The crossbow might be useless now as a projectile weapon, but it wasn't entirely defunct. I held it up, using it as a barrier between me and Cassidy. Her jaws snapped as she tried to tear it from me, but I clung onto it with all my might. I staggered backwards. I couldn't allow her to bite me. The experience with Anna had been bad enough – and I really didn't want to turn into a damned werewolf. I had enough problems as it was.

I struggled with the bow then, when she pulled back a fraction in order to lunge at me again, I thrust it towards her with all my strength. The frame of the bow collided with her muzzle, the wire cutting into her flesh and drawing blood. She whined sharply and fell back.

I scrambled up, breathing hard, gazing at her with challenge in my eyes. As a wolf, she had the upper hand physically. But I was smarter. I *knew* I was smarter.

I dropped the crossbow while Cassidy shook her head, sending drops of blood flying towards me. She lowered the front half of her body, snarling again as she readied herself for a second onslaught. I waited until the very last second and, as she sprang forward, I rolled to my right. She tried to grab me, but I was already up and running.

I didn't aim for the open ground; instead, I sprinted full pelt at the nearest tree, reaching for its branches and hauling myself upwards. There was the sound of ripping fabric as her teeth snapped at my trousers. She was a fraction too late; I was already climbing away from her.

Cassidy jumped up, trying to follow. It was no good. As I'd suspected, wolves were not designed to climb trees.

I manoeuvred until I was standing on a sturdy branch, one arm hooked round the trunk of the tree, then I gazed down at her. Her yellow eyes glared up at me. Suddenly she shook out her fur and transformed, her naked human body quivering with as much fury as her wolf form had.

'I can still come up there and get you,' she spat.

The tiniest smile curved round the corners of my mouth. 'Come on, then,' I said.

Cassidy hissed, then she began climbing. Now that she was no longer in wolf form, however, she was considerably more vulnerable. I broke off a branch and angled it towards her to fend her off. She growled, trying to avoid being smacked in the face as I swung it in her direction.

'Fuck you!'

I ignored her venomous curse and concentrated, ramming the branch downwards and knocking her to the ground. I let my body drop, landed on her shoulders and sent her sprawling. I twisted, keeping my weight on top of hers. She writhed and started to change back into a wolf again. Before she could complete the transformation, I bent my elbow and slammed it into the side of her head.

She paused for a split second, surprised, and then she collapsed underneath me.

From somewhere behind me, someone started to clap. Unwilling to take any chances, I stayed where I was, though I did glance round. Lady Sullivan walked towards me, with several other werewolves – and Lukas – behind her.

'Well, well, well,' she said. 'I wasn't sure you'd have it in you to bring down a wolf, yet you managed it with relative ease.' She looked down at Cassidy's unconscious body. 'I have to offer you my apologies, Ms Bellamy, for the attack that you suffered. It appears you were correct all along. I've heard from the morgue, and there are indeed traces of drugs within poor Becca's system.' She tutted. 'The idea that a wolf of mine could turn rogue in order to get a leg up the rankings is quite disturbing.' Despite her words, Lady Sullivan didn't look disturbed in the slightest.

Lukas's expression was grim. His black eyes were fixed on mine, but he didn't speak.

'She killed Tony,' I said. 'She murdered a police detective.'

'Yes.' Lady Sullivan sighed. 'I rather imagine that is going to cause us quite a few problems. We shall adapt, however. We always do.' She snapped her fingers. Robert and two other werewolves sprang forward. 'We'll deal with her now.'

No. 'She's mine.'

Lady Sullivan's expression didn't change. 'The law is quite clear on this matter.' She raised her head. 'Isn't that right, DSI Barnes?'

'Unfortunately, yes.' Lucinda Barnes moved, stepping into my line of vision. 'Hand over the wolf.'

Hurt and anger flooded my veins. 'What about Tony?'

'I can assure you,' Lady Sullivan said, 'he will be avenged.'

I looked from her to DSI Barnes and back again. 'You've made a deal.'

'We have extracted some concessions regarding the future of Supernatural Squad,' DSI Barnes said. 'The matter has been resolved to the satisfaction of all parties.'

'Apart from the dead ones,' I said sarcastically.

'You will be rewarded for your efforts, Emma.'

I didn't want to be rewarded, I wanted justice. Beneath me, I felt Cassidy stir. I cursed and stood up. Almost immediately, Robert and his wolves grabbed her and hauled her away.

'Detectives are sworn to uphold the law,' DSI Barnes said quietly. 'Whether they agree with it or not.'

I wanted to stamp my feet and scream. Instead, I looked away.

'Go home,' she continued. 'Go home, hug your boyfriend and get some rest. You deserve it.'

Yeah, yeah. I looked up at the sky and the faint streaks of pink appearing as dawn finally arrived. I started to walk away.

Lukas caught up to me. 'That was a dick move, D'Artagnan. You should have waited for me. What happened to "all for one"?'

I didn't answer.

'I know that you're angry that Cassidy will be dealt with by the wolves, but that was always going to be the case. You knew that. The important thing is that she's out of the picture.'

'Yep.'

'You should be congratulating yourself.'

I glanced at him and managed a weak smile. 'Go me.'

Lukas frowned. 'Are you alright?'

'I'm fine. I'll do exactly what DSI Barnes said and go home for a rest.' I bit my lip. 'I do appreciate all the help you've given me, Lukas.'

'Any time, D'Artagnan. Any time.'

I smiled again before picking up my fallen crossbow, turning out of the park and leaving him behind. His words from yesterday echoed in my head: *Just because the deaths occurred within a similar time frame doesn't mean they're related.*

Cassidy had poisoned Anna, murdered Tony and then done the same to Becca. But from what she'd said, she hadn't killed me. Whoever had slit my throat was still out there.

Chapter Twenty-Eight

It wasn't a conscious effort. A combination of bone-sagging fatigue and homing instinct propelled me all the way back to my flat for the first time in days.

With Jeremy already on his way to work, and no handy spare key with a neighbour or hidden in a plant pot, I was forced to wiggle through the open bathroom window to get inside. It wasn't an easy manoeuvre but, once my were feet planted on familiar ground, I exhaled in relief.

God, it was good to be home. I spent several minutes simply walking round, touching stuff and reassuring myself that it was the same place. The knowledge that my home hadn't changed, even if I had, made me feel better instantly.

I sat down on the sofa in the small living room, dropped the crossbow on the floor next to my feet and smiled at Jeremy's briefcase in the corner. He'd forgotten it again. It was surprisingly good to know that things were still the same here. No matter what had happened in the last few days, I could slot back into my old life. Nothing had altered – it was only me who was different.

I stripped off my borrowed clothes and climbed into the shower, setting the temperature to scalding. I scrubbed myself from head to toe, as if I could clean away all the cares and worries from the last few days as well as my curious guilt at walking away and leaving Tony's killer in the hands of someone else.

I don't know how long I spent in the shower. Far too long. When I finally stepped out, my skin was pink and raw. I gazed at my bare face in the mirror. I looked tired but I was still the same old me, even if I didn't feel that way.

I sighed deeply, grabbed the dressing gown hanging on the back of the door and padded through to the kitchen to get something to eat. Food, I decided, then sleep. Once my brain was clear again, I'd figure out what to do next.

The work surfaces were immaculate. Jeremy had obviously been busy while I was away. The thought that he'd been keeping the home fires burning and scouring the flat of any traces of muck only compounded my guilt. I'd make it up to him somehow; I'd do more to live up to his expectations.

There was a fresh loaf of bread, so I grabbed two slices and a plate. I drew out a hunk of cheese from the fridge, and opened the cutlery drawer to retrieve a sharp knife. Absent-mindedly, I grabbed the first one I saw. Then I paused and stared down at it. It was supposed to be part of a set, one that Jeremy and I had purchased when we'd first moved in together.

I opened the drawer again, picked out one of the supposedly matching knives and compared them. The handle on the first one was subtly different: the hard, plastic covering wasn't quite the same shade of black.

I stepped back and sank onto a chair. No. I was crazy. Or paranoid. Or both. I was seeing ghosts where there were none. I turned the knife over and over in my hands. It didn't mean anything. It was just a fucking kitchen knife.

I sprang to my feet and stalked through to the bedroom. The room smelled of Jeremy, his familiar aftershave permeating every corner. The bed was perfectly made, without a single crease on the cover. I flung open the wardrobe and gazed at the neatly arranged shirts on his side. Nothing looked different. Nothing seemed out of place.

Another thought hit me. I whirled round and headed to the hallway. Shoes. Check the shoes.

I crouched down. My spare pair of smart work shoes were there, together with my running trainers and a rarely used pair of wellies. Jeremy's brogues were missing; no doubt he was wearing them. His trainers sat where they always did.

I picked them up and examined them. Usually they'd have a vaguely unpleasant whiff of foot odour that I often teased Jeremy about, much to his chagrin. These trainers didn't smell of anything. Like the knife in the kitchen, the shoes were brand new. They didn't look like they'd been worn.

It didn't mean anything. He'd been shopping. So what? I licked my dry lips and realised that my hands were trembling. I mentally slapped myself. Get a grip, Emma.

I stood up on shaky legs, returned to the living room and reached for Jeremy's briefcase. I sat down, placed it on my lap and gazed at it. I wasn't the jealous type. Besides, I trusted him. I'd never had any reason to snoop through his things.

The briefcase wasn't locked. He'd never know.

I held my breath and opened it. There were a few pens arranged neatly in a row, and several manila envelopes containing printouts of spreadsheets and reports. There was nothing out of the ordinary. I was being completely stupid. I tutted to myself and started to close it again.

And that was when I spotted the phone. It wasn't the state-of-the-art smartphone that was usually glued to his side. This was a cheap throwaway, the sort of phone you picked up in a dodgy little shop when you wanted to communicate with someone without leaving a trace. We'd had a whole day of training at the Academy on crimes that involved the use of burner phones. I stared at it as it peeked out of a small inner pocket in the briefcase. Maybe Jeremy was having an affair.

I'd gone this far. I reached in and slid it out. Then I switched it on.

Only one call had been made and something about the number looked vaguely familiar. Maybe it was to one of his friends, Becky or Tom. Maybe it was to a tall, leggy blonde with a perfect tan and a boring job.

I looked at the number for a long time before I called it.

A warm, sympathetic voice picked up straight away. 'Good morning. This is Dean at the morgue at Fitzwilliam Manor Hospital. How may I help you?'

I threw the phone across the room. My heart was thudding painfully against my chest and I felt sick. I could still hear Dean's voice; it sounded tinny now. 'Hello? Is anyone there?'

I swallowed and stood up, then retrieved the phone. Without speaking, I went straight to the phone's messages. Dean's voice was unsure now. 'Hello?'

I ignored him. The inbox was empty, but I could still recover any deleted texts. I pressed a few buttons and brought up the archive.

There was only one message. I pressed on it and waited for it to appear. When it did, the words on the small screen blurred in front of my eyes. I blinked furiously as I re-read it several times. But I wasn't imagining it. It was right there in front of me.

Apologies for today. Let me make it up to you. Meet me at St Erbin's Church at 10 tonight and I'll introduce you to the main vamp players. You won't regret it. Tony.

My legs gave away. Jeremy. All along it had been Jeremy. He'd bought a burner phone and, when I'd gone for a shower, he'd used it to message me. He'd pretended to be Tony and lured me out to the church. Instead of meeting his own friends, he'd gone to meet me. Afterwards, when nobody came round to inform him about the sad news of my death, he'd used the phone to call the morgue and find out what he could.

My own boyfriend had tried to kill me. I shook my head. No. My own boyfriend *had* killed me.

There was a loud, unmistakable click. I heard the front door open and, a moment later, Jeremy walked in. When he saw me, he froze.

I looked up, my eyes meeting his. 'You forgot your briefcase,' I said. 'I guess you came back for it to avoid another confrontation with your boss.'

He stared at me.

I held up the phone. 'Why?'

'Emma,' he said. 'I...' His voice faltered.

'You didn't see Becky and Tom that night, did you? You went to the church with a knife, a knife from our own kitchen. And you used that knife to slit my throat. You killed me. You fucking *killed* me.'

Myriad emotions flitted across his face, then his jaw tightened and his shoulders straightened. 'How could I have killed you, Emma? Clearly, you're going crazy. You don't look dead to me.'

'Yeah,' I said, 'you didn't expect that, did you? You didn't expect me to rise again.' I laughed coldly. 'You thought you'd made a mistake, didn't you? You thought that maybe, in the heat of the moment, you'd killed some other poor woman.'

'The pressure of work is obviously getting to you.' His calm expression was infuriating. 'Let me call a doctor. We need to get you some help.' He took a step towards me.

I leapt up. 'Don't come any closer,' I snarled.

Jeremy held up his palms. 'Emma, I don't know what's going on with you right now but—'

'Fuck off. Just fuck off.' Then another thought occurred to me. 'When you came to me at Supe Squad, when we sat down together and you reached into your jacket, that wasn't an engagement ring you were going for. It was another knife. You were going to try again. If Lukas hadn't interrupted us, you'd have stabbed me again.' I gazed at him in horror. 'Why? Why did you do it?'

He folded his arms. The sudden switch from panicked confusion to pure ice in his eyes was genuinely terrifying. 'I'm hardly the only one around here with some explaining to do. You *were* dead, Emma. I made sure of it.' He moved closer. 'What the fuck are you? Are you one of them? Are you a vampire?' he sneered. 'I knew there was something wrong with you. I knew you weren't right.'

'Just tell me why,' I whispered.

Jeremy snorted. 'The question you have to ask yourself isn't *why*, it's why not. Do you really think I want a girlfriend who's in the police? Do you know how long I've been trying to get you to do something else with your life, instead of running around playing cops and robbers like a child? It's always been about you, never about me and my feelings. When you wouldn't deign to come out with me and see my friends, I knew enough was enough. It's not my fault – *I* tried to make things work. But you,' he exhaled heavily, '*you* wouldn't listen to me. You always have to do things your way. And all I hear from people is how brave you are. How clever.'

He put on a nasty voice. ' "Emma is so wonderful",' he mimicked. He glared at me. 'Well, you're not wonderful enough or clever enough or brave enough to stop yourself from getting attacked.'

'You're telling me that you slit my throat to teach me a lesson? Because you didn't like my job? And because I wanted to stay home one night instead of going out? Why didn't you just break up with me?'

'Because,' he spat, 'then it would be *poor Emma*. I'd be the bastard who wasn't man enough to cope with your job. People would say I was sexist, that I wanted to hold you back.'

'That's exactly what you were trying to do!' I yelled.

Jeremy took another step towards me. He was less than two feet away. 'I wanted what was best for both of us, but you wouldn't see that.' He tutted. 'Yes, I could have broken up with you, but if you died – if you were killed on the job – it would be so much better for me. Instead of feeling sorry for you, people would feel sorry for me. They'd look after me, help me. For a change, it wouldn't be all about you. Frankly, Emma, if you'd stayed dead, it would have been better for both of us.'

He was psychotic. 'How?' I asked, utterly aghast. 'How do you figure that?'

'You've never been right in the head. Blame it on your parents' death, or on the fact that you're a freak.' He shrugged. 'Who knows for sure? I could have looked after you and made everything right, but you wouldn't let me. Really, Emma, this is all your fault.'

'You're nuts,' I whispered.

Jeremy pursed his lips. 'Yes,' he said, as if considering the idea for the first time, 'perhaps I am.' Then he lunged at me.

His first punch caught me on the side of my head. I reeled, the swiftness of his attack catching me unawares. I stayed on my feet – but only just. Jeremy didn't waste any time. He came at me again. I raised my hands instinctively to protect my head, so he drove an elbow into my stomach.

'I'll be more careful this time,' he said conversationally. 'This time, I'll cut off your head and burn your body. You won't come back from that. This time you'll stay dead, whatever manner of freak you are.'

I doubled over, gasping from the pain and struggling for breath. My fingers scrabbled around, searching for something – anything – that I could use to defend myself. My fingertips brushed against cold steel. The crossbow. It was still on the floor.

Jeremy's hands wrapped around my throat and he started squeezing. I grabbed the crossbow, my fingers curling round it. Then I swung it as hard as I could onto the back of his head. He released me instantly and collapsed to the floor.

I backed away, breathing hard.

'You bitch,' he hissed. 'You absolute bitch.'

I spun round and ran for the kitchen. The knife was lying where I'd left it. I picked it up, gripping the plastic handle and brandishing it in his direction. 'Stay where you are!'

He staggered to his feet. Blood was dripping down from the side of his head. 'Make me.'

'Jeremy...'

'I can work with this,' he said in a morbidly cheerful tone. 'It's good that you hit me. I was planning to make it appear like someone broke in, but now I'm thinking I can say that you succumbed to the pressures of your job and the death of your boss. You went completely nuts and attacked me! I'll still be the innocent, wronged party.' He sucked on his bottom lip. 'It can work.'

'It'll never work.' I shook my head. 'Jeremy, the police aren't stupid. They'll know this was you.'

'You're the police,' he said. 'And you didn't know.' He flashed me a terrifying grin. 'And you're wrong, Emma. It wasn't another knife I was going for when I saw you last time. After you didn't die properly last time, I didn't want to take any chances so I found something more foolproof.'

He went into the kitchen and opened a cupboard. 'I put it here for safe keeping. It's just as well that I did.'

I stared in horror as he took out a gun and pointed it at me.

'You should have made it easier on yourself,' he said, almost sadly. 'You should have stayed dead.'

I ran at him. I had no other choice. I held the knife in front of me and aimed it at his neck. As I plunged it into his exposed throat, he released the safety on the gun and pulled the trigger. I heard the noise and felt the force of the impact in my chest but, strangely, there wasn't any pain.

'Bitch,' I heard him whisper, as the floor rose up to meet me. 'You should have stayed dead.'

Then there was a gurgle and I heard nothing more.

Chapter Twenty-Nine

The smell was both familiar and sickening. Rotten eggs. Sulphur. Fire and brimstone.

'Emma?'

My fingers twitched.

'Emma? Are you awake?' The hope and fear in Laura's voice filled the room.

My hand went to my chest to the very spot where Jeremy's bullet had entered my heart. There was nothing there but smooth skin. I opened one eye and the bright overhead light made me wince.

'Hi,' I said weakly.

I forced myself to sit up. I was at the morgue, in the same room where I'd woken up before and where I'd gazed at poor Tony's body. It was probably the same damned gurney. I looked down at my body, feeling strangely detached. Even the flicker of dying flames emanating from my arms and legs didn't bother me.

'I couldn't be sure, you know,' Laura said. She bit her lip. 'I couldn't be sure you'd wake up again.'

I shook myself. Instead of feeling confusion and horror and fear, I actually felt invigorated. A new lease of life. I almost snorted.

Laura passed me a sheet and I smiled my thanks as I wrapped it round my body. Then I remembered Jeremy and sobered up abruptly. My shoulders sagged. 'Oh,' I said. 'Oh no.' I swung my head towards her. 'Is he...?'

'He's dead.' Her voice was matter of fact. 'He bled out on your kitchen floor. You didn't hang up the phone, you know. I told Dean that if we had any more strange calls, he was to find me. He kept the line open and we heard everything. It's how you ended up here. I made sure that they brought you to this morgue.'

'I can't believe Jeremy did that.' My voice was barely audible. 'He was the one person I thought I could trust.'

'That's not true.'

My gaze snapped over to the doorway. Lukas was leaning against it. On the surface he looked languid, but there was something about the stiffness in his spine that made me think he wasn't as relaxed as he was pretending to be.

'If you'd truly trusted him,' Lukas continued, 'you'd have stayed with him throughout all this. He would have been the first person you told about your resurrection. Deep down, a part of you knew all along.'

My eyes narrowed. 'I did *not* know.'

He pushed himself off from the wall and walked towards me. 'Your subconscious did.' His black-eyed gaze searched my face. 'I wonder,' he said quietly, 'what else is buried inside that beautiful mind of yours.'

I blinked.

He shook himself. 'Anyway,' he said, 'for what it's worth, I'm glad you're back with us.'

'How did you know I was here?' I glanced at Laura, but she shook her head. She hadn't told him.

'Cassidy continued to insist that she hadn't had anything to do with your death, even when she had no reason to keep denying it. It seemed ... prudent to check up on you.' His jaw tightened. 'Unfortunately, I was too late.'

I drew in a breath. 'Where is Cassidy now?'

'Gone.' He looked away. 'I'll spare you the gory details.'

I supposed I should be thankful for that. I nodded and pushed myself off the gurney.

'Here,' Lukas said, 'I brought you some clothes.' He passed me a bundle, his fingers brushing against mine. A shiver of electricity zipped through me. No wonder so many people found vampires irresistible.

'Thanks,' I mumbled.

'We'll have to start a wardrobe for you,' Laura said cheerfully. 'So we're prepared for next time.'

My stomach tightened. 'There won't be a next time.'

Lukas offered me a gentle look. 'Let's hope not, D'Artagnan.'

***

I strolled into the Supe Squad building the next morning. Part of me was expecting Fred and Liza to rush out to greet me with questions about Tony. When I walked into the main office, however, I realised why they hadn't. Sitting on the small sofa and sipping a mug of tea was DSI Barnes. She looked like she was holding court. From the expressions on Fred and Liza's faces, they were a very reluctant audience.

'Ah,' she said, without rising to her feet, 'I was hoping that I'd catch you, Emma.'

'We're going out,' Liza announced. 'Aren't we, Fred?'

He started. 'Uh, yes.' He nodded at me. 'Good to see you, Emma. We heard what happened. Tony can rest easy now, thanks to you. You did him proud.' He spoke gruffly, but there was a ring of honesty to his words. I thought I was fine but before he finished talking there was a painful lump in my throat.

Liza came towards me, took my shoulders and leaned in to kiss my cheek. I was so surprised by her uncharacteristic action that I didn't move. Then she whispered into my ear, 'Stay with us. Please.' She walked out with Fred at her heels before I could react.

DSI Barnes examined the contents of her mug with vague disinterest. 'They don't know about you,' she said, 'if that's what you're wondering. They don't know that you possess the curious ability to un-die.'

I remained where I was, watching her and trying to decipher her agenda from her bland expression. 'Un-die? Is that what you're calling it?'

She placed the mug on the table and leaned back in her chair. 'Well,' she said, 'to call it a resurrection makes it sound like you're the Second Coming. While I admire you, Emma, I don't believe that of you.'

I was hardly going to disagree with her.

'I saw you, you know,' she remarked. 'When you were brought into the morgue this second time. You were most definitely a corpse, so it's extraordinary that you're standing in front of me now. Can you imagine what the world would be like if we could bottle that sort of power?'

I folded my arms.

'Don't worry,' she said, 'your secret is safe with me. I'm not suggesting we start experimenting on you or anything as crass as that.' Her expression grew more serious. 'Don't advertise what has happened, Emma. This is a secret best kept to yourself.'

Despite her hard-nosed façade, she did care about what happened to her officers. I couldn't deny that. 'What do you want, DSI Barnes?'

'Straight to the point,' she murmured. 'I like that.' She met my eyes. 'You know what I want. Your training is almost over. There's the matter of the final examinations, but I'm sure they won't trouble you too much. I want to know what you're planning to do next. You've done well here. Your work into investigating DC Brown's death means that you can have your pick of departments. The entire Metropolitan Police Department is at your disposal.'

'You want me to stay here?'

'Of course I do,' she answered simply. 'But, tragic as it was, DC Brown's murder at the hands – or rather claws – of a werewolf does have a silver lining.' She allowed herself a small smile of satisfaction.

'I've managed to procure an agreement with the clans and the vampires that we'll keep the details of his passing secret in return for greater autonomy for Supe Squad. It doesn't have to be you, although since you're a supe too, it will make it an easier pill for them to swallow.'

I drew in a sharp breath. 'The clans know that I...' I struggled with the terminology, eventually choosing to use DSI Barnes' own word, 'un-die?'

'Oh no. I wouldn't allow that to happen – it would open a whole can of worms. But they are aware that you're different.' She shrugged. 'They are quite impressed with what you've achieved in short space of time. What happens next, however, is up to you.'

Her gaze remained steady. 'If it sweetens the proposition, I should tell you that DC Brown's flat belongs to Supe Squad. Should you choose to take up a permanent position here, the flat is yours for your entire tenure. And you'd be the sole detective here, at least for the time being. No newly qualified detective has ever had such power. You'll effectively be running your own department right out of the gate. Although,' she added with a hint of darkness, 'I'd prefer it if you didn't choose to go down DC Brown's route and accept bribes from the supes in return for your services.'

I started. She'd known about that all along?

'So, Emma,' DSI Barnes said. 'What is it to be?'

I swallowed. It would never have been my choice and I wasn't sure I was up to the task. Without another experienced detective on board, I'd be flying blind. And I wasn't naïve enough to believe that the supes would now fully accept the authority of the human police.

But staying with Supe Squad would be a massive 'fuck you' to Jeremy's memory. It would give me the opportunity to find out what I really was. It would also be my chance to make my mark, especially if DSI Barnes was telling the truth about the supes' more amenable attitude to the squad's existence.

None of those reasons had anything to do with my final decision. Neither did the welcome surprise of free accommodation.

'I met a satyr the other night,' I said. 'He said something that's stuck with me.'

DSI Barnes raised an eyebrow. 'Go on.'

'He said that it's only through truly understanding others that we can achieve peace. I don't understand the werewolves or the vampires, or any of the other supes. I don't even understand why you're so determined to maintain Supe Squad. And that,' I inhaled deeply, drawing air into my lungs, 'is why I'd like to stay.'

The corners of her mouth twitched. 'I'm very pleased to hear that.'

I didn't smile back. 'But if I do, CID doesn't get to take my investigations. I don't care what they think or say – if a crime happens and it involves supes in any way, it belongs to Supe Squad.'

From her expression, she'd been expecting that demand. She might even have been hoping for it. 'Very well.' She rose to her feet. 'I'll make all the necessary arrangements.'

I watched as she picked up her bag. 'Aren't you going to say something along the lines of "I'm sure you won't regret your decision"?'

DSI Barnes laughed. 'Oh, I'm sure you *will* regret it.' She smiled. 'But that doesn't mean it's not the right decision to make.' She nodded and walked out, leaving me alone in the office.

I stayed where I was for a long time. I knew that I was deeply traumatised. From what had happened to Tony, through to Jeremy's betrayal and my two deaths, I had a lot to resolve. Somehow this felt like the perfect place to do that.

I walked to the desk in the corner and sat down, enjoying the warm beam of sunlight filtering in through the window. The familiar shape of Tallulah was just visible outside. I smiled. Then I propped my feet up and surveyed my small domain. Supe Squad was already beginning to feel like home.

About the author

After teaching English literature in the UK, Japan and Malaysia, Helen Harper left behind the world of education following the worldwide success of her Blood Destiny series of books. She is a professional member of the Alliance of Independent Authors and writes full time, thanking her lucky stars every day that's she lucky enough to do so!

Helen has always been a book lover, devouring science fiction and fantasy tales when she was a child growing up in Scotland.

She currently lives in Devon in the UK with far too many cats – not to mention the dragons, fairies, demons, wizards and vampires that seem to keep appearing from nowhere.